# THE MOST DELECTABLE
# MAN IN ENGLAND

"I should get a room at Harker's Inn," he said suddenly.

"Of course you should not. Whyever would you need to do such a thing?"

He said nothing, just stared at her, his eyes dark, nearly black, really. Pru glanced nervously at her lap, smoothing away a nonexistent wrinkle.

And then his hand was at the back of her head, pulling her toward him. Knocked off balance, Pru fell against the hard planes of James's chest. He locked his arms about her and kissed her.

Captain James tasted of darkly steeped tea, and his mouth was incredibly soft against her own. "Mmm," she heard herself moan. She felt him grip her shoulders and knew that he was going to push her away.

Oh, she did not want to be pushed away.

She sighed as their mouths parted and looked ruefully into James's beautiful eyes. "That was so very nice," she said.

James just groaned. "No it was not, Lady Farnsworth. That was carnal and wrong. And that is why I must go stay at Harker's Inn."

### Other AVON ROMANCES

BELOVED PROTECTOR *by Linda O'Brien*
THE BRIDE SALE *by Candice Hern*
HEART OF NIGHT *by Taylor Chase*
HIS UNEXPECTED WIFE *by Maureen McKade*
THE MACGOWAN BETROTHAL: HIGHLAND ROGUES
*by Lois Greiman*
MY LADY'S TEMPTATION *by Denise Hampton*
A SEDUCTIVE OFFER *by Kathryn Smith*

*Coming Soon*

THE LILY AND THE SWORD *by Sara Bennett*
THE MACKENZIES: JARED *by Ana Leigh*

*And Don't Miss These*
### ROMANTIC TREASURES
*from Avon Books*

SOMEONE IRRESISTIBLE *by Adele Ashworth*
TOO WICKED TO MARRY *by Susan Sizemore*
A TOUCH SO WICKED *by Connie Mason*

# MALIA MARTIN

# PRIDE and PRUDENCE

## AVON BOOKS
*An Imprint of HarperCollinsPublishers*

This is a work of fiction. Names, characters, places, and incidents are products of the author's imagination or are used fictitiously and are not to be construed as real. Any resemblance to actual events, locales, organizations, or persons, living or dead, is entirely coincidental.

AVON BOOKS
*An Imprint of* HarperCollins*Publishers*
10 East 53rd Street
New York, New York 10022-5299

Copyright © 2002 by Malia B. Nahas
ISBN: 0-380-81518-4
www.avonromance.com

First Avon Books paperback printing: February 2002

Avon Trademark Reg. U.S. Pat. Off. and in Other Countries, Marca Registrada, Hecho en U.S.A.
HarperCollins® is a registered trademark of HarperCollins Publishers Inc.

Printed in the U.S.A.

10 9 8 7 6 5 4 3 2 1

*This book is lovingly dedicated to myself.*
*You're a whole lot stronger*
*than I ever imagined, babe.*

# Acknowledgment

Special thanks to Julia Quinn for lending me a character from her wonderful books. I can no longer imagine the Regency era without Lady Whistledown and her *Society Papers*.

# Prologue

⌒⌒⌒⌒⌒

1815

There was nothing like being stuck in a dead calm on a moonless night somewhere in the English Channel to screw up a perfectly-timed homecoming. Captain James Ashley stood on the deck of his ship, legs wide to counter the gentle sway, and peered through his looking glass. It was like staring into the wrong end of a musket, darker than death. But James pretended like he could see everything and knew even more, including where the hell they were.

Nothing like a lost captain to provoke a mutiny.

And then he spotted a prick of light, no bigger than his little finger. He thought for a moment that he had certainly imagined the sight, conjured

1

it into being with hope. But then it shone again, stronger this time. Light.

They had reached England's coast. Or at least he had to pray they had.

They'd lost their navigating ability in a freak storm that hit about two hours after they had set sail from Calais. The whole of the day had been spent fighting to stay afloat while winds tore at their sails and waves the size of elephants had washed three of his men overboard. Fortunately, they had been able to save all three, but now the ship limped along in the dark, like a poor ragged street urchin praying for a safe place to sleep.

And there was light.

James shouted to his men, pointing out toward the pinprick of yellow in the blackness. He could see it with his bare eye now.

The men yelled, and movement roused those who had hunkered down to try to sleep. They tightened the rigging, trying desperately to catch any bit of breeze so that the big ship would turn toward the light. Because, of course, now that he needed it desperately, there was not even the slightest breath of wind.

They moved, though, toward the light, and James was finally able to make out a rocky coast-line. But then the light went out completely. He squinted into the darkness.

Something was wrong; he could feel it in the air. James had learned many lessons in his years of being in the military, and number one among them was listening and reacting to his instincts.

"Drop anchor," he said just loud enough to be heard by his first mate.

"Aye, Captain."

Metal clashed against metal as the chain was released, then a splash echoed in the stillness. James put the spyglass to his eye once more. Now he could make out the shoreline, not well, but he could see the jutting blackness of trees against the slightly lighter sky.

He sensed movement, rather than saw it, and trained the glass at a spot just off their starboard bow. "Smugglers," he whispered. James could just make out the light boat skimming across the water toward shore. He swept the expanse of sea about them looking for a larger cargo ship, saw nothing.

The smugglers were probably out culling the water for cargo that had been dropped earlier—casks of whiskey most likely. A shivery thrill tingled at the base of James's skull, and the hairs on the back of his neck rose. "Drop the lifeboats," he said, closing his spyglass with a snap. They could only hope to catch the thieves in the smaller lifeboats. And catch them they would.

He would be going back to London with a double victory, one against the French and one against crime. Damn, it felt good. He actually grinned as he scrabbled down the netting that hung against the side of his ship and into the small lifeboat below.

Grabbing an oar, James helped his men row the boat quickly toward shore.

"What the hell?"

James looked up and saw what one of the men had seen. About two hundred yards ahead of them, the smugglers sat, as if waiting for them. And at the bow of their small skiff stood a man. James could see just the dark outline of the thin figure.

"Do they want to be caught?" asked another of James's men. And then James heard a noise he had heard so many times before; he knew exactly what it was within seconds.

"Holy Mother of God," his first mate whispered.

A flash of light, a thud, and an explosion. James could only stare as his ship caught fire immediately. A huge gaping hole blackened the side of the dark shape of his ship.

And then the telltale gurgle.

"It's going down!" Amazement wreathed with incredulity laced the words that James's second mate cried.

He was right. The *Defender* was going down, and going down quickly.

All they could do was sit and watch. The great ship creaked, then slowly tipped, its bow jutting from the sea. James blinked a few times, closed his eyes tightly once, and then opened them, hoping against hope that he was having a bad dream.

"Where'd the cannon come from?" he heard someone ask quietly.

There was complete silence, and then from the back a youngish voice said, "It was the Wolf."

"What?"

"The Wolf; 'e's magic, 'e is."

"What are you talking about, boy?"

Staring at the slowly shrinking bow of his ship, James listened to this conversation between his men like he was hearing it from underwater. And running through his own mind was the shocked reality that there would be no triumphant return to London.

"See the point over there, jutting into the bay? That's Raven's Head, sure as I live. We're in Gravesly Bay. We're in the Wolf's territory."

"I've heard of him, all right, rumor is 'e could run the king's silver from the royal kitchens!"

Instead of being lauded for his bravery and cunning in battle, James would be the laughing-stock of society. Instead of making his name one to be revered, he'd probably be earning more monikers like the dreaded one society had pinned on him last season.

James closed his eyes, clenching his fists in the material of his breeches and breathing shallowly. He wanted so desperately to rise above his birth. He wanted so desperately for his father, whoever

the man was, to look in the papers and know that
even without him, his son had become a figure of
prominence and esteem. There were more desires, of course, some so keen he had never even
allowed himself to give them complete substance.
Always needs, wants, desires, his life had been
built on them.

And now those papers would surely write bit-
ingly of this horrific night. They would probably
forget entirely his military successes. It had only
taken one terrible rumor to shadow his triumphs
last season. One untrue and horrible rumor, and
the twittering women of the *ton* had attached that
awful title to him.

And now they would have this lovely incident
to stick their claws into. What god-awful name
would they give him now?

# PART I

## Gravesly

# Chapter 1

ᗐᑐ

"The Most Delectable Man in England hunting the Most Wanted Man in England. How catching," Lady Prudence Farnsworth whispered as she peeked around the heavy drapes of the library.

"Do *not* say that word."

Pru glanced over her shoulder at her butler. "Which word? Delectable?"

"No, catch."

Pru laughed softly and glanced back out the window. "Clifton, dear, you do worry too much."

She could actually feel the man's scowl.

"He's come on horseback," she said as she watched the tall man in mud-spattered military dress dismount. "Impressive," she murmured.

"Hmmph."

Pru let the heavy drapes slide from her grasp.

9

"I meant, 'tis impressive that he came the entire way on horseback. Most of the men they send come in coaches, then spend their time here with their doors closed praying for their lives. This one comes with no outriders, a target for all on the back of a horse."

"Captain Ashley is not most men," Clifton said darkly.

"No, Captain Ashley is not most men. He's a famous military hero." Pru grinned at her mammoth butler. "We've seen them before, but we've seen their backs more often."

The military hero's knock sounded at the door.

"His pride's been pricked, this one's has. He's out for blood, and it's careful we need to be."

Pru pulled her shoulders back and smoothed her palms along the skirt of her gown. "We'll follow our plan, and all will go well." She nodded toward the hall. "Now, go let the good captain in. I shall meet with him in the drawing room," she said to Clifton, and whisked herself across the corridor.

"I still say we should make him live in the rooms above Harker's Inn," Clifton grumbled as he stomped toward the front door.

Pru, of course, knew that it would never do to have the captain living at Harker's Inn. She had immediately offered lodging when she had found out that Captain James Ashley was on his way back to Gravesly.

It was the least she could do out of purely civic pride.

Pru heard the creak of the front-door hinges and jumped the last few steps into the drawing room. The low rumble of a very male voice echoed down the hall behind her, and it caused a strange flutter in the depths of Pru's stomach.

The captain was terribly masculine, the low timbre of his voice and strong silhouette attesting to this fact. It made her anxious.

With a quick shake of her head, Pru picked up her embroidery and settled herself on an elegantly shabby settee. Her hand shook a bit as she slipped her needle through the stretched material of a small pinafore she was working on.

Little Emily Sawyer, the baker's daughter, had grown out of the last one she had made—it now adorned Emily's little sister—and so Pru was making her another.

"My lady."

Pru jumped at Clifton's formal address and glanced up. Her butler gave her a piercing look out of his one good eye, then continued, "Captain James Ashley, my lady."

Setting her embroidery aside, Prudence rose calmly, smiled at her butler as he shifted his bulky frame so that she could welcome their visitor, then faltered.

If she had thought the man's voice and stature to be masculine, it was nothing in the face of his swarthy skin, square jaw, and deep-set eyes the color of a stormy sea. He was even taller than she had thought, standing nearly eye to eye with dearest Clifton. His red coat and white breeches were spattered with mud, his dark hair wind-blown, but he still cut quite a figure.

The Most Delectable Man in England, indeed.

He stepped toward her, and Prudence realized that she surely had been standing there with her mouth hanging open. "Captain Ashley," she forced herself to say, "how very good to have you."

"How very good of you to invite me to stay with you, Lady Farnsworth." He took her hand and bowed over it. He had his gloves on, of course, but she could still tell that his fingers were long, his hand large and strong.

She had forgotten to put on her own gloves. They didn't stand much on formality at Chesley House, and she had always hated gloves. She stared for a moment at her own small hand encompassed by the captain's much larger one.

"But, of course, Captain," she said quickly, blinking back up to meet his gaze and withdrawing her hand. "When I heard that Gravesly would be getting such a courageous and intelligent officer to help rid us of smugglers, well . . ." She pressed her hand to her breast and smiled. "Of course, I offered my home for your convenience. I do try to be a boon to my community."

"That is quite admirable, Lady Farnsworth."

Her fingers, the same fingers the tall Captain Ashley had just held, were trembling. With a slight frown, Pru curled her hand into a fist and pressed it tightly against her side. Surely she was not nervous. It had been rather a long time since she had experienced an attack of nerves.

Of course she was not nervous.

"Yes, well," she said finally, her voice sounding faintly panicky to her own ears. Pru stopped and cleared her throat. The captain had a very commanding presence, she realized, and she was certainly not used to being commanded. Pru stood a little straighter and tried to look as daunting as possible.

"I am sure you would like to freshen up from your journey." She glanced at Clifton, who had one bushy eyebrow bunched in a frown, as he glared at the captain.

"Clifton!" she rebutted the man without thinking. At her sharp tone, both men jumped. Pru wanted to groan at her lack of subtlety. What on earth was the matter with her?

"Clifton," she said sweetly, "will take you to your room." She glared meaningfully at her butler and tipped her head slightly toward the doorway.

Clifton's jaw was set at the stubborn angle Pru knew only too well, and she would not have put it past the man to tell the captain to show himself right out the door. "Or, actually," she said quickly,

rushing forward and hooking her arm through
the captain's, "I can show you easily enough."
She could feel the heat of the captain's arm
through his red coat, and she suddenly regretted
her rash action, for now she would have to crowd
through the doorway on Captain Ashley's arm.

That doorway loomed in front of her, looking
very much smaller than it ever had before.

"Do bring the captain's things, Clifton," Pru
demanded, saying a quick prayer that Clifton
would remember that he was a servant.

The doorway.

Pru swallowed tightly, the warmth of the captain's body quite pronounced along her side. She
couldn't remember ever being this close to a man
so tall or warm, or masculine before. There was
Clifton, of course; he was very tall. But she surely
could not remember thinking that he was warm,
or even noticing the timbre of his voice.

Lord, how did the women in society get
through their days always being pushed into close
situations with such gentlemen as the captain?

"I must admit Chesley House is rather small,"
she said, as they stepped toward that tiny doorway. "B-but I have had a room made up for you,
and I am sure that you will find it comfortable."

The captain's hand covered hers, and the contact sent a shiver of some kind of unidentifiable
feeling right through Pru's arm and into her
chest. Her heart did a strange double beat. Well,

fine, she was just going to drop at the man's feet, it seemed, in a fit of apoplexy. At least that would calm her sudden attack of nerves.

Pru frowned at that thought. She *was* having an attack of nerves. How terribly . . . civilian of her.

The captain gripped her hand, peeled it from his arm, and guided her through the doorway ahead of him. "After you," he said softly.

Pru took a deep breath. Oh, yes, of course. They wouldn't attempt to navigate the narrow opening together. Silly woman, Pru chided herself, and stepped out into the hall.

Chesley House was truly only a cottage, nothing as elegant as its name would lead one to believe. And Captain Ashley actually had to turn a bit and stoop forward to get his large frame out into the hall. The baron, her husband, had never had to manipulate his body to get around Chesley House.

The captain cleared his throat, and Pru blinked up at him. He smiled slightly, showing a row of straight white teeth and dimples that dented his narrow cheeks just under the high rise of his cheekbones. The man was too handsome by half. And dangerously masculine.

"Yes, well," Pru said for no good reason at all, and then, realizing that the captain had let go of her hand, and that they stood staring dumbly at each other, she turned crisply and started off at a good clip for the stairway. It probably looked from behind as if she were running away. And, in truth, she was doing just that.

Worrying her bottom lip, Pru led the way up the stairs toward the captain's room. Goodness, the man was not at all what she had expected, she thought.

Of course she knew of his exploits, that he was thought a hero to God and country, at least until he had lost his ship a month ago after confronting the Wolf.

Still, she had not expected Captain James Ashley to have disturbingly intelligent eyes, or such a command to his presence, or to be so . . . well— she dared a furtive glance over her shoulder only to look right into Captain Ashley's stormy gray eyes.

She faltered as they stared at each other, and then, tightening her grip on the skirt of her gown, she turned and continued quickly up the staircase.

She just had not expected him to be so incredibly masculine.


Lady Prudence Farnsworth was not at all as he had pictured her in his mind, James thought, as he watched her unpadded bum sway before him.

This was no doddering old widow he would be staying with, but a young woman, not even in her thirties if he guessed right.

A young woman with golden hair and the soft-

est brown eyes he had ever seen. They had immediately set him to thinking of a mink's pelt he had
once handled.

When he had first entered the drawing room,
he had to admit, his gaze had gone from her wide
mouth, to her incredibly small waist, and straight
to her very nicely curved bosom. Basically, Lady
Prudence Farnsworth was intensely feminine.

But, of course, he had been around beautiful
women before.

He had just never had to live with one.

James watched her as she reached the top of
the staircase and scooted down the hall as if there
were sharks snapping at her heels. Lady
Farnsworth stopped before a tiny doorway, hesitated, then pushed the wooden portal open. She
stood very straight and gestured into the room.

He smiled slightly as he brushed past her, and
noticed once more the light feminine scent of
Lady Farnsworth. It was not any cloying perfume
or bath soap, but rather an airy scent like that of
an ocean breeze with a touch of lavender. He
liked it.

James frowned fiercely at this thought, for he
should be concentrating on the duty before him
and not the scent of a woman. It had been a very
long time since James Ashley had been diverted
by emotions of the heart or weaknesses of the
flesh, and it had only had to happen once. He had
learned a valuable lesson.

With a shake of his head, James turned his thoughts to what he wanted to accomplish in Gravesly.

His superiors had given him only a month, since this was technically not his job. He was a captain in the navy, but of course he had no ship to command and thus was doomed to work behind a desk. But he had proposed that he be allowed to go out and bring down the Wolf.

The notorious criminal was quite a thorn in the side of England, so James was given the permission he needed to try and salvage his dignity by bringing to justice the man who had sunk one of His Majesty's royal ships.

He just had not been given a whole lot of time to accomplish his task, and so he had to stay focused. Now, James glanced around the small room. He gave a sigh at the thought of sleeping on the tiny bed, and went to push aside the lacy curtains.

He had noticed as he rode up to Chesley House that Lady Farnsworth's home had a lovely view of the town below and the sea beyond. Unfortunately, the lady had put him in a room that afforded him only a sliver of a view of the woods behind the house.

"I hate to seem unappreciative, Lady Farnsworth," he said as he surveyed the dense woods. "But you would not happen to have a room toward the front of the house?"

She blinked at him, her brown eyes round and

terribly innocent. "Well, of course, Captain, there are two rooms at the front of the house. One is mine, though, and I thought it very imprudent to put you in the other . . ." She stopped suddenly, her eyes raking him from his toes up to about waist level, then moving away to stare determinedly out the window.

"It has an adjoining door to my own," she whispered.

"Ah." James let the filmy curtain drop, hoping the action would hide the sudden tremor in his hand.

No doubt he was losing his mind when just the suggestion of having an adjoining room with a woman made him hard as a rock.

Sexual attraction zinged about the room like a hail of falling stars, not good. It was really too bad that Lady Farnsworth had not turned out to be the doddering old widow he had believed her to be, because now, on top of everything else, James had another problem.

He took a very deep breath, folded his arms over his chest, and contemplated that problem.

The problem swallowed hard and threaded her fingers together at her waist, shifting her weight slightly from one foot to the other. "Of course," she said tremulously, "Clifton is below stairs, as well as Cook and Mabel. And Tuck and Paul live in the attic, so there is no worry of . . . of . . ." Obviously it was beyond her to finish her sentence.

James felt his lip twitch and bit hard at the inside of his cheek. Truly, he felt the strangest urge to laugh aloud. Very strange indeed, seeing that he could not remember laughing aloud . . . well, since he was a child.

"I am gratified that my reputation will remain unsullied while I reside in Gravesly, Lady Farnsworth."

Lady Farnsworth's brows climbed an inch, and her rosy-lipped mouth opened in a slight "O."

Clifton barged in then, pushing past the still-unblinking Lady Farnsworth, shooting a distrustful glare at James, and dropping his old leather bag unceremoniously on the bed.

"Here you be," the man said gruffly, and turned on his heel, stopping short in front of his mistress.

There was another one that he had never expected. This huge, bald butler with the black eye patch: a pirate gone astray.

They all stood in silent contemplation of one another for a moment, then Clifton did a very strange thing, indeed.

"C'mon then!" the man demanded, and pushed the gaping Lady Farnsworth from the room. Turning, the man beetled his shaggy brows. "You let that poor gel be!" he said, and pulled the door shut with a bang that set the window to rattling.

James stood quite still for a moment. He

blinked, then actually pinched an inch of skin on his hand to make sure that he was awake. Nothing around him faltered or began to swim into reality.

He was awake. He was at his new post. And he had just experienced a very strange welcoming.

# Chapter 2

"**C**lifton! How could you?" Prudence wailed to her butler's back as he marched down the stairs.

The man grumbled something she didn't hear, turned around the banister, and started toward the back of the house.

"We must act as normally as we can, Clifton! And that was most decidedly *not* normal."

Clifton stopped so abruptly that Pru plowed right into his back. She straightened as Clifton turned and glared at her. "Weren't nothing normal to the way that man was looking at you."

Pru blinked. "Whatever do you mean?"

"Nothing." Clifton turned and stomped down the hall, leaving her to stare after him.

At the door to the kitchen, Clifton turned. "I've enough trouble afoot that I don't need to be protecting your virtue on top of it all."

"Virtue? What on earth are you talking about?"

"That man was looking at you like you were a woman!" Clifton nearly snarled.

"And how should he look at me? Perhaps he should see me as a dog? A cat?"

"He should see you as Lady Farnsworth, very much above himself, and definitely not someone he can look at like . . . that!"

"You are being absurd, Clifton." The look on her butler's face told her he didn't find his state-ment at all lacking in sense. "Really, Clifton, I *am* a widow." She lowered her voice a little. "I have no virtue that needs protection." She could feel heat suffuse her face, and she decided in that mo-ment that she absolutely hated Captain James Ashley for making her blush. For it was entirely his fault that Clifton would bring up this most uncomfortable subject.

Clifton growled some unintelligible retort, swirled around, and pushed through the door of the kitchen.

Pru stood staring at the door for a moment, as the full impact of Clifton's words hit her.

The captain had looked at her as a man staring at a woman.

Pru glanced down at her fingers clutching the folds of her gown. They trembled, still.

Slowly, she lifted her hand. She had found her-self staring at the captain as well. And she had trembled at his touch. It had not been nerves at all, she thought. Rather, it had been attraction. She had never in her life been attracted to a man.

Her very good friend, Leslie Redding, had spoken of the feeling, and Pru had always wondered, and, yes, wished to have her heart beat a bit faster than normal, her senses shiver.

"Goodness," she breathed slowly, and pressed her shaking palm against her breast. "Goodness."

She no longer hated the captain. Rather, she was very much in awe, actually, of the first man to whom her body had finally reacted. But, oh, did it have to be the captain?

Pru made a soft sound of sadness. "Of course, you would pick the one man I could not possibly have anything to do with," she said to her stomach.

"If you want him to think you're normal, quit talking to yourself."

Pru looked up to see her butler's large, bald head sticking around the kitchen door.

"Oh!" Pru twitched her skirts and pounded down the hall, as Clifton disappeared once more. She threw the door open, enjoying the crack of wood as it banged against the wall. "Clifton Rhodes you are insufferable."

Her butler was sitting on a stool with his back to her, and he didn't move an inch at her reprimand. Cook looked up from her work, though. "I have dough risin', and if you two keep your stompin' up, it'll fall, sure enough. Get out of my kitchen if you want to keep actin' like children."

"Sorry, Delilah."

"Hmmph." Cook went back to her mixing.

"You"—Pru pointed her finger at Clifton— "follow me." And she walked as quietly as she could out the back door, making sure that Clifton followed. Pru picked her way through the gardens and out to the stable. When Clifton entered and closed the door behind him, Pru propped her hands on her hips.

"Now, we have already spoken of what we must do while our guest is in residence, Clifton. We must, *must* act like a normal household."

"I don't like the looks of that man," Clifton said stonily.

"Well of course you don't! And I don't either." Now that wasn't entirely true, but with Clifton staring at her every expression, Pru surely did not want to dwell on the idea that she found Captain Ashley's looks rather appealing. "But looking at him as if he were Lucifer himself and shoving me through doors is not going to accomplish our goal in the least."

Clifton just scowled.

"Now, we must remain calm at all costs." Pru took in a deep breath and let it out slowly. "I think we definitely bungled our first meeting with Captain Ashley, and we mustn't allow that to happen again."

Still, Clifton said nothing.

"And we must also remember that part of our plan is to have me keep near him."

"That part of the plan is now changed."

"Oh really? So we should just let the man prance about the countryside without any knowledge of his whereabouts?"

"I'll stay near him."

Pru tapped her fingers against her hips for a moment of silence. "I am not sure, Clifton, that will be possible."

Her butler folded his beefy arms over his barrel chest and scowled.

"I rather think that having you tagging after him will make him suspicious. And that is what we are trying to avoid, are we not?"

"When we spoke of this before, I didn't know the man was a rogue."

"Oh, please, Clifton, he is not a rogue."

"Right, then, why would society pin him with a name like the Most Delectable Man in England?"

Obviously men could not see what women did. Delectable was the perfect name for Captain James Ashley.

"You're leavin' tonight!" Clifton suddenly thundered.

"What?"

"Tonight, I say, you're leaving for a visit to your aunt's up in York."

"You jest, Clifton. We have a very serious mission ahead of us."

"*I* do, not you." Clifton pointed his crooked finger at her. "I see your eyes going all dewy and unfocused. You're fallin' for the rogue, like all the rest of them society ladies."

"For shame, Clifton. I have complete control of my faculties." She pushed all thoughts of the captain from her mind and tried her best to look as serious as possible. "I am good, Clifton, you have told me so, and you cannot take that back. You know that I can do this, and I will not allow you to take this mission from me." She took a step closer to her good friend. "Yes, the captain is a pleasing person to look upon . . ."

Clifton looked suddenly as if he were about to erupt.

"But," Pru said quickly, "this town and these people are more important to me than any man. And so is the Wolf." She stared into Clifton's one sky-blue eye.

Her butler blinked, then nodded. "Fine, but you have no idea how persuasive a man of the captain's ilk can be."

"Persuasive or not, Clifton, I think I have proven myself to be a woman of intelligence and focus. I will not allow the Captain's charms to

sway me in my duty. It is his persistence in finding the Wolf that we must worry about, not the
outside chance that he might fancy me."

Clifton seemed about to rebut her conclusions,
but they were interrupted by Tuck. "Oh, excuse
me, milady," the boy said as he stopped just inside the now open stable door.

"Do not worry about us, Tuck, we are just having a bit of a conference."

As if finding his lady conferencing with the
butler out in the stable were an everyday occur-
rence, Tuck nodded and swaggered over to the
stall that housed the captain's horse.

"What are you doing with Ashley's horse?"
Clifton demanded.

"The captain ordered me to bring it 'round,"
the boy said as he led the gelding out of its stall.

Clifton made a soft sound of disgust. "And
what are you supposed to do when the captain
tells you he's going out?"

Tuck hauled a saddle up and over the horse's
back. "Supposed to tell you or Lady Farnsworth,"
he said nonchalantly as he secured the saddle beneath the gelding's belly.

"Well . . ." Clifton was obviously exasperated.

Tuck looked at him as if he were daft. "And I
just did." He rolled his eyes.

Clifton let out a huff of breath, hunching his
shoulders around his ears.

"Tuck, put the captain's horse back and hitch

up the wagon instead. I'll take the captain wherever he wishes to go," Pru said.

"You will not."

Pru glared at her butler. "I shall go inform the good captain that I was just going wherever he intends on going," Pru said to Tuck, with a pointed stare at Clifton.

"Well you can't do it in the wagon," Clifton said, a triumphant tone to his voice. "It's full."

"Oh." Pru tapped her finger against her bottom lip.

"It's all in baskets, though," Tuck said. "Just like we talked about, Lady Pru, I put it all in baskets to look like offerin's to the poor." He stopped for a moment, then cocked his head to the side. " 'Course they're a might heavy."

"Perfect!" Pru cried. "I shall take the good captain with me as I deliver baskets to the poor."

Clifton looked as if he would be sick. "You can't."

Pru clicked her tongue against the back of her teeth. "Oh, come, Clifton, it's not as if I'm taking an entire shipment into London. I'm just taking baskets of tea to the poor."

Her butler mumbled something beneath his breath and stomped out of the stable.

"What died in his bed?" Tuck asked.

Ignoring Tuck, Pru followed her butler, but veered off toward the front door when Clifton went through the garden. She took several deep breaths as she went, girding herself for another meeting with the captain. Only this time she was going to be calm. This time she was going to act like any unsuspicious widowed lady might act. This time she would be normal.

There was something very strange about Lady Farnsworth, James thought, as he watched the woman come up her own front walk. He had already noted that she was talking to herself as she walked. And then just before she reached the door, Lady Farnsworth stopped. She took a deep breath, closed her eyes, and ran her hands down the front of her dress.

James squinted at the sight. His gaze snagged on the woman's hands as they pressed against her lower stomach, then smoothed down to her thighs. He was rather sure Lady Farnsworth had no idea he watched, and he was almost positive that she had no idea how provocative her actions were.

With a shake of his head, James moved away from the sitting-room window. "Provocative my ass," he whispered to himself as he heard the front door open. "You have quite a problem if you think a woman drying her hands on her dress is provocative."

"Captain?"

James turned quickly to see the petite Lady Farnsworth framed in the doorway. She glanced around quickly, obviously looking for the person to whom he was speaking. Wonderful, now *he* was talking to himself.

"Lady Farnsworth," he said with a smart bow.

"Did you need something, Captain?" She took an audible breath and stood a bit taller. "I meant to ask if you wished tea before . . ." Her words tumbled to a halt, and she fluttered her fingers in the air.

Before her butler acted like a threatening father, James thought?

"Are you hungry, Captain?" Lady Farnsworth asked, an almost desperate look in her soft brown eyes.

"Actually, I've asked that my horse be brought around. I'd like to see the town, check on the officers at the excise station."

"Oh, well, then you must allow me to drive you. Your horse is probably overtired from your journey, and I had just meant to go into town." She smiled sweetly, but then ruined the effect by yelling rather loudly, "Clifton!"

The man was at the sitting-room door within seconds suggesting, perhaps, that he had never been very far away. Or had even been listening from the hallway?

"Yes, milady?" he asked, eyes downcast. It was much too demure a pose for the huge man James had seen shove Lady Farnsworth from a room.

"My baskets for the poor are ready, are they not?"

The butler said nothing.

"Good. Have Tuck load them into the cart. I shall be escorting our good captain into town."

This announcement earned James a sharp glance of disapproval from the one-eyed butler. James straightened his spine and returned the butler's look with a hard stare.

When the butler had finally given him one more piercing glare and left the room, James said, "Really, Lady Farnsworth, I do not wish to inconvenience you."

"Not at all, Captain!" the woman returned merrily. He followed her out into the hall, where a maid handed the lady her bonnet and a cloak. "I had planned on delivering my baskets before supper." She tied her cloak around her shoulders. "And I can show you around much better than you could show yourself, I daresay."

"Of course," James agreed, not at all sure he wished to deliver baskets to the poor. He must show the town of Gravesly his ruthless, military self. Being this woman's fetch and delivery lad would certainly undercut that image. "But, really, Lady Farnsworth, I could not . . ."

"Nonsense!" the woman said with a command that rivaled that of any admiral to whom James had been privileged to answer. "I shall show you around Gravesly and take you to see our valiant excise officers."

James took a deep breath. He was accustomed to ordering hardened seamen around, but he had never learned how to manipulate women. That was certainly obvious from the reputation he had in London. James actually winced at the thought. "Thank you," he said finally, with a small inclination of his head.

A cart clattered up the drive then, and Lady Farnsworth's maid opened the door. The boy, Tuck, jumped from the driver's seat of the rather sturdy-looking wagon.

James automatically went to take the reins from the young groom, but Lady Farnsworth got there before him. "I can drive, Captain." She smiled.

I do not like this one little bit, James thought, as he glanced from the top of Lady Farnsworth's pert little bonnet to the baskets sitting in the back of the decidedly large cart. This would be a very bad image to present to the citizens of Gravesly, rolling into town on the passenger's side of a wagon filled with doily-covered baskets. The least he could do was drive.

"I insist," he said with a tight smile, and held out his hand.

Lady Farnsworth looked ready to argue, but stopped when Clifton came barging onto the steps of the house. "My lady," he said, his tone implying that he would once again try to prevent the whole exercise. James was actually glad to see the man. Perhaps he would be given a reprieve on his basket-delivering duties.

"Fine then," Lady Farnsworth said smartly. She handed over the reins and hiked herself up into the wagon.

It all happened so quickly that James stood staring in shock at the woman as she pulled herself up. When he finally realized that he should help her, she was already halfway to her seat. Still, being the gentleman, James stepped forward and raised his hands. Unfortunately, Lady Farnsworth was much more spry than any woman James had ever helped into a wagon, and by the time he put his hands to where her elbow had once been, he encountered the curve of her bottom instead.

He pulled away quickly, his head a bit fuzzy as his fingers tingled and his mind concluded that Lady Farnsworth had a very lovely derriere. Plunking herself upon the seat, Lady Farnsworth stared down at him with rounded eyes, a red blush creeping up her neck.

From behind him, James heard what sounded like muted laughter and turned to see Tuck striding quickly for the stable. And then, *bang*, a noise like the retort of a gun had James twirling around and jumping up to cover Lady Farnsworth. It was only as his arms went around the woman that James realized that the sound he had heard had been Clifton slamming the front door as if the hounds of hell had come knocking.

That man did like to slam doors. Odd behavior for a butler.

"Captain?"

James looked down to find the source of the small voice huddled in his arms. He should have pulled away immediately, of course, and if he had been in his right mind, he would have. But, still feeling as if he inhabited a dream, James held Lady Farnsworth for a fraction of a second longer. He registered the fragility of her frame, the loveliness of the soft eyes looking up at him and, again, the faint scent of lavender that clung to her.

"Excuse me," he said finally, and dropped his arms from around her. "I thought..." He stopped, for he did not know what he thought.

They stared at each other for a moment.

She turned to look forward and surreptitiously scooted about an inch away from him on the bench. "Shall we go?"

His fingers curled around the reins, which were still in his hands, but he stared at Lady Farnsworth's profile a second longer. She was a beautiful woman, but this type of tension would never do. He needed his wits about him, and he certainly did not need anything happening between himself and a widowed wife of a baron.

Above anything, James steered himself very clear of scandals and bad behavior.

. He had spent his life with the specter of scandal shadowing his name, and he had no wish to darken it further.

"Lady Farnsworth," he said finally. She glanced at him from the corner of her eye. "I think, perhaps, that I shall seek shelter at an inn in town. I had no idea that Chesley House was so . . ."

"It is not grand enough for you, Captain?" she asked, her back stiffening, her head turning so that she looked, once again, fully into his eyes.

"No, my lady, not at all! It is just that I do not wish to inconvenience you in any way."

"And the only way that will happen, Captain, would be if you force me to have one of my servants remove your things to Harker's Inn."

James took a deep breath. He glanced behind them at the baskets, wondering how he would explain to this woman that he must concentrate on his work, and having her around would interfere with that goal in ways he was only starting to realize.

He looked back at her, his gaze drifting to her full pink lips before he forced himself to look into her eyes. A man could surely swim in such large dark pools of innocence.

God, he was turning into a jelly-spined poet, of all things. "I have a very important job to do here

in Gravesly, Lady Farnsworth, and I can't be . . ."
*What? What couldn't he be? Pining after Lady Farnsworth like a lovestruck schoolboy?*

"Yes, Captain?"

"I must focus on my job," he said, his concentration evaporating completely as the tip of Lady Farnsworth's tongue slid out and wet the bottom corner of her mouth. For such a prim and proper woman, Lady Farnsworth had the lips of a well-used courtesan.

The moment that thought crystallized, James nearly groaned. Surely this situation had gotten out of control if he had such thoughts in his head.

". . . It would seem to me."

James caught the last of Lady Farnsworth's sentence and realized that she had been speaking to him about something. And now she gazed at him expectantly as if she awaited a response.

Of course, he also realized that he had just spent the last few moments staring heatedly at the lady's mouth. He would most definitely have to remove himself from Lady Farnsworth's home, and hopefully her company.

"Don't you agree, Captain?" she prompted him.

"I agree?" he said, thinking that such an answer could never get him in trouble.

"Good, then, it is settled. Now, Captain, shall we go? We'll be delivering baskets in full dark if we do not start soon." She nodded toward the reins in his hand.

What was settled? he wondered, as he turned his gaze deliberately away from Lady Farnsworth and urged the horses forward.

"I am sure you will find Chesley House much more conducive to concentrating than Harker's Inn, Captain. The fellows that frequent that establishment are terribly loud."

Ah, *that* was settled. If his men could see him now, they would surely laugh him right out of England. The great Captain Ashley befuddled by a woman who did not even reach his shoulder.

The horses seemed to know their way, as they turned toward town at the main road with no direction from him. Trying desperately to focus his own thoughts on his duties, James asked, "What do you know of the smuggling hereabouts, Lady Farnsworth?"

"Nothing at all!"

A rather strident answer.

"What I mean to say is, I really am not the one to give you that sort of information, Captain. I am woefully ignorant of the trafficking of untaxed goods."

"Ah."

"Turn here, please. We shall visit the Widow Leland."

James obliged his passenger and turned the horses down a rutted lane that ended at the front door of a small cottage.

"Surely you know a bit about the smuggling,

Lady Farnsworth?" James tried again to get any information he could. "It is quite prevalent in the area."

Lady Farnsworth fluttered her fingers in a gesture that James found strangely un-Lady-Farnsworth-like. In the little time he had been in her presence, he at least realized she was not at all the fluttering type.

"Really, Captain, I know very little. In fact, I only know what everyone else in the country knows. The smugglers send out our wool on French vessels without putting them through customs, and receive goods like tea and whiskey in the same manner." She shrugged prettily. "I am sure I have never seen any untaxed goods. Since the incoming tea and alcohol usually go straight to London, you have probably seen more of the end product than I." She batted her lashes and then pointed. "There is the dear Widow Leland now."

James pulled the wagon to a halt as the Widow Leland came out to greet them, and all James could think was that the poor of Gravesly were rather better fed than the poor he had seen in other parts of the country.

James jumped down and bowed to the round Widow Leland when Lady Farnsworth introduced them. The woman looked as if she had just seen the devil himself come creeping from the wagon.

"I brought you a basket, Mrs. Leland," Lady Farnsworth said quickly. She shoved the article into the woman's hands.

The Widow Leland looked completely flummoxed. Her beady dark eyes peered from Lady Farnsworth to him, then down to the basket. She reached for the edge of the lace-edged covering.

"No!" Lady Farnsworth grabbed Mrs. Leland's hand and they stood there for a moment. "My dear, Mrs. Leland." Lady Farnsworth kissed the woman's fingers. "It would embarrass me so to watch you open my gift. We will just be on our way now."

As a young boy, James had accompanied his mother as she gave baskets to the poor. She most certainly hadn't kissed anyone's hand. And she had usually chatted a while, taken tea.

Lady Farnsworth turned a wide smile upon James as the Widow Leland ran back into her cottage as fast as her squat legs would take her, and all of his thoughts just flitted right out of his head.

That smile must have gotten Lady Farnsworth anything she wanted as a child, as a wife, as well. She had sweet little white teeth that made one want to explore them with one's tongue.

"Well, that was lovely," she said airily, and held out her arm for James to help her up. He cupped his fingers under her dainty elbow, took in a deep, lavender-scented breath of her, and helped her to her seat.

Perhaps part of her allure was the fact that she seemed a bit off kilter. One moment she acted nervous and flighty, the next she took charge like a flint-eyed admiral.

James boosted himself up to sit next to the mystifying Lady Farnsworth. He glanced at her, and realized that he really could not do that anymore. She was chewing at her bottom lip, and it nearly made him run them off the road. He was certainly not acting like himself.

Perhaps he had been drugged.

James closed his eyes for a moment, shook his head, and tried to regain his composure. He could remember waking up that very morning at the inn where he had slept, putting on his breeches and coat, staring at himself in the mirror. What had happened to that stalwart focused captain of only a few hours ago?

He had never in his life been so out of control of a situation. And he had led men into battle, for the love of God.


Poor, dear, Captain Ashley. Prudence glanced at the man over her teacup. She could feel the energy that exuded from him; it seemed to bounce off the walls. He was going mad with inactivity.

It was very bad of her to do this to him. "Do go on, Mrs. Redding," Pru urged the woman sitting across from her when that woman deigned to take a breath.

"Oh, of course, I intend to, Lady Farnsworth, for I was much horrified at the turn of events after Paul, the butcher's son, tried to cheat me out of a full quarter pound of lamb," and she was off again.

Poor Captain Ashley.

He shifted in his seat, his gaze roving the room. And then his gray eyes caught her watching him. For a moment, he just stared, like no one had ever stared at her before in her life. A tremor raced along her spine, and heat suffused her body as if the temperature in the room had just risen a good twenty degrees.

The reaction stunned her, and frightened her, for she had never felt anything like it before. She blinked just as Captain Ashley jerked his head so that they were no longer in each other's line of vision. Pru's teacup clanked against the saucer as she placed it quickly on the little table at her side.

This attraction business was rather a hard thing to get used to.

Captain Ashley stood suddenly, and she jumped. Leslie did not seem to notice, for her litany continued nonstop. Ah, Leslie Redding was good at this. The captain prowled the room, his presence so commanding it was hard to believe that Leslie did not even glance at him.

He stopped before a window, pulling aside the drapes with a large brown hand. She was sure that she had never noticed a man's hands before.

Captain Ashley's hands made her feel very light-headed, his *hands*, for goodness sake.

"Is that the Station House?" he asked suddenly, interrupting Leslie, and causing Pru to blink.

"Excuse me, Mrs. Redding," he said quickly. "I did not mean to interrupt. I was just wondering if that is the Station House, there"—he pointed with one of his long, masculine fingers—"on the cliff."

"Why, yes, yes it is," Leslie answered, her troubled gaze swerving to intercept Pru's.

"You ladies wouldn't mind, would you, if I walked over there?" He had already started for the door, so it didn't seem he was going to wait for their answer. "I will probably be back before you're finished, Lady Farnsworth." And he was gone.

Pru's shoulders slumped as she let out a long sigh.

"This is going to be dreadfully difficult," Leslie said, staring at the door through which the captain had just left.

"We will handle it."

"Well, of course, there is that." Leslie turned a worried look on Pru. "But I was actually referring to this, this . . . thing between the two of you."

Pru buried her face in her hands. "It is obvious, then?"

"Quite."

Pru looked at her friend through her fingers. "As you know, Leslie, I have never been in this situation before. And, God knows, I would much rather it happen with someone else. Is there a potion I could take? A remedy, perhaps?" If anyone knew of a potion or remedy for such a malady it would be Leslie Redding.

"Oh, if only there were." Leslie sighed, pushing back a strand of dull brown hair laced with gray that had fallen out of the coil at her neck. "I most certainly would have taken it long ago."

Pru went quickly to sit next to her friend. She draped an arm around Leslie's ample shoulders. "Well, at the very least, I must push this . . . thing with the captain from my thoughts. I really must keep my mind on business."

"And you can, Pru, I know you can. You are the strongest woman I have ever known." She turned and hugged Pru. Prudence loved to be the recipient of one of Leslie's embraces; the woman was soft and always smelled of baking bread.

"I am just a bit sad, though," Leslie said, "that you cannot act upon this attraction to the captain. He is very much attracted to you, dear. I could sense it in the air. And it would be so good for you to be loved."

Pru pushed away. "What a silly thing to say, really! I am loved."

Leslie smiled and winked. "Ah, but to be loved in the way the captain would love you is something every woman should experience."

"You mean . . ."

Leslie waggled her brows. "I mean that every woman should have a lover like the captain somewhere in her life."

Taking the captain as a lover, the very thought made Pru dizzy. "It will happen again," she said without much conviction, "with someone else." Of course, she had lived thirty-one years before it had happened at all.

"At least I know now what the attraction part feels like," Pru said with a bit more excitement. "Perhaps now that I've felt attraction, I will be able to feel it more easily with someone else?" Not a lot of conviction rang through that statement. Pru sighed.

Leslie shrugged, but there was not a lot of hope in her gaze.

"You can feel it for more than one person, that much I know, at least," Pru said urgently. "I mean, look at you . . ." She stopped mid-sentence, completely mortified with herself.

Leslie just smiled halfheartedly.

"Oh, dear, Leslie, I am sorry."

Leslie waved her hand. "Don't worry your pretty head over me. Patrick, my long-lost love, worshiped me enough to make up for my current heartache." She stood quickly. "And, anyway, we should not worry about such things now." She went to squint out the window. "You should go after him, Pru. The thought of him in the excise station gives me the willies."

"Oh, Pimpton and Lyle are probably at Harker's anyway. He will find an empty Station House and nothing more. But I shall take my leave and meet him there, anyway." Pru stood. "I am sorry, and do hope you don't take offense that I told the captain you were one of the poor. But, of course, we *have* no poor in Gravesly."

"Thanks to you."

"Oh really, Leslie, I hardly deserve . . ."

"Of course you do." She bustled forward and helped Pru on with her cloak. "But what of tonight? The captain could not have chosen a worse day for his arrival."

Pru stopped for a moment. "Yes, 'tis a smugglers' moon."

"The schooner is sure to come into harbor tonight."

Pru closed her eyes. "I guess I shall think of something."

"Wait!" Leslie Redding turned on her heel and ran into the kitchen, returning almost instantly. "Here." She thrust a jar of what looked like dust at Pru. "Put a pinch of this in his tea, and he'll sleep through till morning, I promise."

Pru stared at the jar. "Oh, goodness, you want me to drug him? What if I kill him?"

"A pinch'll do him, no more, and if you're careful, no harm will be done, Pru." Leslie shook her head. "I'm afraid it's necessary. If the boys don't

get that schooner unloaded tonight, it'll be bad
for us."

Pru took the jar from her friend. "Pray for us,"
she said as she walked out the door.

"Don't you go out with them, Pru, not tonight."

Pru just waved her hand and swung herself
into the wagon. She stowed the jar of sleeping
dust carefully beneath the seat since she had forgotten to bring her reticule, and slapped the reins
against her horse's back.

Her heart thumped against her ribs as if she
had just run at least a mile. She had always
dreamed of an exciting life. In those dull days
when she was living with her elderly parents, she
had always wondered what it would be like to be
a heroine in one of the novels she kept hidden beneath her mattress.

She surely had adventure now. But she suddenly wished for a dull, boring life as she set off
to drug the captain.

# Chapter 3

James squinted through the eyeglass at the horizon. He saw nothing, but that didn't mean there was nothing out there. A noise made him swing around, and there in the circle of the eyeglass were Lady Farnsworth's kissable lips. James blinked and lowered the implement.

Lady Farnsworth was riding up in front of the Station House. As James continued to watch her through the window, she pulled the horse to a stop and sat for a moment. Finally, with a visible sigh, Lady Farnsworth hooked the reins around the brake and jumped from the wagon.

James pushed the telescoping eyeglass together and set it on the table, took one last look at the deserted Station House, and went to meet Lady Farnsworth at the door. The last thing he needed now was to be alone with the woman in a room with two unmade beds at the ready.

He was through the door before Lady Farnsworth had even mounted the first step.

"Oh, Captain Ashley," she said quickly. "Are you finished here, then?"

He stared down at her for a moment. A crisp breeze rose from the ocean, tugging loose strands of the lady's golden hair. One bit settled just at the corner of her delectable mouth, and James had a most unwanted urge to reach out and smooth it away.

And then he would definitely wish to place his thumb where the errant strand of hair had been, perhaps even bend down and brush his lips against her skin. God, to move his mouth and actually kiss her would probably be a wondrous experience. He had never in his life seen a mouth more made for kissing, among other things.

"The officers are not in residence," he answered harshly, and descended the stairs, keeping his hand on the railing opposite the one against which Lady Farnsworth leaned. He hesitated for a moment, but then his gentlemanly breeding demanded that he offer his arm.

Lady Farnsworth blinked for a moment at his proffered elbow. James held his breath and very nearly winced when she finally laid her fingertips lightly on his sleeve, for he could feel her touch right down to his groin. For the love of God, when had he turned into such a randy goat?

He would give his fortune to have Lady Farnsworth turn into the doddering old widow he had thought she would be.

"The men would be at Harker's Inn most probably," Lady Farnsworth said, as he handed her into the cart.

"Ah," was all James could manage to say, as he had just seen a flash of leg. Her legs actually rivaled her mouth in beauty. As soon as possible, James extracted himself from all contact with Lady Farnsworth and walked as slowly as he could around the back of the wagon.

He chanted as he went: focus, focus, focus. And when he finally climbed up to sit next to Lady Farnsworth, he had begun to add numbers in his head. "I'll go to Harker's then. You may leave me there, Lady Farnsworth, I'm sure I can find my way ho . . . back to Chesley House."

Or, perhaps he would just sleep at Harker's. In fact, James decided, he really ought to make sure that he did not spend much time in Lady Farnsworth's company. He would keep late hours searching the beaches, and then sleep most of the day away at Harker's. He, of course, could not snub the lady's generosity, and would have to spend a few nights having supper with her, but he could certainly control his lust for a few hours at supper.

James kept his eyes forward as he slapped the reins against the gelding that pulled the cart. Except for the directions she gave him to the public house, Lady Farnsworth kept quiet as they jolted over the rutted road. Still, though they did not touch, James could actually feel the woman sitting beside him.

This was truly an awful predicament.

James had been attracted to women before, of course, but nothing like this. Holy Mother of God, all he could think about was ... James shook his head sharply. He would not even put that abstract idea into a clear thought. He started doing mental lists, fervently. If he were going on a voyage to France, what provisions would he need? That went a bit too quickly, so he began on a voyage to the Colonies.

They pulled up to Harker's Inn much too soon. Pru still hadn't decided on a plan. With every bounce in the road, she had held her breath, wondering if the sleeping potion beneath the seat would break, or, God forbid, roll out of the cart.

Captain Ashley jumped down and nearly threw the reins at her when they stopped. Should she leave? Perhaps she could return in her disguise? No, no, that would be folly. He was sure to recognize her. Her disguise was only meant to protect her in darkness and from a great distance.

Pru gripped the reins in her hand, then glanced up as the captain said something and turned to leave her. Dusk had fallen. No, she must do this now, here, quickly.

She urged Beauty around the side of Harker's, to the posting yard. Little Artie came scurrying up to her as she jumped from the cart. "Aya, Lady Pru, comin' in for a bit o'a nip?" He peered up at the darkening sky. "Not much time."

"Sh, Artie. There's a new man about." She fished the sleeping powder from beneath the seat.

"Ah, the one the Wolf gave the slip to?" Artie winked at her. "He'll be bustin' with hurt pride and all, now, wouldn't he?"

Pru rolled her eyes. She now wished that the Wolf hadn't been quite so eager to show up the great Captain Ashley on that cold night months before. "Just put Beauty up for me, Artie, and be careful with your words."

She could only pray that the whole town would be more careful. Their good fortune had caused some to forget now and then that they still had to be very careful. Pru held the jar against her waist and hurried up to Harker's. Her legs felt rubbery as she clattered over the cobblestone street.

And she knew now, most definitely, that it was not nervousness causing the strange reaction.

With a heavy sigh, Pru glanced toward the heavens. The clouds had gone very white against the darkening sky, and she could no longer see very far down the lane. It was getting late. She had to hurry.

To hide the jar of sleeping potion, Pru shifted it behind her when she entered the back of the busy pub. She saw Captain Ashley immediately. Through the hazy smoke, she could see the back of his dark head and wide shoulders.

Of course, his height and breadth were not the only reasons she found him so quickly. There was the . . . thing she had spoken of with Leslie. There was something about the man that just drew her attention, probably the same something that had her standing on legs that felt no stronger than a newborn colt's. She let herself stare at the man's wide back for a long, lovely moment, then straightened and forced her mind to concentrate on her objective to get the man foxed.

She sidled around the bar, shaking her head quickly when anyone looked as if they would call to her. Pru reached Josh Harker, finally, and caught his attention. "What's he drinking?" she asked.

Josh knew of whom she spoke without asking. "Havin' a pint with the officers."

"Put a pinch of this in with his next." She passed over the jar. "Just a bit, mind."

Josh held the jar up and peered through the glass. "What is it?"

Pru quickly pulled Josh's arm down. "It's sleeping potion from Leslie."

"Ah." The man nodded sagely. "Good idea, Lady Pru!"

Pru smiled, not a little proud. It had taken a while for the people to accept her in the baron's place. But they had, and it always felt good when they praised her. "Thank you, Josh." She grinned.

"Not to worry." Josh pushed the jar beneath the counter. "I'll make sure this bloke'll be goin' nowhere this eve." He cocked his head toward the back door. "Should probably be goin' now, Lady Pru. It's getting late."

Pru glanced once more at the captain. "Just a bit will do him, Josh," she said again. "Don't hurt him."

"Of course not, milady. Us here at Gravesly, we wouldn't hurt a fly."

Pru patted the hairy arm that protruded from the man's rolled-up sleeve. "And we're going to keep it that way," she said, and slipped out the back without ever being seen by the great captain.

"Josh Harker, you killed him!"

Harker looked up from cleaning glasses behind the bar, his face going ashen behind his dark whiskers. "He's dead, then?"

Pru shook her head quickly. "No, but he's not awake yet."

Harker glanced out the mullioned windows of the pub. It was past noon, the sun was already dipping toward the horizon. Pru sighed and climbed onto one of the stools between Paul, the butcher's son, and Mrs. Witherspoon.

"Afternoon, Lady Farnsworth," Mrs. Witherspoon said between sips of her ale. The woman was the oldest resident of Gravesly and made sure she stopped into Harker's every afternoon for her daily pint. "The good captain isn't farin' well, then?"

"No, Mrs. Witherspoon." Pru narrowed her gaze on Josh Harker. "How much of that sleeping potion did you give the man?"

"Well, seein' as the captain is such a big fella and all . . ."

"Oh, dear, Harker, I told you to give him just a pinch."

The pub owner rubbed his beard. "He's still breathin', though, right?"

Pru felt like groaning. The men had carried the captain home last night before going out to meet the schooner, and he had been snoring away ever since. She had waited for him to wake up all morning, and now she just couldn't contain her fear. "He hasn't moved, Harker. Leslie said that he should have wakened this morning."

"Well, he had a couple pints with the stuff, maybe he'll come to later this evening."

"I hope so. We'll have to figure out some other way to deal with the captain, because I absolutely

refuse to use that potion ever again, on anybody."
Pru held out her hand. "Give it over, Harker, I'm
going to bury it somewhere."

Harker disappeared for a moment beneath the
bar, then straightened and, with a sheepish expression, handed over the jar. "I'm right sorry,
Lady Pru."

Prudence took the potion and shoved it in her
reticule. "It isn't your fault, Harker. I'm the one
who decided to use the stuff. Now, I just want
everyone to start praying that the captain wakes
up soon and is no worse for wear."

"Yes, ma'am," Paul muttered.

"Of course, Lady Farnsworth," Mrs. Witherspoon said. The old lady slapped a sixpence on
the polished wood of the bar. "Good day to you
all." She slid off her stool and hobbled toward the
door.

With Mrs. Witherspoon knowing, Pru could be
assured that the entire town would be praying for
the captain before the hour was up.

"We've got the last payment just in, Lady Pru,"
Harker said.

"Good." Prudence sat up straight and took the
packet Harker handed to her. "Call a meeting
tonight in the cellar and we'll distribute the mon-
eys. Then we'll get that shipment of whiskey we
brought in last night ready to go out on the road."

"And if the captain wakes up before then?"

Pru grimaced. "I'm sure he'll not be up to going out tonight at any rate."

Paul was tallying figures as she and Harker spoke, and he pushed a piece of paper toward her. "Here's the total weights, Lady Pru, and all the shipments sent to London in the month."

"Thank you, Paul. I'll go count the money and make sure our London backer isn't cheating us like he's tried to do so many times before."

Harker shook his head. "Tightfisted bastard." He glanced up and reddened. "Excuse me, Lady Pru."

Prudence shrugged. "It's true. The man takes 60 percent of our profit as it is; you would think that would be enough for him."

Paul took a long pull of his pint and tapped the glass against the bar. "Do you think we could ever figure out who he is?" he asked.

"And what?" Harker returned to his job of cleaning glasses. "Kill him?"

Pru frowned. "Don't even speak of such a thing in jest, Harker. You know I don't like that sort of talk."

"Sorry. You know, Paul, the man's most probably some society fop. Could even be a peer, no offense Lady Pru."

Prudence nodded.

"He's way beyond our influence."

Prudence fingered the money pouch in her

hands. There was a contract signed by her husband and the mysterious Mr. Watson of London in her study at Chesley House. She had read it over and over again, amazed, actually, that her husband had ever entered into such a commitment. Mr. Watson had put up all the funding to start her husband's smuggling venture and was to receive 60 percent of all profits, forever. That seemed quite unfair to Pru. On top of it all was the fact that the man controlled the money completely.

Mr. Watson took control of everything after their goods went into London. He never sent her receipts on how much he was getting for the goods, only a packet of money and an assurance that it was 40 percent of their profit. Prudence tried to figure on what they should be getting with the tallies Paul gave her, and it did seem as if they should receive more. But there was absolutely no way that she could be sure.

Of course, they did have complete control over the goods that Gravesly put *on* the schooner. They sent out wool seasonally, without sending it through customs, and received the money directly from the French captain of the schooner.

Still, Pru always made sure that she carefully showed exactly how much went out and how much they received and sent 60 percent of that to Mr. Watson.

It was rather telling, she thought, that the town made much more on their outgoing products then on their incoming ones. She sighed and tucked the packet of money under her arm.

"Well I'll see you here later, then, and bring news of the captain."

"Sure hope the man wakes up," Harker muttered as he shined up a glass with his rag.

Prudence said another prayer to that effect as she left the pub and waited for Artie to hitch up Beauty for her. She had been praying, actually, since she had gotten home that morning. The sun had just been coming up, the day promising to be bright and lovely. She had been quite proud of herself, really, for pulling such a coup with the great Captain Ashley in their very town.

And then Mabel had informed her that the Captain had not even stirred, and she had begun to worry.

Now Pru took up the reins of her cart, said a hasty good-bye to Artie, and pushed Beauty into a smart trot. She had worried herself into a small fit, really. Her heart seemed to be working rather more rapidly than it should, and she could not keep her hands from shaking.

She had called in the doctor that afternoon, and he had just shrugged and said that the captain was sleeping.

Pru had heard of people going to sleep and never waking up. They hadn't died, their hearts kept beating, but they just never opened their eyes again.

Of course she did not want the captain to be in Gravesly, he was quite a hindrance to their work. But she certainly didn't want the man to sleep away the rest of his life.

The thought of those soft gray eyes never opening again, the dimples never deepening his cheeks made Pru inconceivably sad.

She pulled into the graveled circle before Chesley House and jumped from the cart before Beauty had even come to a complete halt.

"Still asleep," Tuck said without her even having to ask.

She groaned and took the stairs to the front door two at a time. Clifton was in the hall looking for all the world like the scariest pirate ever to wield a cutlass.

"Don't you keep worrying about him, Lady Pru," he said, as she dumped the money packet and sleeping potion into his large hands.

"Of course I'm going to worry, Clifton, don't be absurd." She stripped off her gloves and threw them on the side table. One of them slithered right over the shiny surface and plopped onto the floor.

"Damned things," she muttered, and bent to retrieve it.

"I've got it, Lady Pru," Mabel assured her, bustling in.

"Thank you, Mabel." Pru yanked at the ties

that held her cape around her. "Has he moved at all? Has he moaned, anything?"

Mabel glanced quickly at Clifton, but her butler just frowned darkly.

"What, what has happened?"

"He's been groaning a bit," Clifton said. "But you don't need to think about it at all, Lady Pru. We can take care of the captain. Looks like you've got some work to do." He held up the money.

"I'll just go check on the captain. I'll be down in a moment." Pru draped her cape over Mabel's arm and ignored Clifton's protests.

"It isn't seemly, I say," her butler grumbled.

"And when did I begin to be seemly, hmm, Clifton?" She gave the man a large smile and ran up the stairs. The hall upstairs was eerily quiet, the shadows long in the pretwilight. Prudence automatically slowed her steps and tiptoed to the captain's door.

"Captain?" she called quietly. She held her breath, hoping, but no sound came from the other side. Pru turned the handle and pushed the door open slowly. It was dark in the room, the shade still pulled. She blinked, becoming more accustomed to the darkness before entering.

Prudence took a chair from the corner and placed it carefully beside the captain's bedside, then sat and stared at the man.

Clifton had changed him the night before into a

nightshirt; his uniform had been laundered and hung in the clothespress. He was tucked nicely into the small bed, though his feet did stick out a good half a foot. Pru glanced wryly down toward the bottom of the bed, where the captain's toes made a tent of the covers.

She remembered the look on the captain's face when he had first seen this room. She had realized immediately that the small bed would not be at all comfortable for him. But what was she to do? There was a larger bed, of course, her husband's. Clifton had nearly burst a vein when she had suggested putting him there last night.

Pru sighed. She could remember going to her husband on the nights he had asked her to. He had been a small man. Of course, she wasn't huge, so it had never mattered. He had been a few inches taller than she, perhaps two, and portly, his hair just a ring of white going from one ear to the other.

She had loved him dearly, of course, and had gone to him whenever he asked. She would enter the room, extinguish the candles, and climb into the huge bed, where her husband made a short round lump under the covers. And then she would lie back as he pulled up her nightgown and got on top of her.

He would kiss her when it was over, always, and tell her, "thank you." And then she would sleep with him. She liked to sleep with him, and had missed that part of it since he died.

With a shake of her head, Pru dismissed her reminiscences. A lock of the captain's hair had fallen over his forehead, and Pru leaned over automatically to push it back. She stopped, though, when her fingers touched his skin. He was warm. She pushed the hair back and put her hand against his cheek.

His beard had begun to grow; it bristled against her fingers. She rather liked the feeling. She trailed her fingers down over the captain's jaw to his neck, then farther. Just above the neck of his shirt a tuft of hair peeked out. Pru let her fingers linger there for a moment, wondering if his chest would be covered with the dark springy hair.

She took a deep, quavering breath, and forced herself to pull her hand away from the captain, linking her fingers and placing them in her lap. She watched him sleep quietly, his chest moving slowly up and down.

Her legs were trembling.

Strange.

And her own chest was heaving as if she had just run along the beach. And suddenly she thought of what it would be like to have Captain James Ashley in the room that connected to her own. To walk into that room in her nightgown and see this large, dark-haired man in the big bed.

She didn't think she would want to put out the candles, and she certainly didn't think that she would delay getting into bed next to him. And she rather thought that his hands would never fumble with her nightgown or that his kisses would be slobbery.

Pru heard herself moan softly as she stared at the captain's hand against the coverlet on the bed. His hands were very lovely, and she closed her eyes for a moment and pictured them, his fingers strong and tanned, skimming up the white softness of her stomach.

She felt a strange quiver low in her belly and opened her eyes quickly. Pru shook her head and stood.

This would just not do. She could not sit beside the bed of a man who might be dying for all she knew, thinking salacious thoughts.

And she certainly should not be thinking such thoughts about a man who was her enemy. It would be no good for her if she allowed herself to have any soft feelings for Captain Ashley.

She really had to leave the room. She really must not spend another moment looking at his dark hair against the pillow, or the curve of his lips, or the hard edge of his jaw.

But she couldn't quite force herself to leave. For another long moment, Prudence stood at the captain's bedside looking down at the thick fan his dark lashes made against his cheekbones.

Then with a quick glance at the open doorway, she leaned over and pressed a kiss to his lips.

She pulled away quickly, of course, not wanting anyone to see, or the man to wake up while she took liberties with him.

Really, if she weren't headed for hell already, she certainly would be now.

But, goodness, that small touch had been lovely. It had lasted a scant second and, really, she had barely pressed her lips against his at all. But, oh, Pru sighed and lifted her fingers to her mouth. It would be awfully nice to do such a thing when he was awake.

# Chapter 4

J ames was having terrible dreams. There were a bunch of men, obviously peers, standing above him, laughing as he lay prone, unable to move. "You've proven yourself the bastard that you are, Captain Ashley," one of the men spit at him. And then a large man in the back of the crowd began to laugh, and the awful sound went on for what seemed forever, each great bellow like a fist against his head.

He wanted to stand, straighten his red jacket, tip his hat at its haughty angle, and glare at the men down his aristocratic nose, but he could not move at all. The agony made him groan, everything he had spent his life obtaining was crumbling in that very moment.

England's peers were seeing him brought low. The Ashley name was trampled yet again.

66

And then a cool hand against his forehead and there, hovering above him, an angel. 'Twas no pure, heavenly angel, though, but an angel with a mouth that made him instantly hard. He reached up, and brought her toward him, and she came. Their mouths met in a tangle of heat and wanting, and he rolled her beneath him, and was inside of her instantly.

Her legs went around him, he could feel her feet against his buttocks, her breasts against his chest, her hair and soft breezy scent surrounding them like a cloud. And they were naked, and he was thrusting deliciously into her, and it was perfect. His climax was thunderous. He sighed heavily, his entire being relaxed.

And then the man's voice, "You have the same carnal soul as your slut of a mother." James's body went stiff. He opened his eyes, tried to stand, but, again, could not move. And now he lay naked before the eyes of men he did not know. He knew, though, in his heart, that his father stood in the crowd. But, since he had no idea what the man looked like, or even his name, he could not pick him out.

The roiling emotions went on and on, dragging James through crashing pain and pulling him up to the heights of ecstasy. He knew that if it didn't end soon, he would die, or at least he would wish to.

And then he opened his eyes and realized that

he was finally in a real place, and that it had all been in his dreams. James blinked up at the ceiling of a very normal room. His head ached like he had downed a whole barrel of ale. He wanted to rub his temples, and for a moment, he was afraid that he wouldn't be able to control his own limbs. But the dream was truly over, for when he willed his arm to move, it moved.

He sighed heavily, covering his eyes with his hand.

"James?"

He stiffened, but then relaxed, for it was not the voice of the treacherous crowd of peers, but the light, feminine voice of Lady Farnsworth.

James parted his fingers and peeked out to see the woman hovering over him. Her hair hung down about her shoulders, and she wore a dressing gown. Truly, she made him think of a mermaid. Her hair was naturally wavy and long, hanging about her like a rippling gold curtain. Her nightgown was buttoned right up to her chin, but it was of a soft blue color, and she obviously wore nothing underneath, for the lush globes of her breasts bounced against the fabric when she moved.

And she had called him James.

Dear God, had they . . . ? James tried to sit up, but this time his limbs did not follow instructions, and he just flopped a bit on the bed. His head felt as if someone were banging it with a mallet. "Stop the pounding," he heard himself say.

Her hand went against his forehead, and it was cool just as in the dream. Or had it been a dream?

"Oh, dear James, I am so very sorry," she said earnestly.

What? Oh, dearest Lord, it hadn't been a dream. He lay very still, letting her hand soothe some of the pain.

"Does your head hurt?" she asked, and he could only groan in answer.

"I shall get a compress." She stood, her lovely, cool hand leaving his forehead. "And tea, I shall have Cook make tea." And she was gone.

James managed to open his eyes again. He was in his room at Chesley House, his feet hanging over the end of the little bed. James smoothed his hand down his chest and realized that he wore a nightshirt, not his, for he usually wore nothing to bed. He closed his eyes again and tried to remember how he had gotten to this point.

Surely he had been hit in the head or even shot at point-blank range? James winced as the hammer banged away at his brain.

The door opened, and, without looking around, he knew it was Prudence Farnsworth. She pulled a chair up to his bedside, the scratch of the legs against the wood floor reverberating in his head like thunder. "I just . . . well, I never . . ."

the woman said, and then stopped as she laid a wet cloth over his forehead. She held it there with a gentle hand and peered into his eyes.

"Are you all right?" she asked finally.

Now there was a good question. James thought for a moment. "What happened to me?"

Lady Farnsworth blinked and took a deep breath, then she looked away. "Well, um . . ."

"The last thing I think I remember is having dinner with the other officers." James stopped suddenly. "Was I hurt? Was I shot?" He went to sit up, but Lady Farnsworth murmured softly as if to a child and held him down.

"No, Captain, you weren't shot. Now, calm down and lie still." She turned the cloth so that the cool side was against his head. "But you've been sleeping like the dead for two days."

"Two days!" James sat up, the cloth slipping from his forehead and hitting the bed with a wet *plop*. The room spun about him, and he closed his eyes, keeping himself balanced with his hands against the mattress. "What the devil is going on?"

"When the officers brought you home, I thought you had imbibed. But then, well . . . my goodness, you slept and slept, and groaned and made noises, and I thought you had been possessed!"

James opened his eyes. Lady Farnsworth swallowed audibly. "I was very worried. The doctor said you seemed fine, that you were just sleeping."

Wonderful, the doctor had been called. Now

the entire town of Gravesly knew that Captain James Ashley had been torn asunder by a couple of pints of ale. James sighed deeply, then blinked at Lady Farnsworth. "Two days, you say?"

She nodded. "Two days."

There was no way that he had gotten drunk enough to sleep for two days. He could remember drinking two pints, only two pints! Of course, someone easily could have put something into one of those pints.

"The Wolf!" James cried and stood. He swayed, and the room turned black for a moment, but he felt Lady Farnsworth slip an arm around his waist.

"Captain, you really ought to get back in bed."

"By God, the man has humiliated me yet again." It wasn't until he heard the words that James realized he had said the last aloud. He frowned and closed his eyes as Lady Farnsworth helped him sit on the bed once more. She sat next to him, her arm still around his waist and her hair brushing his shoulder.

He opened his eyes again, noting the darkness of the room, the candle at his bedside. It was night. Had he truly slept through two entire days? Easing from Lady Farnsworth's embrace, James stood again, only this time he did the deed slowly.

Lady Farnsworth folded her hands in her lap

and scooted away from him self-consciously.
There was a tap at the door, and she bolted for it
as if shot from a cannon.

Clifton stood at the door, a tray in his beefy
grip. "So, he's up." The man glared at James as if
he wished him dead. "Now you can go to your
own room, Lady Pru. I can take care of the captain right enough."

Clifton's tone made it sound like his offer to
"take care of the captain" meant throwing James
right out the window.

"I don't approve of you in his room at night,
Lady Pru, especially with both of you dressed for
bed." The big man dropped the tray onto the little
table by James's bed. The dainty cup rattled
against its saucer, and the teapot shimmied dangerously.

Lady Farnsworth gave her butler a scathing
look. "That will be all, Clifton," she said determinedly.

"Oh, no, it will not," the man shot back.

James put a hand against his forehead and
groaned.

Lady Farnsworth was at his side in a second.
He smelled her first, that tantalizing, heady scent,
then felt her strong arm around his waist.

She was awfully strong. He looked down at her
for a moment. She was not an overly tall woman,
and she certainly wasn't a large woman. James
placed his hand carefully on Lady Farnsworth's

shoulder as she helped him to the bed. He could feel her arm beneath his fingers, and it was like touching a steel pole. The woman was very strong indeed.

Smoke was surely going to start pouring from Clifton's ears if the man kept glaring so, but James could not have cared less. He didn't even care that he had to let a woman help him toddle over to the bed. He knew when to accept help, and this was certainly one of those times. He had been brought low once again. This time, unfortunately, there were physical side effects.

He would have to take care of himself and get his strength back, for Captain James Ashley was not going to be humiliated by the Wolf again.

Pru helped James into bed, plumping some pillows behind his head so that he could sit up. Then she pulled the bedcovers up to his chin, shot Clifton a pointed look, and bent over the tea tray to pour. "I shall retire as soon as I have the captain settled, Clifton," she said. "There is no need for you to stay."

"There is no need for *you* to stay, Lady Pru."

Pru huffed an exasperated breath and shoved the teacup into James's hand. "I am not about to tear off my clothes and jump into bed with the man, Clifton!"

There was a choking sound from the bed, and then tea spewed out all over Pru's nightgown.

She blinked down at herself, and then over at James.

"Excuse me," he said with as much dignity as he could obviously muster.

Pru wiped the worst of the tea away with her hands and turned a glare upon her butler.

Clifton gritted his teeth for a moment, then left without another word. A blessing, that.

Sighing deeply, Pru tilted her chin in the air and sat primly on the edge of the chair beside James's bedside. Sometime during the last two dreadful days, the captain had become James in her thoughts. She had believed that she had killed him, and she had sat alternately praying and cursing the man to get well. When one prays at another's bedside, not to mention the small indiscretion of a stolen kiss, formality wanes quickly.

Pru folded her hands together tightly on her lap and leaned forward toward the man in her guest bed. "How do you feel?" she asked earnestly.

James had recovered from the choking episode, it seemed. He swallowed a gulp of tea and placed the cup squarely back on its saucer. "Better," he answered shortly.

Pru searched his face for a moment, not sure of what she looked for, but dreadfully scared the man was going to go to sleep again and never wake up. "I did think you were going to die," she said then.

James rubbed at his temples and made a soft sound of pain. "At the moment, I have to believe death would be a rather nice thing to happen."

"Oh dear." She pulled her chair closer and put her own hands to James's temples. He stiffened for a moment, but then as she pressed her fingers rhythmically against the sides of his head, James relaxed slowly. "I am so terribly sorry," she found herself saying.

" 'Tis not your fault."

Pru bit on the edge of her tongue. It most definitely was her fault, though Josh Harker had a bit of the blame as well.

"Still, I do feel terrible for what you have gone through, Ja . . . Captain." She let her fingers wander into his wavy, dark hair. He had truly lovely hair. Pru had been combing her fingers through the thick softness of it this last night wondering at its steely blackness.

He let out a low moan that made Pru jump, her hands stilling as James blinked up at her. He looked just as surprised as she felt.

"Sorry," he said, his voice sounding a bit hoarse.

He looked very much like a schoolboy caught stealing a tart, and Pru laughed nervously as she straightened and put her entwined hands back in her lap. She glanced down at James, hoping that he had closed his eyes again, but those gray orbs were staring at her, into her.

Pru tried to look away as nonchalantly as possible. The attraction between them had become almost palpable in the last few moments. It was as if the very air between them trembled and waved like the flame of a candle. It was magnetic, hypnotic and, at the same time, thrilling and very, very hot.

"I should get a room at Harker's Inn," he said suddenly.

"Of course you should not. Whyever would you need to do such a thing?"

He said nothing, just stared at her, his eyes dark, nearly black, really. Pru glanced nervously at her lap, smoothing away a nonexistent wrinkle.

And then his hand was at the back of her head, pulling her toward him. Knocked off-balance, Pru fell against the hard planes of James's chest. He locked his arms about her and kissed her.

The candle flame Pru had thought of earlier turned into a raging inferno within seconds, and with a funny-sounding moan, Pru closed her eyes and just gave in to this new experience.

It was truly lovely, and so much more exciting than the dry kiss she had pressed to his sleeping lips.

Captain James tasted of darkly steeped tea, and his mouth was incredibly soft against her own. And then his tongue swept out, tracing the seal of her lips. She opened on a shocked intake of breath, and he entered her.

Her dearest husband had never kissed her thus. Even the small kiss he had pressed to her mouth after lovemaking had always seemed rather chaste. Everything from those moments with her husband had always left Pru feeling like she had missed out on something important.

But now, suddenly, with this man, kissing had become Pru's favorite activity in the world. Tentatively, Prudence touched her own tongue to James's as she placed one of her hands against his thinly covered chest. She allowed herself to seek out that small tuft of hair at his neck and twine her fingers in it.

"Mmm," she heard herself moan.

Prudence pressed her upper body against James, enjoying the feeling of her softness against his strong chest. Pru had a sudden consuming need to strip away James's nightshirt and see him. She moved back slightly, and his arms unlocked from around her. She felt him grip her shoulders and knew that he was going to push her away.

Oh, she did not want to be pushed away.

She sighed as their mouths parted and looked ruefully into James's beautiful eyes. "That was so very nice," she said on a sigh.

James just groaned. "No it was not, Lady Farnsworth. That was carnal and wrong. And that is why I must go stay at Harker's Inn."

She ignored the last part of his statement, curling her fingers into his nightshirt. "Carnal, yes, but wrong?" she asked. "How can something so wonderful be wrong?"

"You are too truthful for your own good, Lady Farnsworth."

She pushed away from the delectable Captain James Ashley and laughed deeply.

When she stopped, James was looking at her darkly. "How can a widow be so innocent?"

"Oh, Captain Ashley, I am far from innocent."

"But you cannot see attraction for what it is. You cannot see what folly it would be to allow ourselves to continue on in such proximity."

Pru's amusement fled. Oh yes, she could see. More than James would ever understand, she could see. "We are adults, Captain Ashley. Surely we can control ourselves." Even as she said the words, Pru could not stop from staring at James's wet lips.

"Or perhaps," she said, feeling like someone had put her in a trance, "we should just act on the attraction? Put it behind us, so to speak?" She looked up into his eyes, to see that he stared at her as if at a changeling.

"Truly, Lady Farnsworth, you speak your mind." He closed his eyes, shook his head, then winced. "But your idea just shows your inno-cence more completely. Acting would not put anything behind us, but rather make it ever so much a part of our present."

Pru was listening, barely. With his eyes closed, James was at her mercy. She could look at him all she wanted, and she definitely looked. At the moment she was marveling at the space between his collarbones. It pulsed with each beat of his heart, and she wanted to place her lips there. She wanted that with an intensity that stunned her.

He opened his eyes, and their gazes locked. James Ashley had the longest, darkest lashes of any man she had ever seen. And the way he looked at her with his storm gray eyes made her very sure that taking him as a lover would never leave her feeling as if she were missing something important.

"James," she began, but he stopped her with a small shake of his head.

"You call me James and sit beside my bed nearly naked."

Pru frowned and glanced down at the nightgown she wore. It covered every inch of her skin, more than any gown she owned.

"This is never going to work, Lady Farnsworth. I have a job to do here, and I must concentrate on that task. I must insist that I leave your home in the morning."

Prudence sighed. "Captain, you have been through quite a harrowing experience, and I must insist that you stay under my care until I am sure you are well again."

They stared at each other in stubborn silence.

Pru chewed at her bottom lip for a moment, then licked at it when she realized that she could taste the captain on her mouth.

James closed his eyes on a groan.

"Does your head still pound, Captain?" she asked worriedly.

"Among other things," James muttered.

She pressed her hand against his forehead, but he stiffened. "You must leave," he said through his teeth.

Prudence let her fingers linger in the captain's hair for just a moment of pure bliss before returning her hands to her lap. "Do you wish for anything else before I leave, Captain? More tea, perhaps? Another compress?"

"No." He still did not open his eyes.

Prudence stood with a sigh. "There is really no reason you must go to Harker's, Captain. We are both adults, we . . ."

"Good night, Lady Farnsworth."

She did not want to go. She would rather sit all night in the hard-backed chair watching Captain Ashley sleep than crawl back into her empty bed. "Good night, Captain," she said finally, and snuffed out the candle.

# Chapter 5

❧❧❧

**"N**ew plan," Pru announced quietly the next morning, as Clifton sat in the kitchen cradling his coffee.

He glanced up at her and frowned. "New plan? But this one is working very well, indeed." The butler chuckled. "I think we should just keep the man drugged for a while until he gets spooked and leaves."

Pru shivered. "No. I shall never use another potion on another human. I have just spent two days very sure that I had killed him."

"So what is your new plan?"

"Since he is convinced that he must remove himself to Harker's Inn, we shall allow the captain to go there. We'll have to keep him here for another night at least while we move the wool from Harker's cellar to our barn, but as soon as

81

that is done, we can let the good captain go and stay at the inn."

"Excellent plan," Clifton said, and took a long drink of coffee.

"And I shall take him as my lover."

Coffee spewed out in all directions as Clifton coughed and sputtered.

"I thought this all over very carefully last night," Pru said quickly before Clifton could begin thundering. "It is a lovely plan."

"It is the most ridiculous thing I've ever heard!" Clifton thundered.

"There is an obvious attraction between the captain and me. You have commented on it yourself, Clifton. And Leslie has noticed it as well . . ."

"So this is all *that* woman's idea. I should have known!"

Pru shot a dark look at her butler. "Oh, really, Clifton, don't be rude. It was my idea entirely. Now," she said quickly to keep Clifton from running off on the unhappy tangent of Leslie Redding.

"I will act upon this, this . . . thing between the captain and me." Pru smiled brightly and twirled about. "I will put myself up as a distraction! I do think it is a brilliant plan."

"It is beyond stupid."

"Oh, come, Clifton, distraction from the main activity always works."

Clifton's cheeks were the color of ripe apples.

"This is preposterous! I will not sacrifice your virtue for a distraction!"

"Poppycock," Cook said quietly.

Pru and Clifton turned as one to stare at Delilah.

The old, grizzled woman looked up from the dough she had been pounding. "Lady Pru's a widow, last time I checked. And in my book widowhood means a woman's hard-won freedom." Delilah punctuated this statement with a vigorous nod of her head.

"That is blasphemy," yelled Clifton.

"Blasphemy, Mr. Eurel Clifton Rhodes, is how young bucks can go about hopping into bed with anything that pleases their eye and women have to wait for some old doddering fool to marry them. There's not a woman in this town that would begrudge Lady Pru's indulgence with a man like that beautiful captain, and there's not a man in this town that won't be happy for her distractin' him."

*Bang!* She thudded her fist into the floury dough on the counter and continued her work without looking up again.

Clifton stood with his mouth gaping.

"Of course, Lady Pru, there's also not a person in this town that'll admit to what they truly feel. So you keep it discreet, and you can go on and do anything you wish."

"Well, then, that's settled." Pru smiled. "And here comes Leslie now, such perfect timing."

Clifton turned to look through the glass panes of the back kitchen door. " 'Tis a god-awful mess, is what it is," he grumbled, and hurried for the hallway before he had to greet Leslie Redding. "Don't you go doing anything foolish until we've talked this over!" And he slammed the door behind him.

"I guess Eurel saw me coming?" Leslie said as she let herself in the back door.

Pru just rolled her eyes. "A more stubborn creature does not inhabit the earth."

"Actually, I can think of someone." She laughed and took over Clifton's stool. "How is the captain this morning? Any signs of life?"

"I'd say," Delilah said with a chuckle.

Pru felt her face heat.

"What happened?" Leslie asked.

"I am going to distract the captain from his hunt for the Wolf," Pru said quickly before Delilah could answer.

"Really?" Leslie looked from Pru to the cook and then back to Pru. "Would this distraction have anything to do with the thing we talked about the other day?"

Prudence bit her lip.

"Ah, well, that will distract him sure enough." She tapped her finger lightly on the table a moment. "It could be dangerous, though, Pru."

She laughed. "Dangerous I can handle."

"No, Pru, I'm not just talking about physically dangerous, though there is that. I am worried for your heart."

"Well, then, I shall keep my heart out of the experience," Pru said decisively.

Delilah and Leslie gave each other the, "Oh, we know so much more than she does," look. Pru sighed. "I really am not a child, though you two sometimes act as if I am. I can take care of myself. In fact, I can take care of this entire town. Have I not proven this?"

"Of course, Prudence, it's just that . . ." Leslie stopped and touched the back of Pru's hand with her weathered fingers. "I know how it feels, that excitement and thrill of a man you find attractive, especially the first. But it is hard for a woman to keep her emotions out of the experience, and it can cause much pain."

Pru nodded and turned her palm up to clasp Leslie's hand.

"And this is a dangerous man, as much as you wish to make light of that fact."

"I do not make light of it, Leslie. If I didn't think it would be best for all, I would not propose this plan."

Tuck stuck his head through the back door. "Thought you'd want to know that the captain is standing out front, bag in hand, waiting for me to bring his horse 'round."

Prudence frowned. "Well, this will never do. I need him to stay for at least one more night."

"He can't feel much better. You should insist on taking him to the doctor up in Brighton," Leslie suggested.

"That'll take you today and tomorrow at least," Delilah pointed out. "The boys can move the stuff from Harker's while you're gone."

"And I can start in on my new plan," Pru said, jumping up from her chair.

"What plan is that?" Tuck asked.

"None of your business," all three women said at once.

Tuck shrugged amiably. "So you want me to hitch up the carriage then, Lady Farnsworth. Might take a while; haven't used it in a year. It'll need a good airing out."

"Thank you, Tuck," Pru said. "I'm going to go change into my traveling clothes. Leslie, can you find Mabel and ask her to pack me a small bag?"

"You ought to take someone with you, Lady Pru," Delilah cautioned as she placed a cloth over her dough while she left it to rise. "It's not right you two going off alone like that."

"Isn't that the point?"

"Pru, you do need to keep up appearances, dear," Leslie said. "We understand, and most everyone else will as well, but they won't if you flaunt it in their faces."

Prudence tsked and rolled her eyes. "Well, then Leslie, why don't you accompany us?"

She smiled. "I would love to, dear, especially because I am rather sure that there is no way you are going to get out of this town without Clifton going along, and you will definitely need me to keep him out of your way if that is the case."

With a shake of her head, Prudence laughed. "All right then, off we go. Hopefully I shall be able to outwit Clifton and crumble the captain's defenses while the boys move our wool out of Harker's cellar. This shall be an interesting night in Brighton, I daresay."

The woman had turned into a general again, and now he sat in a very badly sprung carriage sharing a torn leather seat with Lady Farnsworth and staring into the one good eye of the biggest butler in England.

Leslie Redding sneezed, and, if possible, Clifton's scowl deepened.

"I'm terribly sorry," the older woman said, her words muffled. "I can't stop sneezing."

She had said the same thing after every single sneeze in the last hour. And there had been many.

Lady Farnsworth leaned over and placed a gloved hand on her friend's knee. "I'm sorry, Leslie. This old carriage is so musty. Do you think you ought to ride outside?"

Mrs. Redding's face brightened considerably. "That is a lovely idea, Lady Pru. It is warm enough, I'm sure."

Lady Farnsworth knocked on the roof with the handle of her parasol, and the carriage slowed, bouncing horribly. James barely contained the need to hold his head still with both hands. He felt, truly, like he had awakened to a nightmare.

There were surely small men inside his brain with pickaxes intent upon rendering him absolutely senseless. And, obviously, they had done their job well, for here he sat in a carriage getting farther and farther from Gravesly and, more importantly, the Wolf, with every jolting movement.

When Lady Farnsworth had come charging out the front door of Chesley House insisting he go to Brighton with her, it had felt like an attack of French proportions. And since his senses were addled, he had found himself in a coach bound for Brighton within ten minutes of the attack. Adding to that humiliation, James could have sworn he had politely refused Lady Farnsworth at least a dozen times.

He really needed to be less polite with Lady Farnsworth, or he would never get his job done.

The carriage came to a halt, finally, and James opened the door and jumped to the ground without waiting for Tuck to pull down the stairs. He helped both the women alight, then stepped out of the way and just took in great gulps of fresh air.

They would be away from Gravesly for two whole days at least, add to that the two days he had been incapacitated, the day he had spent handing baskets out to the poor, and he had nearly a week on his new assignment with not a thing to show for it. Or rather, he had himself been brought low to show for it.

Loud voices brought James's attention back to the people assembled at the side of the warm, dusty road.

"Clifton, just do as Leslie wishes, and be done with it, man," Lady Farnsworth was saying with a shake of her head.

The butler looked as if he were about to tear the woman's head right off her pretty little neck. He had never seen a servant level a more insolent stare at his employer. "Right, then, fine," the man shouted, and a couple of grouse took flight from the field in front of them. "But I don't like this one bit."

"Clifton Rhodes, is there anything that you do like?" Leslie Redding said as she went to the front of the carriage. Clifton followed her, grumbling, of course, then stood like a big dumb ox as the older woman obviously waited for assistance to mount the stairs to the top of the carriage.

James kept a sigh behind his teeth as he stepped forward, but he stopped abruptly at the glare from Clifton. The butler then took Mrs. Redding's arm in a rather painful-looking grip and nearly threw the woman up to her seat. The man followed her up as he muttered, of course, under his breath.

With a frown, James glanced around and realized that Lady Farnsworth had already taken her seat back in the carriage and Tuck stood waiting for him to enter as well.

He stood staring at the dark opening of the carriage as if someone had just asked him to walk the plank. Good God, he was now going to be alone with Lady Farnsworth in that small carriage for a good hour at least. Perhaps two if Mrs. Redding could stay atop the carriage that long.

James had a small hope that Tuck would follow him up the stairs, but of course the boy merrily folded them back up and closed the door. A bounce at the back told James the footman had jumped on the tiger's stand behind the carriage.

Keeping his gaze from Lady Farnsworth, James sat across from her and tried to find a place for his legs. The carriage started off with a jerk that made James groan out loud.

"Does your head pain you terribly, Captain?" she asked.

"It is fine, really, Lady Farnsworth. I really do not see why we have to go all the way into Brighton for the doctor."

"I insist, Captain. It was horribly worrying when you slept so long. What if something is terribly wrong? What if you suffer a relapse?"

James had heard it all at Chesley House, of course, and berated himself now for even starting up the argument once more. The woman had her mind set on taking him to the doctor. So he would go, and return as quickly as possible.

He hadn't expected to have to endure a cramped, jolting carriage ride with Mrs. Redding, Lady Farnsworth, and—worst of all—Clifton. But now that he was alone in the carriage with Lady Farnsworth, he even wished Clifton back.

"Would you like me to rub your temples for you, Captain?"

That sounded incredibly wonderful, actually, but he would not allow any more close contact with Lady Farnsworth. His body was obviously not going to help him stay away from her, so he must put his mind to it. "Thank you, no, my lady." He folded his arms, slouched down against the squabs, and, leaning his head back, closed his eyes.

He had thought that closing his eyes would effectively cut out the picture of Lady Farnsworth looking more than lovely in a chocolate brown traveling dress. He had already noticed how the dress fit rather snugly across her bosom and tapered just enough to show her slimness. And, of course, the color brought out her eyes and contrasted perfectly with the golden color of her hair.

Yes, closing his eyes should have helped tremendously, only the picture did not fade in the least and, on top of that rather unfortunate happening was the fact that now his olfactory senses were more alert, and the scent of lavender seemed to swirl around him like a cloud.

He suddenly began conjuring thoughts of opening all the small dark buttons that closed Lady Farnsworth's traveling dress up to her neck. And, most definitely, he would let her hair down.

James opened his eyes with a snap.

The lady across from him smiled. James frowned. This was all very bad.

"Perhaps we should converse?" Lady Farnsworth said softly. "It might help pass the time."

Nothing was going to help, of that James was very sure.

"I hear you have a lovely home in London. Do you enjoy the city?"

"Not really."

Lady Farnsworth nodded. "Well that would seem a good reason to buy a home in town, then."

"How on earth did you hear about my house?"

"I like to keep abreast of the news," Lady Farnsworth said.

"My home is news?"

"It is in *Lady Whistledown's Society Papers*."

James nearly groaned out loud. "Tell me you don't get that horrible piece of filth all the way in Gravesly."

His traveling companion shrugged prettily and smiled. "I have it specially delivered."

"Lovely."

"I find it terribly interesting, and I very much enjoy Lady Whistledown's sense of humor."

"The woman is a menace." The author of *Lady Whistledown's Society Papers*, whoever she was, had been the one to put abroad Lady Jersey's insistence on calling him the Most Delectable Man in England last season.

Hearing the name whispered among a few ladies of the *ton* had been devastating. Seeing the horrible moniker in print had been something out of his worst nightmares.

He would now have to surmise that Lady Farnsworth knew of the name he abhorred. James sighed.

"Why don't you like London?" Lady Farnsworth asked, thankfully turning the subject.

"I did not say that I don't like it. I said I don't enjoy it," he answered.

Lady Farnsworth looked terribly perplexed. "Aren't they the same?"

"No," he said.

She drew her brows together, obviously exasperated with his short answer. "What on earth is the difference?"

"I like London," he found himself saying. "There are amusements and interesting things and places to see, but at this point in my life I just don't enjoy it."

"How very strange."

He was saved from answering because at that moment they rolled over a particularly large rut in the road. James's head banged against the back wall of the carriage, and he let out a tremendous groan.

"Oh dear," Lady Farnsworth said, moving quickly to sit beside him. "Are you all right? Did you hurt yourself?" She reached out, threading her fingers in his hair and feeling the back of his head.

Her fingers on his scalp felt good, very good, *too* good. James pulled away from her quickly. "I'm fine, Lady Farnsworth, really," he said.

"You didn't sound fine."

He didn't feel fine. Never in his life had he experienced such an overwhelming sensitivity to another person's presence.

She did not return to her seat, but stayed beside him. They were not touching, but he could feel her, smell her, hear her. He just might be going mad.

"James," she said softly, laying her gloved hand against his arm.

"Yes," he answered without moving, barely breathing in fact.

"What are you waiting for?"

James waited for a beat of silence to go by and then said, "Excuse me, Lady Farnsworth?"

She leaned toward him. "What are you waiting for in your life that will allow you to enjoy London?"

James frowned. He had been expecting something else entirely. "When I am settled I think I will enjoy it," he said, and then wanted to take back his words. She had befuddled him, truly. He never spoke of personal matters with anyone.

"Settled?" she asked softly. "But you have your home. Do you mean married?"

"No." James sat up a bit. "Really, Lady Farnsworth, I am not sure what I mean at all."

"You know I have always thought it a shame that people wait for something to happen before they enjoy themselves," Lady Farnsworth said, smoothing the wrinkles from her gloves.

"I mean it seems that young people are always awaiting the time when they are older. And young women await the time when they are married. And then they await their children, or wealth or whatever they have decided will make them happy. It seems to me that we ought to enjoy the moment for what it is, don't you think?"

"Of course, but it is rather easier to do so when you are settled, isn't it?" James asked. "I mean, when you know who you are."

"Know who you are? Who doesn't know who they are?"

Now he really had said too much. For some odd reason being with Lady Farnsworth made him say too much, do too much, and most definitely feel too much. James turned to glance out the window. How much longer until they reached Brighton, he wondered?

"Oh." He heard the soft noise from behind him, but continued to stare out the window.

"I am sorry, Captain. I think I understand, and I didn't mean to hurt you."

"You didn't hurt me, Lady Farnsworth. That's quite absurd, really."

"Right, of course it is." Lady Farnsworth was blessedly silent for a moment, then she asked, "So, what is something you *like* about London?"

James let out an audible sigh. He turned forward in his seat and stretched his legs out in front of him. They were hours still from Brighton. "The opera," he said finally.

"Mmmm, I've never heard an opera."

"There are some that are very beautiful. I enjoy the music."

"So there *are* things that you enjoy?"

He furrowed his fingers through his hair. "I like music," he said. He was not sure why he told this woman anything at all. There was not another soul on earth at the moment who knew of his liking for music.

"Really?" Lady Farnsworth smiled slightly.

That was a lovely sight. Her full lips turning

up at the corners, her chocolate eyes going all velvety.

James nearly groaned out loud. What on earth was his problem?

"The only music I have ever heard is when the men on the docks sing ditties."

"You must be jesting," he said, truly amazed.

Lady Farnsworth just shrugged. "I've never been to London, and there aren't very many opportunities to attend an opera or such in Gravesly."

James nodded slowly. His mother had adored music. One of his only good memories of childhood was lying in bed while his mother sang to him. Her voice had been beautiful, her range incredible.

James decided it would be best if he slept, or pretended to at least. Talking to Lady Farnsworth made him want to explain things that were better left unsaid. "I do not mean to offend, Lady Farnsworth, but I am tired and have a horrible headache. Would you mind if I slept?"

"Not at all, Captain," Lady Prudence said, and settled back against the seat. "I think I shall rest as well." And with that she leaned her head against James's shoulder.

He sat for a moment without moving, and then with a sigh, he leaned his own head against the back of the carriage and closed his eyes. But he didn't sleep. To the contrary, he was very much awake, his entire body attuned to the pressure of Prudence Farnsworth's head against his arm, her skirt touching his thigh, and her scent tickling his nose.

# Chapter 6

**R**ichard Von Schubert, Viscount Leighton, slipped past the ramshackle-looking group just climbing out of the oldest carriage he had ever seen and pushed through the doors of Brighton's Seaside Inn. It was a horrid place, really, but the most delightful young man pulled pints at the bar, and Richard had found himself frequenting more often than not.

He had been in Brighton for a fortnight and was planning to return to London soon. The season had begun in earnest and Prinny had already left the seaside town for the bigger city, thus taking most anyone of interest with him. Richard had stayed a few extra days mostly to see if anything came of the young buck at the Seaside Inn.

He peeked through the doors to the public room, but didn't see his quarry.

"I am glad the doctor has pronounced you fit, Captain. I have been terribly worried. But I do think this little trip was a good idea," a woman's voice said from behind him.

"Of course, Lady Farnsworth."

Richard blinked, straightened, and turned around quickly. Lady Farnsworth? Of all the interesting coincidences.

The group that had just entered the inn were the very same shabby-looking lot that had been exiting the carriage that looked ready to die when he had entered.

The captain was none other than Captain James Ashley. Richard had met him a few times, the first being many years before in India. Poor man was too honorable for his own good.

Richard eyed the small blond woman intently. Lady Farnsworth. He could not possibly let this opportunity slip by. His grandfather would probably fall over dead when Richard told the old man that he actually had done something worthwhile in Brighton. Smoothing his green jacket and pink waistcoat, Richard moved forward. "Captain Ashley," he said brightly.

At his greeting the man turned a pair of tired-looking eyes on Richard.

The captain blinked, and then recognition hit. "Viscount Leighton," he said coldly.

Goodness, but Captain Ashley held a grudge ever so long. It was not as if the chit in India had been worth anything anyway. One day Ashley would realize that Richard had done him a huge favor with that one.

"Imagine meeting you here, Captain!"

"Imagine," the captain said, obvious sarcasm edging his voice. "May I present you to my hostess, Lady Farnsworth."

The lady smiled. She was lovely, truly, with soft eyes and a wicked-looking mouth. Richard took her hand and kissed the air above it. "Viscount Leighton at your service, my lady."

Captain Ashley actually seethed beside him. Richard nearly laughed aloud. The captain really needed to learn to use a bit more common sense when choosing his love interests. Poor man was led around by emotions, truly.

"And these are companions from Gravesly," Captain Ashley said.

Richard glanced up at a huge, bald man with a black eye patch. Good God, nothing like flaunting the fact that you were not quite law-abiding. He'd bet this was the infamous Eurel Clifton Rhodes.

"This is Mr. Clifton Rhodes and Mrs. Leslie Redding."

Richard dipped his head in the mammoth man's direction, then kissed the air above a matronly woman's hand.

"My lord," they both said, obviously stunned at being introduced. He knew that Clifton was Lady Farnsworth's butler, so he'd guess both people were servants. Rather out of place for the captain to introduce them, but Richard really didn't care much for places anyway.

"Lady Farnsworth of Gravesly," he said, tapping his finger against his bottom lip. "I can't say that I've had the pleasure. Have you ever been to London?"

"No, my lord," the lady said.

"Well, goodness, my lady, you ought to. The place would become ever so less dreary."

Lady Farnsworth's lovely, pouty lips turned up into a smile that would tempt the holiest of saints. "How kind of you, Lord Leighton."

Captain Ashley was getting ready to plant him a facer. "Would you like to join me?" he asked, enjoying himself immensely. "I was about to get a bit of supper in the public room."

The captain looked as if he would rather pull his fingernails out from their moorings.

"That would be lovely, Lord Leighton. I am absolutely famished."

Mrs. Redding shook her head. "Mr. Rhodes and I ate while the captain was seeing the doctor. I'll just go on up to my room, thank you."

"Why don't you make sure Leslie gets to her room, Clifton." Lady Farnsworth nodded to her butler.

The large man scowled, but turned and followed Mrs. Redding.

Richard could tell the captain was torn—either

protect his lady or escape the villain. "You've been to see the doctor, Captain? Are you ill?" he asked innocently.

Captain Ashley shook his head quickly.

"Took a pint at the inn at Gravesly that didn't sit well with him," Lady Farnsworth said. "But, as he is my guest, I did want to make sure that it was not anything else."

"Ah." He would bet there had been something foreign in the captain's pint. The town of Gravesly, it seemed, was doing a fine job of keeping the captain diverted from his duty. "Well, should we? I am very near starving." Richard pushed through the door into the public room. He hoped to glean just enough information from the captain and Lady Farnsworth that his grandfather would leave him alone for at least a week.

Viscount Leighton was quite an interesting character, Pru thought, as the man finally took his leave. Obviously quite a fop, with his outrageously bright clothes and flamboyant manners, but very intelligent as well. Pru watched the viscount depart the public room, then turned her attention back to the captain. He had taken off his coat and opened his waistcoat, and he looked about ready to drop into his soup.

"You must be tired, Captain."

"I must be," he said, and actually laughed. She did like it when the man relaxed a bit. His dimples showed on such an occasion, and they were quite endearing, really.

Pru smiled and bit at her bottom lip. It seemed that the good captain had allowed himself to get a bit drunk. The viscount had been quite an entertaining dinner companion, and Pru had found herself talking with the man throughout much of their meal. The captain, on the other hand, had stayed very silent, and at some point had switched from drinking ale to a dark, earthy-smelling brandy.

Goodness, whatever was she to do with a drunk Captain Ashley? Prudence actually felt herself grin. "Shall we adjourn to our rooms, Captain?"

Dimples creased the captain's stubbled cheeks, and he nodded, taking up his glass when he stood. He took a step toward the door, but wobbled a bit, so Pru quickly grabbed his coat and placed herself at his side. "Careful," she cautioned.

James slugged down the rest of his brandy and tried to place the glass back on the table. It missed by a foot at least, thudding to the carpeted floor. "Whoops," the captain said, and dipped as if to retrieve it.

Pru slipped her arm around his waist. "Ah, no, Captain, someone with better balance will pick it up, I'm sure."

The man actually laughed again. If she had thought him handsome before, it was nothing compared to how he looked when he smiled and laughed. His gray eyes resembled sparkling raindrops rather than stormy rain clouds, and his entire face brightened.

Pru let the man use her for balance as they left the public room and started up the small staircase. At the top they ran into Leslie.

"Well, goodness," Leslie said, startled.

Pru eyed the door her friend had just come through. "That wasn't your room," she said.

Leslie waggled her brows. "No, dear, while you were downstairs I have been hard at work driving dear Clifton mad."

"Lord, what a frightful thought," Captain Ashley said in mock horror. "Frightful" came out sounding more like "fiseful."

Leslie blinked, and Pru giggled.

"The captain has imbibed, I'm afraid."

"Well, lucky you," Leslie said dryly. "But I'd suggest you hurry along, because your ever-committed butler would probably lock you alone in your room if he saw you now."

"Come along, Captain," Pru said, and started down the hall once more.

"Do be careful, Prudence," Leslie called after them.

Pru just waved and kept walking, the thought of Clifton seeing her making her hurry her steps.

The captain fumbled for his key for a few moments while Pru said a little prayer that Clifton would stay tucked away in his room for at least another moment.

"Well, good night, Lady Farnsworth," the captain said, shoving open his door. He tripped into the room and fell nicely right on top of the small bed, leaving his door wide-open, with the key still sticking out of the lock.

Leslie came up behind her then, and they both stood staring into the captain's room. "Well, this is quite a dilemma, isn't it?" Leslie asked with a low chuckle.

"It is," Pru said. "You know, I feel rather bad. I mean, I don't know the captain all that well, but I know that he will be very upset with himself in the morning. And he'll be horrified if I allow him to do anything that he will really regret."

She felt Leslie nod beside her. "Yes, he is quite a gentleman. I have to say, I was rather thrilled when he introduced me to the viscount as if I were some lady of the court."

Prudence turned to glance at her friend over her shoulder. "It was lovely of him, wasn't it?"

Leslie turned her mouth up in a smile that didn't quite reach her eyes. "Yes, lovely." She looked over at the now snoring Captain. "It made me sad, though, that we have to be at odds with the man. He makes me want him to succeed, but, of course, we can't let him."

Prudence followed her friend's gaze to the captain. "Yes, I do know what you mean."

"And now I worry for him as well as you with this new plan of yours."

"Oh come, Leslie, this is the Most Delectable Man in England we're speaking about. It's not as if I am out to seduce an untried boy."

"Yes, yes, I know. But, I must say, he doesn't seem at all as I thought he would be."

They both watched the captain silently for a moment. "Well, I certainly cannot let this opportunity slide by," Pru said. "He's relaxed and a bit tipsy, this is the perfect moment."

"Perhaps a bit too relaxed," Leslie commented.

The captain let out a snore that seemed to shake the windows. "Hmm, yes, I see what you mean."

"But if you must try, you must try," Leslie said. "Though I do feel as if I ought to protect one of you. I'm just not sure which."

Pru laughed. "All right then, off with you. I will let you know how it went in the morning."

Leslie gave Pru a hug. "Good luck, then," she said, and turned on her heel. Pru watched her friend find her own room without once looking back, then turned to stare again at the sleeping captain. Voices on the stair made Pru jump into the room and close the door quickly.

It was dark, suddenly, but instead of lighting a candle, Prudence just stood inside the door and let her eyes get accustomed to the gloom.

She had no idea what she was going to do and

had to curl her fingers into her skirt to keep them from shaking. One would think, after all the things she had done in her life, that she could seduce a man without becoming so scared she couldn't move.

But here she was, feeling very much rooted to the spot.

The captain grunted and breathed deeply, his snores stopping for a moment. Well, there was no time to waste. The deeper into sleep he got, the harder it would be to rouse him.

Pru went and sat down on the side of the bed. "Captain?" she said softly, touching his shoulder. He didn't move.

"Captain," she said a bit louder.

He snuffled and lifted his head, then looked over at her. She could see that he blinked a few times in the dark, then he plunked his face back down in his pillow.

She sighed. It didn't look like the captain was going to make this any easier for her. Not that he had made anything easy from the moment she had met him. Prudence stood and quietly started undressing.

When she had peeled off her outer layers and stood only in her chemise, she took a deep breath, held it for a moment, then clenched her hands and climbed onto the bed next to the captain.

She lay there for what seemed forever, waiting for the man to realize that there was a nearly naked woman next to him. Unfortunately, it didn't seem to register in his fogged head.

She had never had to seduce her husband, and she had absolutely no idea how one would go about such a thing. Prudence frowned and tried to remember something of her days as a wife that might help her now.

But the only thing that came to her mind was the lovely memory of James Ashley kissing her. Just the thought made her stomach flutter and her legs feel strangely weak.

Perhaps she just needed to kiss him again, the way they had kissed before. Prudence turned onto her side and stared at the back of James's head. He was facedown on the bed, his arms straight down at his sides. This was going to be rather difficult. She sat up. First she was going to have to turn him over somehow.

Prudence knelt next to James's body on the bed and, reaching across him, tried to pull him over. She groaned and pulled, but the man didn't budge. Pru quit trying with an exhausted sigh. She was strong, but she didn't have the right leverage to move someone so heavy.

Obviously, she needed a new plan. Pru sat staring down at the captain again. He wore his hair short, but it was lovely and thick. She tapped her finger against her knee, then touched the nape of his neck. He was warm, and it felt strangely good just to touch him.

Prudence swallowed against a funny lump in her throat and threaded her fingers in the captain's hair. She heard a sound, and realized suddenly that it was the captain. He had groaned.

She blinked and flexed her fingers against his scalp.

"Mmmm." He made the sound again.

Prudence had an idea. She leaned over and pressed her mouth against James's neck. His skin was smooth and warm and held a scent that she had noticed on him before. It wasn't anything she could think of, rather a mingling of musky soap and wind and man.

Pru slipped her tongue out and tasted him. She heard another sound and realized that it was her own. She moved down so that she lay against James's side and continued her exploration of the back of his neck.

She had never realized that such an activity could be so intriguing. She nipped at his ear and nuzzled his nape. Then she pulled up the back of his shirt and slipped her hand beneath it.

The captain groaned again, and turned. She found her hand sliding around his side and finally coming to rest on his flat stomach. She trailed her fingers about, realizing that she rather wanted to kiss him there as well. She had never thought of kissing a man anywhere but his face, but that seemed so very limiting now.

Especially when she found a trail of wiry hair

that started at the hollow of the Captain's neck, whirled around his navel, and wisped down to the waistband of his pants.

James groaned again, and Pru glanced up at him. His eyes were still closed, but a smile played about his mouth.

"Captain?" she asked.

"Mmm, yes," he murmured.

Well it seemed he was awake, at least. She had felt strange kissing and touching someone who was fast asleep.

"Um, Captain," she said again, hooking her fingers under his waistband and feeling a bit light-headed. "I was thinking that, well, perhaps, I mean . . . that is to say."

Prudence took a deep, calming breath. "I am, of course, not a maiden, being a widow. But in a town like Gravesly, I am rather restricted. I was wondering, though, if you wouldn't mind . . ."

The man threaded his fingers in her hair, pulled her to him, and kissed her.

Her first thought was elation that her plan was most definitely going to work, and then all thought completely fled as he opened his mouth over hers and took her. Yes, this is what she wanted. She kissed him back with an abandon that made her giddy.

His hands moved around her and down her back to cup her buttocks, and he pulled her tightly against him. She could feel him hard against her stomach, and the light-headedness from before whirled into complete dizziness.

"Oh my," she said, as he left her mouth and tongued his way down her throat, his large hands squeezing her buttocks.

"Mmmm," he said again, nibbling along her collarbone. Every nerve ending in her body sang with anticipation. She could feel her nipples rigid against the cloth of her chemise. Prudence shivered, her heart beating like a drum against her chest.

Being a diversion to the captain was going to be quite thrilling.

"You smell divine," he murmured, his mouth dipping to taste the skin just above her décolletage.

"Oh my," she said on a sharp intake of breath, leaning her head on her neck to give the captain better access to her breasts. His tongue left a devastating trail of heat, and Prudence knew that she wanted the man to strip her down to nothing and slide his tongue all over her body.

She felt a bit shocked at her own thoughts, but quickly dismissed her prudishness. She could not be a prude and accomplish her goal.

Prudence wiggled her arms between them and fumbled at the buttons of the captain's breeches. Lord, who knew it would be so hard to get a man out of his pants. She yanked and pulled, and then pushed back slightly to try and get his breeches undone.

"Goodness," she said breathlessly. "I never imagined this could be so exciting. I'm shaking so." She tore at one of the buttons but could make no headway.

And then she heard another strange noise from the Captain and glanced up at him. His eyes were still closed, his mouth slightly open.

"Captain?" she said.

He didn't move at all. And then she heard the noise again and realized that it was a snore. James had fallen asleep, again.

Or he had never been truly awake.

Prudence placed her hands on his chest and shoved against him. "Captain!"

The man fell over on his back, snoring even louder.

This just wasn't going to work. Prudence sighed loudly and lay for a while next to him. She would just have to try again when he was sober. A pity, really.

She pushed up from the captain's bed, threw her clothes over her head, and stood watching the man sleep. It didn't matter. She knew that he was attracted to her, and he knew now what she wanted of him. She was sure that later they could pick up where they'd left off.

With a nod, Prudence let herself out of the captain's room and went to her own.

# Chapter 7

~~~~∽⌒⊙⊙⌒∽~~~~

**N**ot wanting to tempt fate by spending an-other second in Lady Farnsworth's intimate company, James left Chesley House the moment they returned home from Brighton. He did not even say good-bye to anyone, but grabbed his case and saddled Devil himself as Lady Farnsworth did battle with her butler in the kitchen.

Lady Farnsworth had been in a foul mood their entire ride home, and his head had felt even worse than it had after being drugged. He could remember nothing from the night before except their unfortunate meeting with the vile Viscount Leighton, drinking too much in the public room, and then dropping facefirst onto his bed.

It was early afternoon now as James rode through the steep cobblestoned streets of Gravesly, his uniform smartly pressed and his posture erect. His head throbbed with each echoing step of his horse, and every once in a while he felt his stomach heave, but with a determined effort, James kept himself in the saddle and showed the town of Gravesly the man they should fear.

"Oh, Captain, dear, are you feeling better?" the smallest and oldest woman James had ever seen yelled up to him from the stoop of a seamstress's shop.

James actually looked behind him, wondering how many captains could possibly be prowling Gravesly's streets.

"You just stay right there, dearie. I've got something for you." The woman waddled back into her dark shop. James stared after her, then leaned forward in his saddle to peer at the doorway of the woman's store. There, whittled into the doorframe, was the form of a wolf's head.

James blinked just as the old woman returned.

She held a jar of some strange substance. "Here you go, luv, this'll cure what ails you." She pushed up on her tiptoes and reached toward him, still only coming to Devil's withers.

James peered about the street, wondering if this could possibly be a trap. No one lurked in any shadows, so he swung his leg carefully over Devil's rump and slid to the ground.

"Thank you, um . . ."

"Mrs. Witherspoon, that's me," the lady said

obviously delighted as she handed over her cure-all. She patted his hand. "We all heard you were feeling a tad under the weather."

James had bent forward so that he could hear the old woman, when her gnarled fingers grabbed his suddenly. "Goodness, man, you're still hot to the touch."

Before James knew what Mrs. Witherspoon was about, the old woman took his face between her hands and pulled his head down. And then she pressed her leathery lips against his forehead and held them there for a full minute.

James wanted desperately to pull from the woman's embrace and put some distance between himself and this elfin menace, but his manners kept him still beneath her ministrations.

"Ah no, boy, you've just the right feel to you," she said, finally releasing him. "You've got warm hands, though." She wagged a bony finger at him. " 'Tis a good sign, I think." She nodded. "A good sign." And she hobbled around and went back into her shop.

James straightened, smoothed his white waistcoat, and flicked a piece of lint from his red coat. Then he tucked the foul-looking stuff Mrs. Witherspoon had given him into his saddlebag.

Lovely, he was now a patient to the old and widowed. James frowned as he took Devil's reins and led him up toward Harker's Inn.

"Captain!"

"Captain!"

"Captain!" a chorus of little voices showered over him from above.

James squinted up and saw small faces poking out of an upstairs window.

Hands joined the faces, waving. James once again looked around suspiciously, wondering if the sinister Wolf would actually use children to make him look up and then come at him from below.

"We're sorry you were sick," a little girl in long dark braids singsonged.

"Really, really sorry," another child piped up around a thumb that hung at her mouth.

"We want you to have our Sickly-poo," a boy said, and tossed something from the window.

Alarmed, James watched some dark object come hurtling at him. Instead of catching it, he stepped out of the way, but it just plopped innocently on the ground and rolled over. A much-loved stitched face stared up at him with button eyes. James carefully bent over and plucked the stuffed rabbit off the cobblestones.

"He'll make you feel so much better, Captain, he's magic."

James gazed back up at the angels in the window. "Uh . . . well, thank you."

There was a bit of a commotion from above, and the children turned into the room and disappeared. And then an older face appeared. Not old, actually, but adult at least. A woman smiled down at him. "Ah, Captain, I wondered what had the children all excited. So glad to see you up and about."

"Thank you," James said lamely.

"I see the children have lent you Sickly-poo."

James stared down at the pink rabbit still clutched in his hand.

"He'll do wonders for your constitution, Captain." The woman winked at him. "He's magic, you know. You can just return him downstairs when you're done. I'm Mrs. Sawyer, and my husband is the baker." She smiled again, pointed toward the shop at eye level to James, then retreated within the upstairs room and drew down the sash.

James glanced at the storefront. Through the paned windows, he could see a man placing loaves of steaming bread on a tray.

The man looked up, caught James's eye and waved. James waved back.

His superiors in London had warned him that the town of Gravesly probably wouldn't take kindly to him. Had they been wrong, or was he walking into some sort of trap?

Just as he was about to turn away, James spied the likeness of a wolf carved into the top of the bakery door. He stopped and stared, then peered around the empty street. Obviously he had found the Wolf's hunting grounds. Now, he just had to find the lair.

James heard banging above him and glanced up to see the three children's faces mashed against the window. They were waving, so James managed a crooked smile. Then with a heavy sigh, he tucked Sickly-poo into the satchel with the stuff that was probably another dose of poison and started up the road once again.

"Aya, Captain! Heard ya been sick."

Obviously the entire town knew exactly who he was, why he was there, and that he had been sick after two pints of ale. Wonderful. James stood very straight and gave his best captainly look to the man who now hailed him.

The spindly little man in front of James shook his balding head. "Now that's just too bad. Your first night in town, and you get sick." The man smacked his tongue against the only two teeth in his head.

"You goin' on into Harker's, are you? Well, I'll take your horse. The name's Franklin Arthur Telmann Sariston, but you can call me Artie." He sauntered over and took Devil's reins. "And this is a right beautiful horse."

James took his pack from Devil's back as Artie murmured soothing sounds to the beast.

"If you get to feelin' ill again, Captain, you just come to ol' Artie." Artie started leading the horse away. "I've got a special brew, my grandfather's own recipe, you know, that'll fix you right up faster than any highfalutin' sawbones."

James nearly groaned, but he waved obligingly to Artie and took the steps two at a time to the front door of Harker's. Just as he was about to go in, though, he noticed something above the door. He hadn't seen it when he had been there before, but it had been darker then.

With his hand on the door handle, James peered up at the shape whittled into the door-frame. And then he frowned. It was a wolf.

Pru finally found James hunched over the can-non that sat in front of old Gravesly Castle over-looking the bay.

"Haven't had much use for that old thing," she said brightly. "The French never invaded."

"Hmm," he said darkly.

Prudence waited for the man to make mention of their intimate encounter the night before, but he just stared out to sea.

"Are you going to say anything, Captain, about last night?"

He glanced over at her. "I must apologize, Lady Farnsworth. I promise I do not make a habit of drinking too much, usually." He shook his head.

Prudence blinked. She had begun to wonder as they rode in silence on the way home if the cap-

tain even remembered what had happened between them. Now she was rather sure he could
remember nothing. Damn. She would have to
start at the beginning again.

"Josh Harker says you have put in at the inn,"
she said, deciding to go at this thing straight on.

"I do think it better if I did not reside in your
home."

"And, of course, you are right, Captain."

He turned slowly to look at her. "You agree
with me now?" he asked, a hint of suspicion in
his voice.

"Oh yes. It will be ever so much better to conduct an affair off the premises of my home. No
one would ever suspect."

"Excuse me?"

"Oh, dear, I have gotten ahead of myself. I tend
to do that when I'm nervous." She smiled. "Truly,
I have never done this before, as I'm sure you can
probably tell. I must say, though, Captain, that
your reputation has preceded you, so I know that
you, on the other hand, have a wealth of knowledge and experience." She was rambling. Pru
stopped and took a deep breath. She *was* nervous,
and she did so *hate* being nervous.

The captain stood looking at her as if she were
a talking dog. Perhaps she should not have been
quite so straightforward. Who knew that it would
be so difficult to begin a clandestine affair.

Pru smoothed her hands along the front of her

gown and decided to try the same tack she had begun with the night before. "Captain," she said with as much calm and command as she could muster, "I am a widow and thus no untried girl."

She took a step forward. "I am terribly lonely here in Gravesly since I obviously cannot consort with any of the men in such a small town. But now, especially with you comfortably ensconced at Harker's, I think it would be quite perfect for us to strike up a . . . relationship, if you will."

"You cannot be serious."

"Oh, but I am, terribly. You cannot deny your attraction, Captain. I mean last night . . ."

He frowned suddenly. "What happened last night? Did I . . . ?"

She bit her lip. "Well, last night perhaps you didn't realize it was me, but you did kiss me."

The captain furrowed his fingers through his hair. "I thought last night was a dream."

"Last night was lovely," Prudence said, taking another step forward. "Really, lovely. And I want desperately to continue with what we started."

Prudence placed her gloved hand upon James's broad chest. She could feel his heart thumping away beneath her fingers.

James closed his eyes on a groan.

Letting instinct guide her, Pru smoothed her palm up and around James's neck, twining her fingers in the hair at his nape. And then she exerted a bit of pressure on the back of his neck, pulling him toward her. She tilted her head and stood on tiptoe as he leaned forward.

"I think there is so much you could teach me, James," she whispered.

James stiffened and opened his eyes. They were dark like a windswept sea.

"I do not wish to offend," he said, his voice a harsh whisper as he reached up and took her hand from his neck. "But I must decline your very generous offer." He bowed smartly over her hand and kissed the air above her glove.

Pru frowned, very much vexed that she was not going to receive the kiss she had just anticipated. "But why?"

James let go of her hand and stood straight. "Are you to have a temper then, *Lady* Farnsworth?"

His tone held none of the respect he had shown to her thus far, and his gaze was altogether frosty.

Pru took a step backward. "No, actually," she answered. "I have never had a temper in my life, and shan't begin now."

"Good, because there most definitely will be no dalliance happening between the two of us, Lady Farnsworth. I am here on extremely important business, and I will not allow my attention to be diverted."

Prudence frowned, it was as if the man had read her mind. "Surely, Captain, a man of your prowess would not have trouble keeping your mind on your job when the time called for it."

"No, I will not have trouble at all, my lady. And now, I shall bid you *adieu*." James bowed stiffly, his eyes a flinty gray, and turned away from her smartly.

"Well, I bungled *that*," Pru whispered to the captain's wide, retreating back.


"Is there something wrong with me, Leslie?"

Leslie took a sip of tea, and said, "Of course not, dear, you are lovely and full of wit."

"But the Rogue of England will not even lay a hand on me." Pru huffed a great sigh and let her posture slump. "Who would have known that it would be so hard to get a man to have an affair? Surely, with all the dire warnings that my mother used to lecture me with, I thought most men were itching to jump into bed with any woman who would look at them."

Leslie giggled, and the sound made Pru smile.

"Perhaps he isn't the scoundrel his reputation has made him out to be?" Leslie ventured.

"But what of the stories of all the women he has bedded . . . ?" Pru stopped for a moment as her throat felt rather tight suddenly.

"Rumors, all," answered Leslie. "Or, perhaps he has some sort of rule that he does not conduct affairs when he is on an assignment. I've heard men are very much distracted by the deed, and sometimes abstain when they need to keep their minds duly focused on one thing."

Leslie shook her head and cradled her teacup in both hands. "Truly, Pru, we both know that men have absolutely no imagination. You ask them to do two things at once and they panic."

Pru nodded quietly. "So true."

"They think they are so superior, but if you ask me, I think men have something wrong with their brains."

Pru knew exactly of whom Leslie was thinking. "Oh, Les, aren't we a pair?"

"More like *they* are a pair of idiots."

"Of course they are! With women like us just waiting for them to beckon."

A long silence followed that statement, then Leslie said, "Well, now, that makes us sound somewhat pathetic."

"Hmm, yes, sorry."

"More tea?" Leslie asked, holding up the pot.

Pru stared dejectedly down into the tepid brown liquid still in her cup. "No, thank you."

Leslie put the pot down with a clank, stood, and without saying another word, left the room.

Pru just waited for her friend.

"I have just the thing," Leslie said when she returned, holding a bottle of brandy aloft.

"Oh, yes!" Pru laughed, and held out her teacup. "Of course," she said, as Leslie tipped some brandy into Pru's tea. "I have a higher goal here, you know, and I really must think of a way to keep the captain occupied. He is not the sort to be bought off."

"And, it seems, he's not the sort to be distracted."

Pru sipped her drink and sighed deeply. "I did have such high hopes for my plan."

Leslie laughed. "Oh, yes, there is nothing like a plan with a bonus."

Pru rolled her eyes at her friend. "Still, perhaps I should continue my pursuit of the good captain. Even if he continues to reject me, I shall be a distraction, don't you think?"

Leslie downed her share of the brandy in one swig. "Oh, yes, dear, there is no arguing with that. The man cannot keep his eyes off you."

Pru leaned back in her chair. "What a strange thing this attraction business is. It is very exciting, isn't it? But it also makes me sad at the strangest moments. 'Tis probably a good thing I never had to deal with it during my marriage. It seems to me that I would have gone decidedly mad."

Leslie sobered, her green eyes darkening with a touch of sadness. "Yes, it makes you mad, mad in love. And, dear Pru, it is very much worth it."

Pru dropped her gaze to the boarded floor for a moment. She could feel tears threatening the backs of her eyes, and so she breathed deeply and swallowed them away. She felt as if she had begun to live in the last two years, and she absolutely adored her life, finally.

It was not as if she had lived horribly up until two years ago. On the contrary, Prudence had always been taken care of very nicely. Her elderly parents had adored their only child. She had loved them, too, and had been very sad when they had died within a year of each other just after her marriage to Lord Farnsworth.

But, of course, they had known they would probably not live until Pru reached her majority. That had been their reasoning in marrying Pru off early to an older gentleman who could care for her.

And Lord Farnsworth had definitely taken care of her. She had lived with her husband very much as she had lived with her parents: quietly, sheltered, and with nothing to do that would tax her.

With her husband's passing, though, Prudence had been left alone in the world. And because Lord Farnsworth had not anticipated his death, his responsibilities had landed in Pru's lap.

That had been two years ago, and that had been, really, the beginning of Pru's life.

Suddenly, she mattered. Suddenly, Prudence Farnsworth was needed. Suddenly, she made a difference to people. Suddenly, she was really, truly living.

Now, though, a bit of darkness had edged into

Pru's bright world. She had thought that she was living life fully, but could she, perhaps, be missing something else entirely? And could that something else make her happier than she ever dreamed?

"There's nothing like drinking the profits," Leslie said lightly, interrupting the pained silence.

Pru glanced up at her friend and smiled slightly. "Especially when you've got idiots to deal with."

"Hear, hear."

# Chapter 8

It had taken James rather longer than he had expected to get out of town that evening. Mrs. Witherspoon had come toddling after him wanting to know how the tonic had worked, and before he knew it the old woman had talked his ear off for nearly an hour. She had promised some other cure-all as he finally made his good-byes.

He had to smile as he left the road and went to the edge of the cliff. He was actually starting to like Mrs. Witherspoon. It was odd to have someone who actually seemed concerned for his welfare. Odd, and disquieting, and really rather nice all at once.

With a sigh, James closed his eyes and listened. Nothing. The beach below him was quiet. James opened his eyes and scanned the horizon. Nothing.

And then the hairs on James's neck stood on end. Unfortunately the sensation had nothing to do with smugglers, but rather with the memory of Prudence Farnsworth's caress.

Damn. He could not get the woman out of his mind. Anger warred with downright lust as he thought of how she had thrown his *reputation* in his face.

The irony of his life was hideously funny, really.

James made a small sound halfway between a laugh and a growl, but then bit his tongue. He closed his eyes again and listened. Yes, a sound. Someone was coming along the road. James crouched stealthily in the underbrush and waited.

In the darkness, James could just barely make out the form of a person on horseback. Rather late to be out riding.

"Captain, finally, I have been looking all over for you."

James let out the breath he had been holding. "Lady Farnsworth," he said, standing. Frustration, lust, and a bit of confusion tumbled about his head. "How on earth did you see me?"

"Oh, I have excellent vision at night," she said merrily, and dismounted. "Clifton teases that I must have an owl in my family tree."

If there was something he could not imagine Clifton doing, it was teasing someone. "You were seeking me out?"

Lady Farnsworth dropped her horse's reins, and the animal seemed to take that to mean she should not move an inch.

"I brought you a bit of something to eat," Lady Farnsworth said, handing him a cloth-tied bundle he had not even noticed.

James took the offering and just stared at it for a moment.

"I thought you might get hungry skulking about out here."

Skulking?

"Have you seen anything?" she asked, and walked to the cliff's edge.

"Be careful, there, Lady Farnsworth. 'Tis a dangerous place to be in the dark."

"Oh, you don't have to worry about me." She smiled at him over her shoulder.

That was debatable.

"Looks like nothing is happening here." She turned and came toward him. "Would you like me to take you to the bay where your ship went down?"

James winced.

"I think that is where the smugglers usually conduct business."

Actually, he had been trying to figure out exactly where that had happened. The two excise officers were useless. It seemed they spent most of their time at Harker's or asleep. And they had looked at him with openmouthed, vacant stares when he had asked where most of the smuggling activity took place.

"Of course, before we go, you will have to apologize to me for this afternoon."

The woman was obviously mad. "Apologize, Lady Farnsworth?"

"Yes, Captain. You implied that I would have a tantrum because I was not given what I wished, and it was terribly rude of you."

For a moment, James nearly laughed. Dear God, he wanted to lie down and roll with mirth. "I am sorry, Lady Farnsworth, for upsetting you," he said instead.

"Oh, no, it didn't upset me, really, I just found it rather a rude statement."

"Right, well, I fear I was a bit taken aback by your proposition and thus acted rashly."

"I understand completely." She came close to him and patted his arm. "Now, we shall be friends again, yes? And I can show you Gravesly Bay." Lady Farnsworth went to her horse and gave the animal a slap to her rump. "Home, Beauty."

The mare whinnied and trotted off. "Captain?" James turned his gaze from the retreating shadow of the horse to find Lady Farnsworth standing in the road, her arm held out to accept him. "Shall we?"

No matter that she was sacrificing herself as a diversion for the good of the Wolf, Pru could not

remember having a more lovely evening. It was
May, and should have been rather nippy out, but
instead the air was still and, if not warm, definitely not cold. The sky was clear, with a sliver of
a moon and a million stars.

"It is beautiful tonight." She sighed, enjoying
the night as well as the feel of the captain's
strong, warm body next to hers. It was really too
bad that he was so adamant about not doing anything to further their relationship.

"Hmm."

She steered them off the road and over to a
small winding path that cut down the cliff to the
sea. She started to descend, but James stayed her
with a hand on her arm.

She really did love his hands.

"I will go down first, Lady Farnsworth," he
said in that commanding but polite tone he had.

She nodded, but twisted her arm and snagged
his hand. And just like that they were holding
hands as they took the steep path to the beach.
She had never, ever held a man's hand before. It
was truly a wondrous thing.

She could feel his strong fingers wrapped
around hers, the pulse point at his wrist inti-
mately cupped against her own. Mmm, it was
better than clotted cream on warm scones.

They reached the sand, and Pru made sure she
held tight to the captain's hand so he could not
shake her off. "Does it look familiar?" she asked,

pointing out to sea. "That's where your ship went down."

He stood very still. And then he turned slowly and looked up behind them. There on the highest point of land above them and to the right was Gravesly Castle, with its defensive cannon pointing right at them. "I don't remember much of what happened, actually, after the *Defender* went down."

"Yes, I'm sure that was quite a shock."

"Quite," he said with a bit of sarcasm.

"Especially after all the battles you had won against the French."

"So, this is the most likely spot to catch the smugglers?" he asked, obviously uncomfortable with the subject.

Pru smiled into the darkness. "I've heard it said so." *When they're not loading wagons four miles inland in the marsh.* "Where do you hail from, Captain? Every once in a while I detect a rather strange intonation to your words, but for my life I can't place it."

He glanced down at her. It was just light enough that she could make out the darkness of his hair and the planes of his face, everything else was in shadow. "I was born and raised in India. I am surprised you didn't know, seeing that you've heard all the other rumors about me."

"Ah yes," she nodded, and started walking toward the water. "I remember. But now you have a home in London that you don't enjoy."

The captain said nothing, so Pru continued, "It was bandied about that you were looking for a wife last season. Did no one pique your interest?"

"That would be the gossips' conclusion, I'd say."

Pru frowned at James's rather strange answer. "I think you are out of luck, Captain," she said. "There doesn't seem to be anything happening at all along the beaches this evening." She stopped and sat in the sand.

James stayed standing and their hands separated. She sighed as she gathered up her skirts and started rolling down her stockings. "I enjoy holding your hand, Captain. You have lovely hands."

Obviously the man could think of nothing to say to this, for he stayed silent. Pru kicked off her shoes and began rolling down her other stocking. "Take your boots off, James. We can wade."

"No."

"Oh, come. I'll help you." She stacked her shoes and stockings on the sand beside her and turned to kneel in front of the captain. He backed away from her.

"This is not at all appropriate, Lady Farnsworth."

"Of course it isn't." She laughed lightly. "But, trust me, James, being inappropriate is actually very enjoyable sometimes."

She hooked her hand around his ankle and pulled before he knew what she was about. James landed on his bottom in the sand with a thud.

"Ouch!"

"Oh come, it could not have hurt that much."

She could see that he was frowning at her and holding his fingers to his mouth. "I bit my tongue," he said around his hand.

"Ah. I am sorry." She crawled up his body. "Would you like me to kiss it better?"

He went very still, his eyes round and dark and staring into hers.

He had been pursued by many women but had easily turned down the women of the *ton*, much to their chagrin. In fact, it had been the infamous Lady Jersey who had started the rumor that he was so incredible a lover as to be called delectable. She had done it out of spite because he had refused her.

Some men might have reveled in being thought of as a pastry to the more adventurous women of the *ton*. He could not think of anything worse. Lady Jersey had sensed that and used it to her advantage. She was a cunning and viperous woman, truly.

One would think, James contemplated as he stared into the shadows at the woman now trying to bed him, that it would be easy to rebuff the innocent Lady Farnsworth with someone like Lady Jersey in his past.

If only that were so.

James took a deep, calming breath, but, unfortunately, it did not calm him at all. Lady Prudence Farnsworth was on all fours straddling his legs. Even in the darkness, he could make out the shape of her breasts pressing, as they were, against the top of her bodice.

Prudence Farnsworth was not making him feel slightly ill as most of the women in London had. In fact, James felt extremely good at the moment, too good, his heart beating strongly and the blood surging in his veins.

He ought to push away from the lady above him and leave her presence immediately, but someone really needed to teach her a little lesson about men.

James grabbed Prudence, flipped her onto her back, and straddled her hips before she had even taken another breath. "Lady Farnsworth," he said tightly, "you show your stupidity when you tantalize a man on a dark secluded beach." He leaned toward her. "If you were to scream, no one would hear."

"That goes both ways, James," she said with a small laugh, and he suddenly felt his balls held in a tight fist. He sucked in a breath. Again, James noted that Prudence Farnsworth was a very strong woman.

"I warned you before, Captain Ashley, I'm not as innocent as you would think. And I do hate being called stupid."

He moved, and she tightened her hold. It didn't hurt, yet. Still, it was a terribly vulnerable position to be in, and he hated it.

She let go suddenly and smoothed her hands up his chest and around his neck. "I wouldn't hurt you, James. I just wanted to make sure you understood that I am not as innocent as you seem to believe."

James sighed heavily and shook his head. "You are a very strange woman, Lady Farnsworth," he heard himself say. She was rubbing off on him; usually his thoughts stayed in his mind rather than falling from his lips.

"Do call me Prudence," she said softly, and pulled his head down to her. Her soft mouth moved beneath his, and he was lost. Even as he let himself lean against her body and rake her teeth with his tongue, a part of his mind was cringing and swearing and thumping his head in consternation.

Prudence moaned, and a more erotic sound James had never heard. It mingled with the sluice of the waves on the beach and the soft, faint whistle of the crickets. She nipped at his mouth and slid her tongue between his lips.

He was lying against the widowed wife of a baron on the sand of a beach in the middle of the night with smugglers probably making off with thousands of pounds' worth of untaxed goods under his very nose.

And he really did not give a damn.

James slid kisses down Prudence's jaw, traced her neck with his tongue and nibbled at the décolletage of her gown. "Oh God," he groaned, and cupped a breast in his hand. It swelled against the fabric of Pru's dress as he brushed his thumb over her nipple.

"Oh!" she cried, her entire body bucking beneath him.

And James rolled away, breathing hard. He lay for a long time, his face buried in the cool sand, and fought for control.

"Oh why do you have to be such a man of integrity?" Pru lamented prettily.

James could only laugh.

"What is it?" she asked, and he felt her roll against him. "Explain to me why you will not do this for me?" she whispered, her mouth against his ear.

Gooseflesh rose on his arms and he closed his eyes, fighting the temptation to turn over and take her, there, on the beach, with the grit and sand and stars overhead.

"Is it the work you must do? Is it our stations in life?" she asked hungrily. "With all that I know of you, I just don't understand."

James went very still. "With all that you know of me?" he asked quietly.

"Well, yes, I know, of course, about your reputation, everyone does."

"Yes, I am sure they do. And, really, that means you know all about me, does it not?" James pushed himself up and stood. Lady Farnsworth sat staring up at him, her hair hanging in waves about her shoulders, a sleeve of her gown drooping down one arm, and her bare toes curled in the sand. She looked like a sea nymph.

He suddenly wanted her to know, wanted her to know everything. He did not want Lady Farnsworth to think he was just some party toy for London's society women.

But it should not matter at all.

James drew in a deep breath and held his hand out toward his companion. "I shall escort you home, Lady Farnsworth."

Lady Farnsworth folded her arms and leaned them against her knees. She squinted into the darkness toward the sea, but did not move again. "I will go home when I am ready, thank you."

Truly, Lady Farnsworth could be quite a pain in the arse. "I thought you said you do not have tantrums."

He was not sure, but he thought he saw the lady roll her eyes.

"I have decided that you are afraid of me," she said.

"Yes, you are frightful, definitely. Now, Lady Farnsworth, it is not safe for you to be out here alone."

She laughed. "I thought I had proven to you that I can take care of myself." She cocked her head back, her lush hair falling away from her face. "Do I need to show you again, Captain?"

James tapped a finger against his thigh. How on earth had he gotten to this point in his relationship with Lady Farnsworth? He should never have kissed her, obviously. And he most definitely could not allow himself to be alone with her again.

He wanted to turn around and climb back up the cliff, but he could not leave her here. Being a gentleman meant he must not let her stay alone on this dark beach, but if he stayed, he was not sure he would be able to continue to be a gentleman. A quandary, this.

And what had happened to his contempt for all women of Lady Farnsworth's ilk? He made a soft sound of disgust.

"Do you hate me, then, Captain?"

"I hate people born into a good name, who then take advantage of that name to control others." Well, there it was. Why on earth did he say such things to this woman? For one thing, it was like baring his soul to a shark. For another, she would probably call his superiors in London, and he would certainly not be allowed to continue his quest for the Wolf.

Yes, he had a fortune, but he had learned quite early that all the money in the world did not make it all right for a bastard son of questionable parentage to offend a peer.

"I'm sorry," he said shortly.

The woman turned to face the sea again, and shrugged. "Sit, Captain."

With a sigh, he did as the lady wished.

"Tell me, James, am I right in assuming that the reputation you earned in London as a rogue is quite to the contrary?" She turned her head slightly, glancing at him out of the corner of her eyes. "Or am I truly so easy to resist?"

James said nothing.

"I think I understand," she said quietly.

How on earth could she? he thought. He didn't truly understand himself. And yet, in the carriage on the way to Brighton, she had done this very thing, understood. She had known that she had hurt him, and seemed innately to understand why, even as James sat confounded and reeling.

He shook his head on a sigh. "I do not trust women of the peerage," he heard himself say. God, had the devil taken over his tongue?

Surely, he was possessed. He glanced over at the nymph who sat beside him. She smiled.

Oh, God.

"Tell me about India," she said.

James shook his head, glad she had turned the subject, but hating to think of India. "It is hot."

"Hmmm, your words are so descriptive, Captain, I feel as if I am really there." She paused. "Is your family still there?"

Family. James turned and looked at the path up the cliff behind them, escape. "My mother died when I was ten, Lady Farnsworth," he answered finally.

"Oh."

And though he said nothing else, he knew that Lady Farnsworth understood that his mother had been the end of the only family he knew about.

"Do call me Prudence."

Right, sure, he would call her Prudence, and Clifton would have his head.

"Was there a woman in India who hurt you? Or is she from London?"

James laughed hollowly. "Do you have gypsy blood, my lady? Perhaps you have a crystal ball somewhere?"

She turned, and, instead of keeping his gaze steady on the dark waves, James looked into her eyes. Mistake. She smiled again; he could just see the curve of her full lips and the whiteness of her teeth.

He wished in that moment that Lady Farnsworth was a milkmaid, or the daughter of a baker, anyone within his reach. But she was most definitely no one he could dally with. He stood quickly. "Both, Lady Farnsworth. I have been put in my place on both continents. I will return you to Chesley House now." He said the last with the tone he used for his crew aboard ship. And then he turned and left her.

If she followed, he would be able to behave the gentleman. If she did not, he would have to pick her up and carry her home.

He hoped to God she followed, because if he touched her again, he would probably never let go.

He was deep in thought the next day, berating himself, really, for being such a complete fool with Lady Farnsworth the night before. How on earth could he have let his guard down so completely?

"Good morning, Captain."

James glanced up from the cobblestones to acknowledge the Widow Leland's greeting, then continued his self-castigation. Not only had he allowed a form of intimacy to burgeon between him and the lady, but he had accomplished absolutely nothing in his goal to apprehend the Wolf.

"You're looking well this morning, Captain, I'm so glad!"

James smiled at some woman he was rather sure he had never met.

"We were terribly worried," the little woman of nondescript age and coloring said as they passed one another.

"I am feeling just the thing, ma'am."

The woman stopped, and James sighed. "You do remember me, don't you, Captain? I'm Mrs. Raithespeare. You came by with Lady Prudence to give me a basket your first day here in Gravesly."

"Of course, Mrs. Raithespeare."

"Good, good, I must tell you, Captain, it is quite a delight to have such a nice-looking young man walking our streets. I do hope you will be staying for a while."

The way things had been proceeding, he was probably going to live in Gravesly, hunting the Wolf, until all his teeth fell out. "It's a lovely town."

Mrs. Raithespeare beamed. "It is, isn't it? So much nicer than Rye, but you wouldn't know it to hear any of them talk. You get any of those people by the ear, and they'll let you know at least a hundred times over that Rye was one of the Cinque Ports. As if that has any bearing on anything today, I ask you. The Cinque Ports." The woman made a disgusted sound with her tongue. "That is their only claim to fame, and it happened nearly a thousand years ago."

"Oh, I would pick Gravesly over Rye any day, Mrs. Raithespeare."

"Such a smart young man." She shook her finger at James. "If I were just twenty years younger and unmarried . . ."

"I could only dream of such a thing, Mrs. Raithespeare."

The woman giggled, patted his arm, and moved on up the street. James stood for a moment as he realized that he had just flirted. He never flirted.

With a shake of his head, he continued down the cobblestoned main street of Gravesly. He really needed to plan and be more focused on his work. If he could just take down the Wolf, he would be able to return to London in triumph. No one would dare laugh at him. His name would be said with respect. And then . . . James would not even put into thought the true desire of his heart.

"Captain!"

"Captain!"

"Captain!" Three little voices chorused behind him, and James stopped once more and turned to face the three angelic faces of the Sawyer family.

"Did Sickly-poo work her magic?" the oldest girl asked, hands behind her back, body swaying forward and back.

"Yes, have you taken care of her?" the middle girl piped up.

"Sickly-poo is a boy!" the little boy informed them all adamantly.

James had actually been on his way to return Sickly-poo to the baker. "Sickly-poo did a wonderful job," he said quickly. "I am feeling tip-top."

"We told you he's magic!" the little boy beamed.

James took the stuffed plaything from his pocket and held it out to the little boy. "I only wish that I had known about Sickly-poo before.

He would have been a great help to the officers injured in battle."

"You fought the French?" the little boy asked eagerly, cradling his stuffed rabbit close to his body.

"Do tell us all about it, Captain," the oldest girl demanded.

"Children, do not bother the captain."

James looked up to see Mrs. Sawyer emerge from a small shop across the street. "Oh, they're no bother," James said quickly, actually amazed that they truly weren't.

Mrs. Sawyer laughed. "Well then," she said merrily. "You could not be speaking of my little urchins."

"He is, Mother! And he is going to tell us about fighting the French."

"That's just lovely, Tim." Mrs. Sawyer smiled at James. "But I'm sure the captain is terribly busy."

"Oh, please!" the girls cried together.

"Emily, Rachel, you mustn't beg," their mother remonstrated.

"It is quite all right, Mrs. Sawyer," James said quickly. "I do not mind telling the children stories."

"Well, then, you must at least allow me to offer you dinner. Could you come this evening?"

James blinked. The three children were begging with their eyes as Mrs. Sawyer waited for his answer. "Of course," he said finally.

"See, children, we will have Captain Ashley for dinner, and he can regale you with his stories."

"Hurray!" All three of the children danced around James and clapped their hands.

"Come now, children." Mrs. Sawyer held out her hand and Timmy grabbed hold. "Until this evening, Captain." She grinned at James and marched off with her charges.

James stood watching after them with the strangest feeling in his chest. He was not sure exactly what it was, but it felt a bit like an ache. He had grown up without many friends, and definitely as the pariah of the community.

Though his maternal grandfather, Robert Frederick Ashley, had been extremely wealthy, the man had not been a peer, and so the upper society of Calcutta had ignored him and his daughter.

When Mr. Ashley had died and his daughter had given birth to a bastard child, she had been absolutely shunned. The middle-class English population had treated James like some sort of disease that one wouldn't want to get too near.

At the age of ten, James's life changed completely. His mother died, and James inherited his grandfather's fortune. From then on, James had friends. They were slimy, two-timing thieves. But they paid attention to him.

All along, James yearned for acceptance. He had thought, once, that it was within his reach. With his commission in the navy, and, of course, his money, James had secured the hand of Melissa Rutland in marriage.

She had been the daughter of the Honorable Mr. Tobias Rutland, a younger son of a younger son of an earl. Mr. Rutland had grudgingly given his blessing to the marriage. Obviously, the man's blue blood ran a bit cold at the thought of James's parentage, but he was quite ecstatic at the extent of James's fortune.

Still, James had learned a valuable lesson. Money did not overcome all obstacles. All it had taken was the arrival of Viscount Leighton in India for Mr. Rutland, and the fair Melissa, to forget that James existed.

It had been humiliating, especially since they broke off the engagement without any real commitment from the viscount. James had left India, not so much heartbroken as world-weary.

If his experience in India had not taught James to distrust the peerage of England, his time in London most definitely had. He trusted no one.

But he still yearned for acceptance.

He had thought to accomplish that goal on English soil. Unfortunately, London society thought him an interesting enigma, with his great heroics in battle, uncertain parentage, and rigid manners. Still, they had never truly opened their ranks. And certainly his one true desire had not been met, yet.

The navy had been the only place where James

had felt accepted and respected. Until now, in this town which was supposed to revile him for hunting down one of their own.

Perhaps it was a trap?

James watched the Sawyer children skipping down the lane and shook his head. He had never before in his life been invited to dine with a family. He was actually looking forward to the evening, and he hoped with all of his heart that it was not a trap.

# Chapter 9

**P**ru was in a deadlock with her butler. They stood several feet apart in the parlor, arms akimbo, eyes glaring.

"Swords or pistols?" Pru demanded.

Clifton rolled his single eye skyward and made a strangled sound deep in his throat.

She should not have teased him, but he was soft beneath his crust, and he made her laugh when he got riled. "Well, I can think of no other way to compromise, so we shall have a duel," she said.

"Don't be ridiculous!"

"Sorry to interrupt," Tuck singsonged through the open doorway. "But Mrs. Sawyer's here to see you." The boy continued on down the hall and Sarah Sawyer came into view, delicate brows knit together over her light eyes.

"Sarah! I am so glad you have come. I have a pinafore all made for Emily, and I've meant to bring it to you."

Sarah hesitated, her uneasy gaze on Clifton. "Is this a good time?" she asked.

"Of course." Pru nodded at her butler. "Clifton and I are just having a bit of a row, but that's quite normal."

"I just wanted to let you know that I have invited your captain to dinner tonight."

"He's not *her* captain!" Clifton roared.

Poor Sarah looked as if she might scamper off like a scared rabbit. Pru wanted to clock Clifton on the side of the head. Instead, she went quickly to take Sarah's arm. "Come in, Sarah, we shall have tea." She gently steered Sarah toward a chair. "Do tell Mabel to bring tea, Clifton."

The man stalked off grumbling about captains sent from the devil, and Pru sighed with relief when he finally rounded a corner and she could not hear him anymore.

"So, you have invited the good captain to dinner, Sarah. That is lovely of you, really."

"I thought it a wonderful way to keep him occupied. And, actually, the children absolutely adore him."

"A perfectly smashing idea, as we have a long night ahead of us. Of course"—Pru frowned as she sat next to her friend—"the men need to haul some wool out of the basement of Harker's. That *is* rather close to your house." She tapped a finger against her chin. "How long do you think you could keep him?"

Sarah threaded her fingers together in a nervous gesture. "I don't know, Lady Pru, and I do not believe I would be able to detain him if he wanted desperately to leave."

"And if you did try, he might become suspicious."

Sarah's eyes rounded in fear, and Pru realized she should not have said that last bit. "It would probably be easier if you had someone else there as well . . ." Pru stopped suddenly, her mind running on ahead of her. "I just had a wonderful idea." She stood and paced for a minute. "It will be tricky, but I think it will work perfectly."

Young Mabel entered with the tea tray.

"Ah, Mabel, I've had the most wondrous idea, but it all depends on you and Delilah."

"Yes, milady," Mabel said as she set up the tray on a little side table. "If I may be so bold, I'd say Delilah can handle anything you need her to do. And if I do say so myself, I've become quite versatile since I've been in your employ." The thin girl nodded her mousey brown head at Mrs. Sawyer and straightened. "What shall we be up to now, milady?" She grinned at Pru.

"Could we have a party together for this very night, do you think?" Pru asked.

Mabel tapped the toe of her sturdy boot. "For how many people, if you don't mind my asking?"

"The whole town."

Mabel tapped her toe some more. "Hmmm, that would be a right good number. The guest of honor, I'm guessing, would be your captain?"

It was interesting that the entire town was starting to think of James as "her" captain. She actually enjoyed the sound of that. It probably was a bad thing that she liked hearing it. But, then, she tended to be bad lately. "Captain Ashley will be invited and will spend his evening much occupied."

"He seemed interested in telling the children stories of his time in France, perhaps we could persuade him to entertain us all," Mrs. Sawyer interjected.

Pru clapped her hands. "Brilliant, Sarah, and while he is entertaining us, we can have the men rotate out. The captain will never even know that there was ever anyone missing at any given time." She twirled and giggled. " 'Tis perfect!"

" 'Tis stupid!"

"Oh, Clifton, you have become the worst of worriers." Pru sighed as she elbowed her way past her butler. She plunked the barrel full of potatoes she held down in front of the fire and sat on a stool. "It will be a marvelous evening. We will keep the captain diverted from his goal and get our own accomplished with no fear of detection."

"And that is your problem right there," Clifton roared. "There ought to be great fear of detection."

"Oh, Clifton." Pru took a paring knife to one of the potatoes.

Mabel hustled in with a pile of folded linens. "All ironed, starched and ready to beautify a table," she announced, stacking the tablecloths on a counter. "I'm off to town to make sure everyone has their orders right. Unless *you* would like to, milady. I could peel potatoes instead."

"Oh no, Mabel, you go." Pru grinned. Mabel had on her best dress, and her hair was all done up in a tight coil at her neck. Pru was rather sure Mabel's first visit would be to Paul, the butcher's son.

"I don't like this one bit," Clifton grumbled.

"You have to make sure that the men go out in indiscernible shifts, Clifton, and make sure they know to stay away for short periods of time. You'll be able to get the whole shipment out of Harker's and to the beach. I am sure we will all sleep better knowing that it is gone, and I know the entire town will be happy to have the crop out and money in their pockets."

"And I am sure that no one wants to rot in a London prison," Clifton said. "I say we suspend all business until Captain Ashley is well away from here, and the sooner that happens the better."

"You know we cannot do that, Clifton."

"Well, then, at least you should stop running the transports."

Pru looked at the potato in her hand and realized that she had whacked the thing down to a white nub. She threw it in the fire, where it plopped into the ashes, sending out a poof of soot. She stared for a moment at the ashes that lay on the hearth, then looked up into Clifton's dear face.

He had opened the door the first time she had ever come to Chesley House. Pru could remember standing there with her parents, waiting to see the man that she would marry. She had been sixteen, and had never before left the small town of Larkshire. And now she was an entire hour away from her home knocking on the door of a man thirty years older than she, who would wed her the very next day.

And her first sight of her new home had been a man a full foot taller than she, with arms the size of ham hocks, a head that shone like a gazing ball in the sun, with a black eye patch strapped across his face. Pru had nearly fainted at the sight.

Now she trusted that man completely, and loved him even more than she had loved her parents. And, in the last two years since her husband had died, Clifton had given her a new life to which Pru clung with all the tenacity she had within her. Because, truly, before the moment Clifton had revealed her late husband's work and asked her to continue it, Pru had not lived at all.

"You did not ask me to quit before the captain arrived. You believed in me then," she said, and immediately hated the pathetic words.

"Prudence," Clifton said on a long-suffering sigh, "you can do anything you put your mind to, 'tis not you I'm afraid of. But I *am* afraid of the power he could have over you."

And without putting it into words, they both knew of whom and what Clifton spoke.

Out of the corner of her eye, Pru saw Delilah quietly put down her stirring spoon and discreetly leave the kitchen.

"You do not show much confidence in me if you think I would allow him to have power over me."

"You are naive, Lady Pru, and do not understand the sway this kind of thing can have over a man's, or a woman's, mind," Clifton said solemnly.

When he had said the word "naive," Pru had bristled, but because of Clifton's demeanor and tone of voice, she stopped herself from making a cutting remark.

Clifton turned away from her and stared out a window. "I fear for the people of Gravesly, yes, and so I worry about this new man. I do not fear your ability or have any less confidence in you. I do, however, fear for you as a woman. The attraction you trifle with is something you do not understand."

"He speaks true, Pru."

Prudence had been so intent on Clifton's speech, she had not heard Leslie enter the kitchen. Her butler turned quickly and stared at Leslie for a silent moment. Then he bowed slightly. "I must get things ready," he said quietly and left through the back door.

Leslie stared after him with a bemused smile curling her lips. "I do know how to scare that man off, don't I now?" She sighed, her bodice straining across her heavy bosom.

Pru turned to look at the back door, which had clicked softly shut after Clifton's retreating figure. Her mind was awash with thoughts of the captain and his power over her, and along with those fears, the shock of Clifton's searing glance at Leslie churned and roiled about. "You both think me so naive, but I do finally see that you are wrong, Leslie."

The woman lifted her brows and turned her gaze upon Pru.

"You think Clifton hates you, that he runs from you, because he abhors you."

Leslie frowned at Pru's words.

Pru laughed without much humor. "It is funny, I think, that I should be the one to see this, when you are the one who sees all. Surely you must notice that he runs from you because he has feelings for you."

Leslie made a sound of disgust. "Yes, dear, feelings of pure hatred."

"That man looked at you like you were the last drop of water on a desert island just now, Leslie. I have seen that look only once before in my life." Pru's stomach tightened just from the memory.

Leslie stared at Pru, then blinked. "Goodness," she said as if she had just seen a vision of angels.

Pru bit her lip, but couldn't stop the small giggle that escaped.

Leslie plopped down upon a chair. "Really, Pru, you are not jesting with me, are you?"

Pru laughed outright and shook her head. "No, Leslie, there was no misunderstanding the look in Clifton's eyes just now."

Leslie nodded, her gaze thoughtful. "I do believe you are right, Pru. He runs from fear, not hate." She sat up, determination glinting in her eyes. "Get that man back in here right now."

Pru's laughter died a sudden and silent death. "Now, I am not sure . . ."

"Go get him."

Pru jumped up off her stool and went to the back door. "Clifton," she called, her voice a bit wobbly. She cleared her throat and yelled again, "Clifton, come here, please!"

They waited quietly, Pru not at all sure that Clifton would heed her call. But then she saw the man stomp out of the stable and come up the garden path.

He stared warily past her and into the kitchen, and stopped before he reached the door. "What do you need, Lady Pru?" The poor man was scared to death to come into the kitchen.

"Clifton, I need you," Pru said, gesturing for the butler to enter. Pru felt Leslie beside her and watched as Clifton's eyes rounded in what could only be fear.

Pru had never seen Clifton afraid of anything. She stood stunned as she realized that her friend was right; Clifton had always run from Leslie Redding because he was afraid, not because he could not stand her.

Leslie put her hand on Pru's shoulder. "You have brought him far enough," she said, and walked past Pru into the garden.

The woman went to stand before Clifton, and the butler did not move an inch. The poor man looked as if a poisonous snake had just wriggled out of the house and begun speaking to him.

Only Leslie had not yet said a word.

Pru watched for a long moment, very much intrigued at what Leslie would do, then she realized that she should not be so nosy. Reluctantly, she turned back into the kitchen and sat on her stool. Taking up another potato, Pru scraped her knife over its skin. She kept her ear cocked toward the outside door, but heard nothing at all.

A good half an hour later, Leslie swung through the door with a big smile. She plunked down beside Pru and grabbed a potato. And then she peeled it, humming to herself the whole time.

Pru waited through two whole potatoes before she dropped her knife with a clunk and planted her fists on her hips. "Well?" she asked, exasperated.

Leslie shrugged one shoulder, but did not look up from her task. "Well," she said, "I've given Eurel a few things to think about."

"And . . ." Pru prompted her friend.

"And, I want to thank you for pointing out what I should have seen years ago."

With a long sigh, Pru picked up her knife.

Leslie laughed. "I really did not say much, Pru. I stood really close to him, and looked in his eye, and then I told him that I loved him, and that he should consider himself a hunted man from now on."

Pru blinked. "And I thought I had been forward with the captain."

Leslie threw her now white potato in the basket. "Some situations warrant fast action."

With a nod, Pru went back to her work. "You are a wise woman, Leslie Redding, very wise."

His simple dinner with the Sawyers had turned into a country fair. And he was the star attraction. He sat now in Lady Farnsworth's garden surrounded by a bevy of attentive faces, all wanting to hear of his exploits with the French. And he had to admit that he was terribly flattered, as well as very suspicious.

He had, again, thought trap, when the town decided to honor him with an impromptu party. He wondered if it was a distraction of some sort. He had told the officers, Pimpton and Lyle, to scout Gravesly during the party.

But, truly, the entire town was here at Chesley House. James had ticked them all off on a mental list, and he constantly looked about to see if anyone had gone missing.

He had actually started wondering about Harker, but there he was under one of the lanterns with a woman who had been introduced as Miss Templeton.

"Captain Ashley, what happened then?" a little voice piped up in front of him.

James looked down at the small faces surrounding him and laughed. "Sorry," he said quickly, and returned to his story. Parents ringed their circle, also enthralled with his stories, and beyond them he could see out of the corner of his eye Prudence Farnsworth.

He resolutely kept from staring straight at her, for he was not sure that he could control the emotions that would surely cross his features, lust being the primary one and obviously not something he wanted people to see.

Fear hunkered in his heart as well, and confusion and anger and frustration. And it all had to do with Prudence Farnsworth.

Of course, it was compounded by the fact that he had been in Gravesly nearly a week and discovered absolutely nothing. The only clues that the town harbored a smuggling gang were the images of wolves that adorned every single doorframe in the town.

And those small, carved insignia would surely drive him to bedlam.

A crack of thunder interrupted the end of James's story, and every face in the crowd glanced toward the heavens. They waited a moment in silence.

It was another warm night, too warm, James realized in that moment, the air heavy.

And just like that the sky opened and dumped buckets on the town of Gravesly. The entire lot of them ran for little Chesley House, women taking in trays of food, men grabbing children and slinging them over their shoulders, and the children giggling, screaming, and scuttling around the already muddy garden.

James stood and slicked back his soaked hair so that he could place his drenched hat upon his head. Lyle and Pimpton chose that moment to scurry up the hill.

"Nothing happening, Captain," Lyle said quickly, and ran for the house.

Pimpton just nodded his agreement. James had yet to hear the thin, young man say one word. Perhaps he was mute?

James stood staring back at the dark town, contemplating a quick trip down the hill, but his arm was caught against the warmth of a body.

Without looking, he knew Prudence clung to his elbow. His entire body knew when she was near, every sense taking in her smell, sound, and feel. That he craved to taste her as well made James nearly tear out of her grasp and run.

"Come, James," she said. "Some of the men have brought instruments; we can clear the furniture in the parlor and dance until dawn."

James. She called him James. No other woman besides his mother had ever used his name.

He should probably tell her not to call him that, but he liked the sound of it on her lips.

She tugged on his arm, and they sloshed through puddles to the house. He glanced down at her and realized that her wet gown was plastered to her body. He could see the tight buds of her swollen nipples.

God help him.

Prudence opened the back door, and they entered the dark, slightly cool kitchen.

"You should change your dress," he said.

"Oh no," Prudence laughed. "Everyone is wet, and it isn't very cold. We will dance to warm ourselves, and shan't get sick, I'm sure."

Suddenly James could think of nothing worse than for the entire town to see Prudence the way he saw her now. He stared at her breasts, then the soft swell of her belly and thighs.

"No," he said, his voice rough. "Go. Change."

"But . . ." She stopped, her gaze climbing his own wet chest to burn into his eyes.

They stood just staring at one another for a moment that seemed like an eternity.

She blinked then and took a step toward him, and the scent of her made him dizzy. He felt like he was leaning over the bow of a boat, staring into the dark, swirling waters of the ocean. If he jumped in, he would drown. But he knew he would jump.

Why, he wondered absently? Since Melissa, he had always been able to resist women with titles. At times it had been difficult. Never had it been impossible.

# Chapter 10

Why now? Why now, did his body find the woman that it would surely never be able to resist?

Now, when he needed desperately to focus on his job and bring honor to his much-belittled reputation. Now, when he was so close to the glory he had dreamed of his entire life. Now he was to be brought low by the one thing that had never made a problem of itself.

He raised his hand and placed it against Prudence's throat. It was slender, but strong, and her heartbeat raced against his fingertips. He let his hand drop, his palm covering one of her straining nipples.

She let out a small sound, and he lowered his mouth and kissed her. Her lips were parted, and he touched his tongue to her teeth with a deep, inward sigh. She tasted divine.

He wanted to drown in her.

In that moment, everything left James's mind except the intense desire to lay Prudence out on the stone floor and bury himself inside of her. He shifted the sodden fabric of her dress and cupped her bare, cool breast in his hand as he continued to take her mouth in a deep kiss that would surely be the end of him.

"Goodness," Prudence whispered into his mouth, and then her breath hitched deliciously when he let his thumb track a light trail over her nipple.

All that mattered to him then was making Prudence Farnsworth sigh with pleasure. He tasted her mouth once more, then trailed kisses across her jaw and down her neck.

She leaned back in his arms, her hands buried in his hair as he found her breast with his mouth. It was soft beneath his lips, and he had a moment when he thought that he could possibly stay there forever. But then he found Pru's nipple with his tongue.

She clutched at his head and groaned, and he reveled in the sound.

And then there was light.

James closed his eyes in confusion as light pierced the comfortable darkness around them.

His mind came back to reality quickly, though, and he realized that someone had opened the door to the kitchen. He straightened quickly, pulling Prudence against him and turning so that his body blocked the intruder's view of Prudence's half-naked body.

Prudence had gone very still, her forehead pressed to his chest, and whoever had pushed open the door let it click back into place without saying a word.

James quietly pulled Prudence's dress back over her shoulder and held it in place. Her muscles flexed beneath his fingers, and even in the horror of the moment, James enjoyed the feeling. He enjoyed everything about this woman's body, her lips, her full, firm breasts, her strong, sinewy arms. He could only dream of undressing her completely and tonguing his way down her body to the curve of the stomach he had seen through her wet gown, and the line of her slender thighs.

And then there was the woman, the straightforward approach she had, which terrified him. Yet she thrilled him as no other woman had.

"Well," she said quietly, "it does seem that our lovemaking is always cut short in one way or another. Quite distressing."

"Quite," James murmured against her hair.

"I should probably go up and change now." She stopped and took a deep breath. "You would not possibly want to come with me?" she asked, the tiny inflection of hope hard to ignore.

James closed his eyes. Prudence Farnsworth could shock him like no other woman. And he had been propositioned by the best. It probably had to do with the fact that she was so incredibly innocent.

"Did you see who it was that opened the door?" James asked, rather than think or speak to Prudence about helping her undress.

Prudence shrugged as if it did not matter. "No, I am sure that whoever it was is just as embarrassed as we."

"I have compromised you," James said, and knew in that exact moment what he must do.

"You speak nonsense." Prudence laughed softly. "They will not tell of what they have seen. And, anyway, even if the whole town knew, no one would care."

"I never speak nonsense, Lady Farnsworth."

"Well you are certainly not speaking any sense whatsoever."

"Sense, nonsense, it does not matter. You are a peeress, revered in this town, and I have compromised you, Lady Farnsworth." James stopped and swallowed the lump that had lodged in his throat and threatened now to choke him. "I will, of course, announce our engagement."

"Excuse me?" Prudence cried incredulously. "What on earth are you talking about?"

"I realize that I am beneath you, Lady Farnsworth, but I do have quite a fortune."

Even in the dim room, James could see the shock that rounded Prudence's eyes. "You *do* speak absolute nonsense," she said.

James sighed deeply. "I am speaking of honor, Lady Farnsworth, yours as well as mine. I have never before put myself in the situation that I now find myself, but I would never forgive myself if I just let it go now and did not do the right thing."

"Truly, Captain, you do not have to do something so rash as to marry me. No one will say a word of this, I swear."

"But people will know. At least one person saw us, and I cannot believe that they will not whisper of it. And even if that person does not dare to revile you to your face, your reputation has been compromised. I will not allow that as it is my fault."

Prudence made a sound full of frustration. "Your fault? It is just as much my fault as yours."

James closed his eyes for a moment. "Lady Farnsworth," he said calmly, " 'tis now you who speaks nonsense."

"Well, Captain, I can tell you this very honestly. *I* never speak nonsense."

"Well, you certainly speak no sense."

They stood staring at one another, the silence bearing out their mutual stubbornness.

"Captain, my honor is not at stake, but if this situation upsets you, I have only to offer you escape. You may leave and know that the town will not revile me, and you will not hear of this incident again."

James wanted to throw something. This woman had no idea what he spoke of when he said "honor." "I am not leaving Gravesly, Lady Farnsworth, until I have accomplished my goal and brought the Wolf to justice."

Prudence looked very sad suddenly. She dropped her gaze and stared intently at the floor.

"And now, I guess, I have something else to accomplish." He could see only the top of her head, her hair dark with rain. "If there is one hint of scandal, my lady, I will marry you."

She sighed and looked back up at him. "We would never suit, Captain. You must believe me when I say that."

James felt as if she had slapped him. "Of course not. You are *Lady* Farnsworth. I am *Captain* Ashley."

She frowned and then shook her head. "I will not marry," she said, and, turning on her heel, walked regally out the door, her departure made only slightly less majestic by the sloshing of her sodden shoes.

"So, I hear you were quite a distraction to the good captain last night. The wool is certainly out of Harker's cellar."

Pru glanced up from the book she had been reading. "Tell me the story is not all over town," she demanded.

"Of course it is. The entire assemblage knew of it the second Paul returned from catching you in the kitchen." Leslie sauntered into the sitting room and glided into a chair.

Pru had been about to warn Leslie to make everyone quit their gossiping immediately, but she stopped and stared at her friend. "What on earth is the matter with you?"

Leslie lifted her brows and shook her head as if she had not understood the question. "Why, nothing, dear."

"Nothing? You look as if you have been at the brandy bottle again."

"Oh." Leslie giggled. The woman giggled, for heaven's sake.

"Are you sure you are feeling all right, Leslie?"

"I'm feeling just lovely." She smiled. "I've been speaking with Eurel in the barn for a bit."

Pru winced. "And that has put stars in your eyes? He's in a horrific mood, I can't believe that he was any better for you than he was with me this morning."

"Oh, I am sure he was worse."

Pru shook her head.

"I kissed him."

Pru could not contain the laugh that broke from her throat. "And you are still alive?"

Leslie grinned. "Barely. I just took his growling face in my hands and planted a good one right on his mouth, and you know that man melted like butter in the summer."

Melting and Clifton just did not fit in the same sentence.

" 'Tis just a matter of time, dearest, before I have that man not knowing which way is up."

Pru sighed heavily. How would it be to understand your power as a woman so thoroughly? It sounded very nice, really.

"Anyway, Prudence, the entire town is talking about what happened last night."

Pru groaned as she remembered what they had been speaking of in the first place. "We must warn everyone not to gossip at all."

"Now there is an impossible task," Leslie said dryly.

"No, Leslie, I am serious, deadly serious. The captain was intent on marrying me last night when we were found out."

Leslie nodded slowly. "Yes, well, he does seem the type to be honorable now, doesn't he?"

"I, of course, told him that I could never marry, but he has insisted that if there is a scandal, he will force the issue. And to him, having the entire town in the know would definitely be a scandal." Pru closed her book and leaned against the back of her chair. "What have I done?"

They were silent for a moment, the only sound that of the rain drumming against the windowpanes. Then Leslie said quietly, "Unfortunately, dearest, I do think there is a bit of a scandal. A real one."

Pru glanced at her friend's serious face. "What do you mean, Leslie?"

"Well." Leslie straightened in the seat and smoothed out her dress before continuing, "I do think you have overestimated the people of Gravesly, Pru."

Pru's heart doubled its rhythm as a tiny prick of dread traveled up her spine.

"It was hard, you remember, for them to accept you in your husband's place." Leslie sighed. "But they did, finally. I think, though, that this thing with the captain may just be too hard for them to deal with."

"But I am a widow!"

"True, but even widows must live by society's standards, especially when 'tis a provincial society we are talking about."

Pru covered her face with her hands and groaned. "But you are the one who told me it was too bad that I could not act upon my attraction to the captain. That must mean that others will feel the same."

"Oh yes, dear, they would have. But only if you had been discreet."

Pru peeked through her fingers at Leslie. "Discreet? How on earth can you be discreet in Gravesly?"

Leslie smiled a bit and chewed on her bottom lip. "Well, not kissing him in the kitchen would have been a good start."

"Now you tell me."

"Yes, well, now I must tell you another thing you will surely not wish to hear."

Pru closed her fingers with a snap to cut off her view. "Lord no, it gets worse?"

"Not worse so much as more complicated."

"Lovely."

"I am just wondering if you have given a thought to what a boon this marriage could be to the town."

Pru sat straight up in the chair, her book sliding off her lap and landing with a thud on the wood floor. "You must be jesting," she finally managed to say.

"Well, of course, I am not saying that you should," Leslie said quickly. "I am just voicing a thought that if you were to marry the captain, he would certainly never reveal the Wolf's true identity. In fact, he might just quit his interfering altogether."

"Of course he would not, Leslie. He is a man of incredibly high standards, and he would still find it necessary to resurrect his pride from the terrible beating the Wolf gave it."

Leslie shrugged lightly. "I don't believe he

would, Pru. Think of the beating his reputation would take in London society if, *as your husband*, Captain Ashley brought the Wolf to justice."

Pru felt as if her chest had suddenly filled with water. She gulped in a mouthful of air and tried to breathe.

Leslie reached over to clasp Pru's hands in hers. "I am just stating a fact, Pru, a fact that would solve many dilemmas for you. But, of course, I am not telling you to marry him."

Pru could barely move. "It certainly sounds that way to me," she said quietly.

Leslie shook her head. "I am just voicing a thought that came to my mind, dearest."

"A thought better left unsaid."

Both the women turned at Clifton's dark tone.

Leslie scowled at the butler. "For the love of God, Clifton, for a large man you move on the feet of a cat."

"When Lady Farnsworth is ready to marry again, she will marry someone much better suited to her than a bastard son."

"And what does that have to do with anything?" Leslie demanded. "Rank and status do not make happiness. Love itself can make a happy marriage."

"Love?" Pru asked feebly, but neither Clifton nor Leslie paid her any heed.

"Love!" Clifton said vehemently. "A figment of a woman's imagination."

"Oh, you are so dense, Clifton!" Leslie shook her head and tsked. "And what of the villagers? I have already heard some whispers."

"They would do well not to speak so of their betters!"

"For claiming to be Pru's champion, you are certainly not thinking in her best interest at the moment!"

The two glared at one another furiously, and if Pru had not been so horrified at the situation, she would have laughed out loud. Instead, she stood and took a deep breath.

"Neither status nor love has anything to do with my decision, children. I grew up under the wing of my parents and was shifted from there to the care of my husband, and now, finally, in the last two years, I have tasted freedom and independence. And it is too sweet a fruit to throw away for anything." She glanced from Leslie's sad eyes to Clifton's angry ones.

"I am happier now than I ever dreamed I could be."

For a moment, Pru remembered the fleeting thought she had entertained in Leslie's home a few days before. Was she as happy as she believed? Or was there something else?

But, no, she had been married, and she had been a single woman on her own. And she much preferred being single.

"I shall not marry again, ever." She shook her

head in disgust. "And most definitely I am not going to marry a man who's main objective in life is to take away the only security Gravesly has." Prudence punctuated the end of her sentence with a nod. "And that is the last we shall say on the subject."

The subject of his marriage to Lady Prudence Farnsworth was foremost in the minds of every person residing in the town of Gravesly, it seemed.

James had been trying to get out of town for at least two hours. Harker had been the first to delay him. In fact, an entire bevy of men had bought him a pint and mourned the loss of James's bachelor days. That had been his first inkling that Prudence had been very wrong about the reaction of the town to their tryst of the night before.

As James readied Devil for the short trip to Rye, Artie had spoken to him for twenty minutes about being honorable. The Sawyer children had regaled him for a half hour on the subject of Lady Farnsworth's beauty and grace. And now he was actually sitting in Mrs. Witherspoon's tiny parlor having tea.

"Now, Captain," she said, after setting her teacup back in its saucer. This feat had taken a good five minutes, as the dear woman's hands shook with extreme ferocity. "I must assume that as an officer you are also a gentleman."

"I like to think so, Mrs. Witherspoon." James took a tentative bite of the biscuit on his plate. It was actually quite good, so he took another, more hearty bite.

"Then, of course, we shall be preparing for a wedding?"

The biscuit suddenly became a huge lump of dough going down the wrong way. James coughed and sputtered as little Mrs. Witherspoon thumped on his back with the strength of ten men.

"What I mean to say, Captain," Mrs. Witherspoon continued as she banged on James's back, "is that we all adore Lady Farnsworth and think of her as family." A huge whack followed this statement. "And so we do worry about her."

Mrs. Witherspoon quit beating on him then, and James sat for a moment just breathing. He was rather sure she had set a kidney loose. "Mrs. Witherspoon," he was finally able to say, "I have most definitely asked for Lady Farnsworth's hand in marriage."

"Good, then, are you going to take her away to London? Because that will never do. Oh, no, dear, that will never do." Mrs. Witherspoon dumped at least a half a cup of sugar into her tea and stirred.

"You know Chesley House is hers. Her husband's entailed estate is up near London somewhere. Chesley House was the dower house of his estate. He just loved it so that they spent all their time here. And, of course," Mrs. Witherspoon continued quickly, "we do need Lady Farnsworth here."

James blinked as his hostess poured half the cream into her tiny cup of tea. "Well, certainly, I shall stay until I bring the Wolf to justice."

Mrs. Witherspoon laughed and waved her hand. "Oh, goodness, you are still about that wretched business?" She took a great gulp of her tea and made a satisfied sound deep in her throat.

"That wretched business is all that I am about, Mrs. Witherspoon."

The tiny woman wiggled back against her chair and shook her head at him. "Bringing the Wolf to justice would be the downfall of this entire town, Captain. We would be unable to exist." She took another deep drink of her tea.

"But I shall say no more. I just wanted to make sure that you would do right by Lady Farnsworth." She grinned at him. "It is so nice to have such a handsome man about the place. I am glad you've decided to stay. Now drink your tea, boy."

And James drank.

He was starting to realize that you just did not go up against Mrs. Witherspoon. But he did wonder about the woman's insistence that the Wolf was good for Gravesly.

He was finally able to extract himself from Mrs. Witherspoon's and turned up the street once again to collect Devil from Artie's care.

"Ho there, Captain Ashley." Josh Harker clapped him on the shoulder. "Been drinking sweet tea with Mrs. Witherspoon, have you?"

James laughed. "Her tea must have been extremely sweet."

"Ah, yes, our Mrs. Witherspoon. She likes her sugar and good strong ale."

"It is amazing that she is still a seamstress, the way her hands shake, I mean."

Harker laughed and shook his head. "Oh, she is mostly just the go-between now. People go in and tell her what they need, and she finds someone to do it. Lady Pru has been making the Sawyers' little pinafores since the girls were born."

"Wouldn't it be easier if someone else took over the shop?"

Harker stopped and just looked at James for a moment. "Probably, but then what would Mrs. Witherspoon do?"

James felt as if he were missing something, so he changed the subject. "Harker, tell me, why does everyone in town have a wolf carved into their doorframe?"

A beat went by in silence, and then Harker said quietly, "Think, Captain, of what these people's lives would be like without the Wolf."

"They would be rid of a criminal in their midst?"

Harker shook his head and glanced up the

street, then turned to look again at James. "Captain, smuggling will happen no matter if the Wolf is around or not. I could be hanged for saying so, but the king's taxes make it impossible for normal folk to get by without it. Some of the smuggling gangs around these parts are vicious, greedy people. Captain, if you had gone to one of these other towns, you would probably be dead by now."

James only nodded at this, for he knew it to be true.

"The Wolf has kept our town together. We do not live with murder and crime. And we prosper."

"But smuggling itself is a crime."

Harker sighed, then silently shook his head. "So are starving children, Captain." And the big man turned on his heel and marched down the street.

# Chapter 11

❧〜◦〜❧

**"A**ll right, then, out of bed, the lot of you!" James yanked the mattress out from under Pimpton. The young man rolled facefirst onto the hard wooden floor.

Lyle sat straight up in bed, his squinty eyes blinking at the light of James's lantern.

"You two are about as useful as tits on a hog," James yelled, and butted Pimpton's side with the toe of his boot. "It's prime smuggling time, and you gents are dreaming the night away in your cots. Pathetic."

Pimpton had pushed himself off the ground and now stood shivering in nothing but his underclothing. The rain had finally stopped earlier that afternoon, but it had left a distinct chill in the air.

James made a sound of disgust. "Put your clothes on. We are going out."

The two men glanced at each other as if they were wondering whether or not to do what James had just asked them.

"That was a direct order," he bellowed, his pulse pounding in his neck. "Get dressed immediately. I will wait outside, which, by the way, has turned quite nippy. So make sure I'm not standing too long!" James's voice got progressively louder until he was basically yelling the last few words. He pivoted on his heel, banged through the door, and threw it back on its frame as hard as he could. He absolutely could not abide lazy stand-about soldiers.

Fortunately, Lyle and Pimpton had gotten the message, for they were out the door in two minutes flat.

"Good then," James said, when they came scrambling outside. "I've been along the beaches and haven't detected a single movement or any activity. But I rode to Rye today and the excise officers there said they chased a ship late last night into the Channel. They believe it came from Gravesly Bay, which would mean that they either loaded or unloaded goods in this very town last night."

This information had truly shocked James. The whole town had been at the party until an ungodly hour. He was starting to wonder if the Wolf and his gang were actually of the animal variety, living in caves somewhere. Either that, or they were ghosts, it seemed.

"Now," James continued, "most probably there were goods unloaded. For, even if the ship were here to pick up wool, it would have brought a shipment of something to off-load as well. So now we need to find where the goods have gone." James held his lantern a touch higher and peered at the men before him. "Any ideas, gentlemen?"

Pimpton had a completely blank look in his eyes as if he had not understood a word that James had just said. With a long sigh, James shifted his attention to the slightly more intelligent-looking Lyle. "Well?" he prompted.

"Uh," Lyle said with all the conviction of a gnat.

No wonder the Wolf was so incredibly successful at his illegal undertakings. The excise officers of Gravesly had half a brain between the both of them, probably less, actually. "All right then," James said. "Since I have combed the beaches and found nothing, we shall search farther inland."

Again Lyle and Pimpton glanced at each other as if trying to gauge James's seriousness. "I shall take the road out to the marsh. You, Pimp . . ."

"Oh, no, sir, I shall take the road to the marsh," Lyle interrupted him. "That is to say, sir, I should rather I take the marsh, as it is, er, well, terribly, uh, marshy, sir."

"Marshy?"

"I mean it is very dark there, sir, and hard to navigate. I would be able to do it rather better than you, sir, as I know my way around." Lyle took a deep breath, and James realized that the boy was shaking. He frowned.

"Not necessary, Lyle. I will take the marsh." There was something very strange going on here, and James was determined to get to the bottom of it. "You take the road into town, Lyle. And Pimpton." James stopped and stared at the man for a moment. Pimpton's mouth was open slightly, his eyes a bit crossed, and drool was forming on his lip. Surely, he was touched in the head. With a roll of his eyes, James said, "Why don't you keep watch over the beaches?"

Nothing was going on at the beaches. James was rather sure of that, at least.

"But, really, sir . . ." Lyle started to protest. James just held up his hand.

"When I give an order, I expect direct compliance and definitely no questions. You are dismissed!"

The two men looked as if they both would rather jump from the cliffs right in front of them and dash themselves on the rocks. But they saluted rather badly and took off for the small stable behind the station.

Damn if there wasn't something strange afoot this night.

"You should not be here," Clifton grumbled.

"Oh, please, quit your griping and just work."

Pru hefted another sack from the wagon and threw it down to her butler, who then passed it on down the line of men that stretched through the murky, thigh-deep water to the high, dry ground where they were hiding last night's shipment of tea.

"But if the captain were to find us . . ."

"The captain is out spying on a deserted beach, Clifton." Pru tossed another sack down from the dwindling pile on the wagon. "He has no idea what happened last night. Not even a clue."

"Let's not speak of last night," Clifton snapped.

Pru put a bit more strength behind her next throw, causing Clifton to stumble when the sack hit him at chest level. Pru was tired of all the fuss everyone was making over her tryst with the captain. The men were scuttling around giving her a wide berth and never looking at her directly. It was devilishly irritating.

A whistle pierced the chill night air, and the men below her froze. Pru held her breath, waiting. And then another whistle sounded, long then short. Someone approached, but it was friend not foe.

Splashes, the sound of hooves beating through the marsh. Pru twirled about, squinting through the dark and mist toward the newcomer.

She made out the gold buttons and braid of an officer and her heart stopped for a fraction of a second, then doubled its beat, pumping blood through her body so fast her fingers went numb.

Another second and Pru recognized Lyle. She closed her eyes for a moment and sent a little prayer of thanks toward heaven. Lyle and Pimpton were loyal to money, thank heavens, not the law.

Lyle splashed toward them, yanked hard on his reins pivoting his horse about next to the cart. "He is coming to the marsh."

Pru let out a short burst of air from her lungs, her breath showing white in the icy darkness. They all knew whom Lyle meant.

The men scattered, melting into the night like the moon going behind a cloud. Clifton jumped to the seat of the cart and slapped the reins, as Lyle took off at a hard run.

Pru dropped to a crouch and wrapped her hands around the back of Clifton's seat.

"Jump!" Clifton commanded her.

"No," she said simply, gritting her teeth as they bumped over a rotted log.

"Jump!" Clifton yelled again.

"Quit yelling at me and get us out of here," Pru said tightly.

She heard some rather creative words, but at least Clifton leaned forward into his driving and did not try to speak to her anymore. They bounced along, going deeper and deeper into the marsh, finally pulling the cart into a stand of tall reeds.

Pru jumped out of the back of the cart only after Clifton tied the reins to the brake. Icy cold water seeped immediately through her shoes and breeches, and Pru gave a small gasp. She bit her lip quickly, knowing that any small sound could give them away.

With all the stealth she could muster, Pru lowered herself into the water until it lapped at her neck. The water was like fire against her skin, it was so cold.

She glanced over at Clifton, who had also submerged himself in the marsh water. He pointed under the cart, and Pru nodded. They both moved as silently as they could, parting reeds to get under the cart.

And then they waited in complete silence. True to her name, Beauty was beautiful. She stayed completely still, never twitching or even moving one hair of her gorgeous tail.

And Pru prayed.

They had only had to scatter a few times in the two short years she had been with the gang, and each time she felt as if her heart was going to beat right through the thin wall of her chest and her body would just slump over dead. She hated it more than anything else, and the only thing that kept her halfway calm was praying.

Rather ironic, really. To pray that God would help her perform an illegal act. But Pru was fairly sure that He would. He certainly had so far, and she knew that if she were God, she would definitely see the merits of smuggling for a town that could never survive otherwise.

Her feet and fingers had gone numb with cold when she finally heard the determined splashes coming right for them. Pru closed her eyes, held her breath, and intensified her pleas to God.

The splashes slowed, halted, then started again. Pru felt an almost panicked need to scream. Instead she slowly, silently let out the air in her lungs, and took in another long quiet pull of breath.

He was right in front of them now, and Pru was fairly sure the captain would hear her heart thumping away in the stillness.

He stopped for a moment. His horse whinnied and stamped. Water lapped against Pru's chest.

She heard the soft sound of James's voice urging the horse on, and she knew that he was not going forward, but crossing over to check the tall stand of reeds.

He was not a stupid man, James Ashley, and it was almost as if she could read his mind as he stared at the reeds, just tall enough and full enough to hide someone or something. Perhaps a few of them were bent or broken.

And then she heard a yell. It was close, and accompanied by thrashing water. Pru blinked at the sudden noise. It seemed thunderous after all the silence.

She heard, then, the quick rush of splashes as James turned his steed toward the noise. They had been saved, surely. Pru let out an audible sigh as she listened to James move quickly away from them. He was in pursuit of someone, and as he moved farther and farther away, Pru glanced over to grin at Clifton.

But her butler had vanished.

# Chapter 12

The dawn had come, finally, gray and colder than any May morning before it. Clifton had not returned during the night, and Pru could only pray that he had hidden himself away in some safe place.

Still, Pru had dressed early and stood on her front steps waiting for Tuck to bring the wagon around. She stamped her feet and blew hot air onto her gloved hands.

She had begun to sniffle the night before, and now her nose felt as if it were stuffed with cotton. Her head ached as if someone banged upon her temples with a hammer, and she could feel every tight, painful muscle in her body.

Worse yet, she felt a queer sort of dread she had never experienced before. It did not bode well for the day ahead.

Pru stamped her feet again, wishing she could wear her breeches and wool socks every day. Men had no idea how lucky they were not to have to suffer through cold drafts sliding up their skirts.

She heard the crunch of gravel then, and glanced up to see Captain Ashley riding toward the house. Pru swayed as she watched him, for the man led another horse behind him. And sitting upon that horse like a mammoth warrior was Clifton.

God help her.

James swung down from his horse, his eyes upon the woman before him. She was pale this morning, her eyes large dark splashes of color in a colorless face. He did not relish his task, but he knew that he had to tell Prudence Farnsworth that her trusted butler had been leading a secret life, one that most probably would get the man hanged.

James bowed his head for a moment, and then looked up again. "Lady Farnsworth," he started, then faltered at the flash of anger that brought bright red flags to her cheeks.

"The least you could do now, James, is call me Prudence."

He said nothing for a long moment, breathing slowly, letting the cold air burn in his lungs. A little breath of frigid wind tugged at the bonnet that hugged Prudence's face.

"Prudence, I found your butler in the vicinity of the marsh last night . . ."

"Yes, James, he often walks at night. Is that a crime?" Prudence stared at him defiantly.

"I also came across a shipment of untaxed tea hidden away in the marsh," James said.

"And that means that Clifton put it there?"

James frowned. Prudence was acting rather differently than he would have expected. He had thought that she would cry, berate her butler, perhaps even fling herself into James's arms. That part, actually, was something he had hoped for. Though, of course, he would never admit to such a thing out loud.

"I have a signed confession, Lad . . . Prudence." James patted his chest, where the parchment sat folded in his inside pocket.

"This man, your butler"—James pointed dramatically at Clifton—"is the notorious Wolf, who has been plaguing this town with his illegal acts."

Prudence sucked in an audible breath of shock, her gaze flying to Clifton. "You!" she cried, a look of pure anger emanating from her eyes.

"I realize this is terribly unsettling for you, Prudence. I am sorry to have been the person to break this news to you, but it is necessary. I must take this man and the goods I have confiscated to Rye, where the officers there can transport him to London for his sentencing."

Prudence closed her eyes tightly and went very

still at this pronouncement. James waited for her to get over her initial shock.

He had known she would be upset. But he was also sure that Prudence would soon realize that it was all for the best. Clifton was a menace to the good town of Gravesly and all of England.

Prudence opened her eyes slowly, then turned a penetrating glare on her butler. "How could you, Clifton?" she asked.

"You know why, Lady Pru. And you had better just accept it."

"No," she said dully. "Captain." Prudence turned toward James. "I need to speak with you in private."

"No!" Clifton bellowed.

James winced and glanced back at his captive. The man was twisting about, trying to wrestle the shackles from his hands: an impossible task even for the strong butler.

"Come now, man, you promised to go quietly!"

"Clifton," Pru said calmly, "of course I will not allow this."

James frowned. "I beg your pardon, but you really have no say in the matter, Lady Farnsworth."

"Come, James." Prudence turned and opened the front door of her home.

"I really mustn't leave my prisoner, Lady . . ."

"Come with me now, Captain. Tuck"—the lady nodded to the boy who had just brought the wagon around—"watch over Clifton. Make sure that he goes nowhere."

"My pleasure, Lady Pru." Tuck grinned happily at James's captive.

James glanced from the scowl on Clifton's face, to the boy jumping from the wagon, then at Prudence's back as she went inside her house without another backward look. Again he was struck by the way such a small woman could take complete command of all those around her.

"Might I have your word, Tuck, that you will not allow this captive free?"

"Of course, Cap'n," Tuck said merrily.

Another dark glance at the furious-looking butler, and James turned to follow in Lady Farnsworth's wake.

Pru sat for a moment in the silence of her drawing room and tried to figure out what to do. Of course she would have to tell the captain the truth, wouldn't she?

Most definitely she would not allow him to cart poor Clifton off to jail. That would entail telling him the truth, wouldn't it?

She heard a small sound and looked up into the gray stormy eyes of the man she had wanted to make her lover but had always known to be her nemesis.

Prudence shook her head on a sigh, but the answer to her problem came to her then in a flash of clarity.

"Well, James," she said crisply, "do sit, or I shall surely get a crick in my neck."

He took a deep breath, the jacket of his uniform rising and falling across his wide chest. Then he moved stiffly toward the chair across from her.

"I thought you should understand something before you take my butler in for smuggling."

Captain Ashley frowned.

"The scandal you spoke of the other night has most definitely come to fruition." Pru tried to smile, but felt the corner of her mouth quiver, and so she bit at her bottom lip instead.

She said a quick prayer that her nervousness did not show, and continued, "I'm afraid, dearest Captain Ashley, that you are right, you will have to become my husband."

Captain Ashley's expression was that of a stalwart soldier going into battle. Lovely, she could now count herself as intimidating a prospect as a battalion of Frenchmen.

Most probably she had displayed the exact expression when her parents told her that she was to marry Baron Farnsworth.

"I will be going on to obtain a special license after I take Clifton to the magistrate in Rye, my lady."

That gave her pause. "Really?" He was going

to get a special license without even consulting with her first, as if he knew all along that she would do as he wished?

She frowned, ready to get very upset about this point, but a glance out the window at Clifton in shackles made her stop.

"Of course you will. Good. But, of course, this means that you cannot possibly turn Clifton in to the magistrate."

"Excuse me?"

"I cannot have my butler taken in for smuggling, think of the scandal."

"But . . ."

"And, of course, it would do nothing for your own reputation to have the world know that your wife's butler was a smuggler."

James was looking at her as if she had just sprouted another head, and Pru realized that she had to take another tack, quickly. She had to appeal to the man's sense of honor.

"Captain," she said softly, "I realize that you do not love me." She blinked a few times as if fighting back tears, then glanced quickly at her lap. "But, please, if you will, think of my feelings before you do this terrible thing."

"Lady Farnsworth, I must do my duty."

Prudence stood quickly and went to kneel at the captain's feet. "And where does your duty lie now, Captain? If you are to marry me, I think your duty is with me, is it not?"

James took a deep breath, and Pru took his hands in hers. "I can't have my butler charged with such a horrible crime, Captain. How will I ever hold my head up in this town again?"

"Well . . ."

"The only solution is to let dear Clifton go."

Silence met that statement as Pru held her breath and prayed.

"I can make him give his word that he will no longer associate with the smugglers, Captain."

James stared at her for a moment, then he carefully extracted his hands from hers and stood. She moved aside as he walked away from her and stopped to stare out the gray panes of the window.

Pru took a deep breath and threaded her fingers together. James stayed still for a long time.

Prudence carefully pushed herself to her feet, wondering if she should go stand beside him. She knew there was no action to take but to marry the captain. She could not allow this man to take Clifton to the magistrate. She could not allow him to ruin the lives of every single person that lived in Gravesly.

Still, it was very hard for her to continue. She was throwing her very happiness away. A happiness she had lived with for only a short while. Oh, she did not want to give it up.

And then there was the captain. Pru felt suddenly horrible as she stared at James's wide shoulders. He looked so alone standing there. She thought back to their ride in the carriage to Brighton and what he had said about finding his place in the world.

Part of finding his place obviously involved bringing the Wolf to justice, and she was about to yank that opportunity away from him completely. But, of course, she would *never* have allowed such a thing to happen.

James turned around slowly then, and Prudence stood a bit straighter.

"I shall go obtain the special license and return to Harker's Inn as soon as I can," he said without so much as blinking. "Let me know where and when you would like to be married, Lady Farnsworth." He bowed slightly and left the room, his face a mask hiding any emotion he might be experiencing.

Prudence was not sure whether she had won or lost as she watched the man leave. She felt, though, as if she would like to cry either way.

# Chapter 13

They said their vows three days later in the small garden behind Chesley House with the entire town in attendance. The three days' wait had given Prudence enough time to get over her cold and also allowed James to obtain the special license.

The day threatened rain many times, but it stayed clear throughout the ceremony, though a chill wind chased them indoors soon after Prudence officially became Mrs. James Ashley.

She had given away her name again.

Her new husband was quiet throughout the ceremony and afterward, though he played with the children and entertained Mrs. Raithespeare.

Pru knew that she would have to tell him the truth at some point, but she rather hoped she could slowly win him over to her way of thinking first. He seemed to enjoy the people of Gravesly; perhaps he would understand when she finally deemed it necessary to tell him all of it.

Leslie had insisted that the servants vacate the house so that Prudence and James could spend their first night as husband and wife in complete privacy. Clifton, of course, had been downright irritable about such a thing, but Leslie had managed to cart him away.

Prudence said her last good-byes and closed the door with the knowledge that she was finally completely alone with Captain James Ashley. And it was now completely honorable for the man to ravish her most thoroughly. And though there was much that she would worry about on the morrow, that lovely thought had her gliding up the staircase with a huge smile on her face.

She managed a pirouette as she danced into her room and closed the door. Prudence stopped for a moment and listened. James was in his room adjacent to hers, but she could not hear him at all. With a shrug she peeled out of her clothes and readied herself for the lovely night ahead.

She hummed softly as she washed and then actually began to sing as she brushed her hair. She started to braid the long mass, but then decided to leave it down. Finally, she sat on the edge of her bed and waited for her new husband.

And she waited.

After a while she began to wonder if the man

was waiting patiently for her on the other side of the door. With a sigh, she stood and went to the door that joined their rooms. Pru knocked lightly.

Her husband didn't answer.

She knocked again, and when he said nothing, she pushed through the door. The room on the other side was empty. Prudence stood in the doorway for a moment, then frowned and stepped inside to make very sure that her husband was not in the room.

"James," she called. But he did not answer. With a sigh, she went out into the hall. First she checked his old room, then she went downstairs. By the time she had scoured the house, Prudence was feeling rather perturbed with her new husband.

And she suddenly wondered if the man had bolted. Holding her nightgown above her ankles, Prudence ran out into the cold night to check the barn for James's horse. The first fat raindrops splattered at her feet the second she left the confines of the warm house. By the time she reached the barn she was quite on her way to being soaked.

She was also spitting mad, and freezing as well. She would most probably get sick again, and she just might have to kill James Ashley. She rushed into the dark barn and shoved the doors closed behind her against the whipping wind.

Pru stopped just inside the doorway and waited for her eyes to adjust to the murky dimness of the barn.

And then she heard a noise: a faint rustling just to the right. "James?" she called, her voice a bit thin sounding.

"Right here," he said, and kissed her. She stood for a moment in shock as her husband took her mouth with his. He tasted of dark red wine.

"Are you drunk?" she asked breathlessly against his lips.

He laughed softly. "No." He nuzzled her neck, trailing kisses along her jaw, then tonguing a sensitive spot behind her ear she had never known existed.

"With Tuck staying in town tonight, I came out to feed the horses and made a rather interesting find," he said.

Pru was barely listening. She had been angry, hadn't she? She was nearly drenched, wasn't she? She wasn't truly happy to be married, was she? She honestly could not remember, because every nerve ending in her body was tingling with intense desire, and Captain James Ashley had her pressed against him, his lips flirting with her skin, his fingers wreaking havoc with her memory.

"French wine," he murmured, sucking for a moment at the tender skin just above her collarbone.

"Mmmm," she said.

"So, dearest, I rather think you know more about untaxed goods than you have led me to believe." He kissed her mouth again.

"MmmHmmm." And then she stiffened. Oh

God, one of the cases of wine must have been left in the barn by mistake.

"It is very good wine." Her husband slid his hand beneath the edge of her robe and pushed it off her shoulder.

She shivered.

James stepped away from her, and Pru made a small sound of protest. But her husband picked up something from the ground and gave it to her. "Drink, it helps."

Pru put the glass bottle against her lips and tipped her head back. The dark, fruity wine was like heaven on her tongue. "Oh," she said on a sigh. She did not often drink the wine, just transported it.

"Yes," James said.

"It does help." She giggled.

"Makes you just want to forget all the reasons this is wrong and take advantage of what you can have, doesn't it?" James's voice was like the purr of a cat. A big, dark, beautiful cat.

"Oh yes," she said.

And he kissed her again.

"I have wanted your lips from the first moment I saw you," he murmured.

"They're yours."

"You're wet," he murmured against her.

She shivered. "I'm freezing." Instead of remedying the problem, though, they continued kissing as if that was the only thing keeping them alive.

James ran his hands over Pru's back, her shoulders, her arms. And she wished he would never stop. He pulled the ties that held her night rail closed at her neck, and she arched her head so that he could kiss her skin. Heaven.

"You're beautiful." His hands, those tantalizing hands, pushed her nightgown down to her waist, and then the material dropped to the floor and she was naked.

He stepped away from her, and she wanted to cry. She must have whimpered, because James laughed softly. "Patience," he said, and shook out one of the horse blankets onto the floor.

He took her down right there, the buttons on his shirt abrading her skin. But it did not hurt. Instead it made her feel utterly wanton and absolutely daring, and she just wanted more.

"You're fully dressed," she said, in a mock scold.

"So sorry." He took her mouth, his tongue touching hers and making her cling to him. "I shall strive to fix the problem at once," and he undid the button at the top of his shirt.

She just wanted his mouth against hers, she wanted him to keep touching her, and it was taking way too long for him to get all the buttons undone. Pru reached up and yanked her husband's shirt open. Buttons clattered to the floor, but Pru had already started at her husband's pants.

"I want you," she said, splaying her hands in

James's hair. It was soft and thick, and she clenched her fingers in it, holding his head so that she could kiss him and never stop.

"I feel like I'm drowning," he said. "And it is wonderful."

"Oh yes, let's drown together."

This was amazing, truly. Never had she felt such a dizzying need to let go of all control and just be. Her heart raced as if she had run through the marsh with a heavy barrel in her arms, and her body quivered and trembled and it was all good. All wonderfully, excitingly good.

And the whole world just did not matter.

James was naked, finally, and she pushed against his chest so that she could look at him. "God, you are incredible," she said, and then knew that she blushed. His entire body was muscled and long.

Pru reached down and wrapped her fingers around her husband's manhood. It bucked in her hand, and he groaned. "Oh," she murmured. She had never touched the baron like this. Never wanted to. And now her body wanted to do things she could barely fathom with her mind.

"You are hard and soft and beautiful."

James groaned, a low rumbling sound she could feel against her chest and stomach. She wanted him inside her. She wanted him to envelop her, hold her, take her.

Pru moved her hands around and cupped her

husband's muscled buttocks, holding him against her. She felt wetness between her legs, and she closed her eyes with the strength of need that pounded at her core.

James kissed her again, lightly this time, his lips trailing from her mouth, to her neck, then lower. Pru arched her back, her nerve endings tingling with need. She wasn't sure exactly what she wanted her husband to do, but she knew that every touch was like an exquisite torture.

She wanted him inside her, now. But she did not want him to stop touching her, ever.

"You are beautiful," he said.

Pru opened her eyes. Her husband hovered above her, his mesmerizing eyes dark, nearly black. "Your hair is like a golden waterfall," he said, reaching up and threading his fingers in its length. He traced his finger down one of her arms and across the flat of her stomach.

"Your body is so strong."

Her skin tingled at her husband's touch, and she trembled. She had never felt so fragile before, so womanly, and yet so very powerful. She reached up and pulled James back to her.

He came without resistance. She felt the give of her breasts against his solid chest and let out a small, low moan.

He moved up her body and kissed her again, his mouth gentle but hard and so very good. He traced patterns on her stomach, then went lower, his fingers brushing her most intimate place. She made a funny sound, her breath hitching in her throat. And then he entered her, his finger against a place that made her tremble with a need she did not know she had.

"Come into me," she said against his mouth.

"Oh yes," he said, touching her as no one had before.

"Please," she said, arching against his finger.

He knew that he couldn't, not yet at least. He would be gone the minute he entered her.

James slid his finger inside of his beautiful, strong wife and kissed his way down her neck. He could feel the gooseflesh, and she shivered.

"Are you cold?" he asked, pushing back slightly.

She blinked at him and shook her head harshly. "No! Don't stop, James."

He chuckled. "You like this, then?" he asked, and pulled his finger out slightly only to slip it inside of her again.

Her eyelids fluttered, and she arched her back.

James watched Pru's face, gazed at her neck and breasts as he used her own wetness to rub against the nub he knew would help her find her own release.

Her breasts heaved, lovely round globes crested with tiny pink nipples. He touched the top of one breast with his mouth, the skin cool and smooth, so very soft. Pru shuddered beneath him, and he sought out her nipple with his tongue.

"Oh!" she cried, and he took it into his mouth, flicking it with his tongue.

The wind howled about them, spattering rain against the walls like bullets. Prudence writhed beneath him. He loved the taste of her. A thousand times he had thought her scent would push him beyond control, but her taste did it to him in only a second.

Prudence clutched at his head, incoherent words slipping through her lips as she lifted her hips beneath him. He sucked, taking her nipple far into his mouth, and suddenly he felt her woman's place clench about his finger over and over.

She gasped, her chest heaving as she throbbed against him in a primitive rhythm that made him desperate to thrust inside of her.

The rain had turned to hail, and the entire barn creaked with the onslaught. Thunder rumbled like a great ship rolling out of dry dock.

"I am angry with you, James."

"Excuse me?" he said with a laugh. "I should think you would be ready to lick my boots if I asked."

"Oh you," she swatted at his shoulder. "Must I beg to have you inside me?"

"Did I not pleasure you?" he asked with mock indignation.

She pursed her lips. "Oh yes, husband, you pleasured me." Prudence pushed against him, and he fell onto his back with his wife following to straddle him. He was hard, still, hard and aching as watched Pru's full breasts swing an inch away from his nose.

She shimmied down his body and leaned her forehead against his. "You held back." She flicked her tongue out and licked the corner of his mouth.

James closed his eyes and caught her tongue with his lips. He felt in that moment like he could live on the taste of Prudence for the rest of his life.

They kissed deeply for a moment. He kneaded Pru's back, and then slid his hands down to cup her buttocks.

She laughed and wiggled against him. "I would like you to do that to me again only this time I want all of you, James. I want you to do all of it . . . um . . . with another part of your . . . um . . ." and in the soft glow of the candle James could have sworn that he saw his wife blush.

He chuckled. "If I have finally embarrassed the outspoken Lady Farnsworth, surely the world is about to stop spinning."

She smacked him playfully on his shoulder. " 'Tis Mrs. Ashley, thank you."

"Ah, yes, I had almost forgotten." He squeezed her bottom and laughed when she squealed.

"You ought to laugh more often, husband. When your dimples show you are quite devastatingly handsome."

"And without them I'm quite the ogre, I take it."

"Quite."

James quirked a brow at his wife and moved his hands to her hips. "For that, pretty maiden, you shall be punished by the horrible ogre."

"Promise?"

James laughed again as he lifted his wife and brought her down on his erection. She moaned, gripping his shoulders, and he closed his eyes as he felt her tight wetness take him in.

She moved above him, and he watched her, not caring about anything else in the entire world except this moment and this woman.

Her incredible hair, the color of moonlight on water, rippled around them, cocooning them in a safe space while the cold wind shuddered against the windows. The storm crashed about them, battering the walls and electrifying the air.

He slid his hands up Pru's sides to her breasts and thumbed her nipples. She closed her eyes and leaned her head back in invitation.

He could feel the pounding of his heart and the rushing of his blood in his veins. And then his wife clenched around him, and he let go inside of her. Each contraction of his wife's intimate place brought another pulse of his own, and he closed his eyes and reveled in the ecstasy of the moment.

Prudence dropped across his chest, her legs quivering around his hips. And James felt as if he would never move again.

Sometime in the last few seconds, the wind must have died down, for now there was just a pitter-patter of rain hitting the window. Beauty whinnied from her darkened stall. James sighed and rubbed his hand up Pru's back.

And he tucked the moment into his mind as one that he would never forget. He did not have many memories that gave him joy, but he knew this one would. And he suddenly hoped, with a strange ache burrowing a hole in his chest, that he could have more.

He smoothed his hand against the crown of Pru's head, her hair soft and fragrant. "I have never truly trusted a peer," he heard himself say.

Prudence glanced up at him. "I can understand that," she said, and snuggled against him. And that was all that had to be said. She understood something he barely understood himself.

"They do tend to believe they *are* good and so they don't have to *be* good," she commented.

Exactly. "You say, 'they.' "

She laughed softly. "Yes, I guess I am one of them, aren't I? The daughter of the younger son of an earl. The widow of a baron."

James grimaced. "Earl? I do abhor earls."

His wife chuckled. "Well, some distant cousin I've never met holds the title now, so I guess, technically, I am no longer the daughter of the younger son of an earl." She sighed. "And I am me, James, not one of them. We'll not let any of them hurt either of us, what do you say?"

James closed his eyes and pulled his wife's body closer to him. He was not sure what to say, really. But he knew a hope he had never really felt before in his life.

# Chapter 14

The light was that of late afternoon by the time Prudence finally felt able to throw back the covers and actually attempt to leave her bed. James groaned from beside her, turned, and pulled a pillow over his head.

Pru spent a moment enjoying the view of James Ashley's bare back. The man had a beautiful body, and she loved to look at it. She loved to feel it against her. His shoulders were wide, and his waist was trim.

She especially liked the dark hair that was shaped like an arrow down the center of his chest. The quill sat at the hollow of his neck, then the shaft shot down toward his stomach, where it whirled around his navel and then pointed straight to what Prudence had begun to think of as James's handle to heaven.

She giggled.

Her husband turned over and opened one gray eye. "What?" he asked, his hair sticking out in all directions.

"Nothing," she said, but dived across the bed and landed atop the chest she had just been thinking about.

James's arms went automatically around her, but he groaned. "I could not possibly do it again."

"Hmm, yes, I might have to wait a good hour before I attempt another go at it myself."

James dropped his head back against the mattress. "I have married a wanton."

"Yes, you have, you lucky devil." She shifted about on top of him. "It seems that you have underestimated yourself, Captain."

He cocked one dark eyebrow. "It does, doesn't it?"

Pru pushed away from her husband, grabbed a pillow and threw it at him. "I am not sure I can take your arrogance."

James scrambled up and threw the pillow back at her. "Hmm, I'd say you have no choice."

She whacked him on the side of the head with the pillow, and he went down backward.

Prudence laughed, but jumped away when she saw that her husband had got a hold of another pillow. He slung it at her, and it bounced against her naked breasts.

"Now that is a lovely picture," he said, and grinned.

Nothing in the world was more incredible than Captain Ashley grinning. It made her actually feel faint, he was so perfect. Prudence scowled at him and thumped her pillow over the top of her husband's head. He grabbed at it, but she pulled it away quickly.

Feathers poofed out from the pillow and rained down on them. They laughed and continued their fight for a few more minutes until the entire room was blanketed in fluffy white down.

Finally, James pinned Pru's arms above her head and kissed her, and the fight was forgotten in a moment. She reveled in her husband's mouth, the feel of his large, callused hands against her body and his strong legs pushing between her own.

Her husband had taught her much this night. She knew exactly what to do in order to achieve the climactic release she now craved with every intake of breath. And her husband knew as well. He rocked against her, holding her buttocks in his hands and kissing her so deeply, she thought she might drown.

The feathers flew around them, sticking to her husband's hair and shoulders and making Prudence feel as if they inhabited some dream world come to life. She laughed joyously and arched into her husband's body as the first feelings of release swirled in her lower belly, then tightened her woman's place and crashed through her.

Her husband spilled his seed within her on a great shout and they rolled over together in the soft white down. Prudence closed her eyes and waited while her breathing went back to normal.

James nuzzled against her neck, one hand still cupping her breast. His own breathing slowed, then evened out.

"James?" she asked.

"Hmm," he said, sliding his thumb over her nipple.

She gasped and grabbed at his hand. "No," she laughed. "We must get up. We have to eat."

"We do?" He glanced up at her, a mischievous glint in his eye she had never seen before this morning. "Really? I do think I have found something much more sustaining than food."

Pru rolled her eyes. "No, dearest, this will never do. Food is the only way that we will be able to continue on in this way."

"Well, if it is food that will make it possible to live the rest of my life making love to my wife, then food has just become of utmost importance." James kissed her nose and rolled away from her.

Prudence lay for a moment watching her husband as he found his breeches thrown over a chair and pulled them on. For some reason the words that had just tumbled from James's mouth sounded again and again in her mind. *Make love to my wife. Make love to my wife.*

Love. Wife.

She closed her eyes, and suddenly felt fear. This was real. She was married. Mrs. Ashley. She belonged to another man—a man who might just ruin her.

She smelled the dark musk of her husband, and then his lips pressed against hers. "Up, dearest, we shall eat and then return to our play."

Prudence blinked at James. When he knew exactly who she was, he would understand, wouldn't he? He smiled the smile that before last night had been so fleeting and rare.

She wished he would smile more. She wished he would be like this always. She wished the real world would retreat and never come knocking at her door again.

James pushed away from her, and Prudence sighed. They would eat and return to their play, and hopefully the world would stay away for just a little while longer.

It came knocking way too soon. Though James had her up against the hallway wall before it came. In fact they had just finished when a loud knock came at the front door.

"Who on earth could that be?" James asked.

But Pru knew. " 'Tis Clifton, I'm sure."

James actually laughed as he pulled her dressing gown together and tied her sash. "Then by all means get the door, milady. You have the look of a woman recently tumbled. It will make the man crazy enough to have my head."

Prudence scowled at her husband. "You are altogether a different man from the one I married."

James kissed her so that her knees buckled, and he had to hold her up. "Truer words have never been spoken. Now tell your faithful keeper that we are not finished and to be off." James turned and started for the servants' stair. "Oh," he turned, his expression going somber for the first time since the night before, "and remind him of the promise he gave you. No more Wolf."

Pru bit at her bottom lip and wanted to cry, but she forced herself to nod and turn away from James. "Of course," she managed to say as she went to open the door for the person who was now knocking even louder than before.

Prudence tidied her hair as best she could before she pulled the door open for Clifton, but she knew that he would not be fooled at all.

"Well, at least the two of you are going to get this thing out of your systems, then," he grumbled when he had finished glaring at her with his one blue eye.

Pru frowned weakly, but didn't say anything. She rather thought that she would never get Captain Ashley out of her system. Even now she could smell him on her, and it made her want to run back upstairs, lock her bedroom door against the world, and never leave her husband again.

"What is it, Clifton?"

"There's a problem at Harker's, and you are the only one who is going to be able to handle it, Lady Pru."

Prudence made a disgusted sound in the back of her throat.

"The boys are anxious. They need to know that you are going to be able to stay in control." Clifton lowered his voice. "It seems Captain Ashley has sent communication to London saying that he has taken care of the Wolf. The Marley brothers showed up at Harker's today."

Prudence groaned. "Oh, no."

"Oh, yes." Clifton nodded harshly.

Pru turned and paced away from her butler, then she whirled on her heel. "I'll come to Harker's tonight, late. The only way to show the Marleys that Gravesly is not open for their taking is to get a shipment out."

"My thoughts exactly."

"I'll let them know that I am still in charge, Clifton, give them confidence in that. But I cannot possibly be gone all night. You will have to take care of the shipment."

"Not a problem," Clifton said with a tug on his hat. "Do you want some of that sleeping potion from Les . . . I mean Mrs. Redding?"

"No!" Pru cried, then shook her head and said

in a lower voice. "No, I'm sure I can get him to sleep deeply without that vile concoction. We haven't . . . that is to say, last night was . . ."

Clifton scowled. "All right, all right, I understand. He'll sleep." Without another word her butler turned on his heel and stomped down the stairs to one of Harker's old horses that stood munching weeds from the gravel drive.

Pru sighed as she watched him mount the old roan and clop off down the drive. The real world was back—with a vengeance.

James lay on his side, his arm around his wife, her rump snuggled against him and his hand cupping one of her lovely round breasts. He sighed and settled more comfortably into the soft mattress. He had never felt more satisfied in his life.

The world still existed and there were problems in that world he was not sure how to handle, but for the moment in this room, with this woman, James entertained a feeling he had never before experienced. Happiness. James buried his nose in his wife's hair, inhaled lavender and sex, and closed his eyes.

James came awake slowly, his dream filtering away into reality. He turned over with a contented sigh and stretched. It felt damn good to sleep in a bed that was big enough for his body.

The one at Harker's had been even smaller than the one in Pru's guest bedroom.

Prudence. With a grin, James reached for her in the darkness. His hand encountered a soft pillow, then the mattress. With a frown, James levered himself up on his elbow and squinted at the bed beside him.

It was deserted.

"Prudence?" he called, but she did not answer. James lay for a moment listening, but he could not hear a thing. There was no sound of footsteps on the stairs or the clanging of pots from the kitchen.

James sat up, reluctantly letting the warm blankets slide away from his body. The floor was cold beneath his bare feet, and he winced as he stood up. He had to admit, though his home in London was not somewhere that he yearned for when he was away, it was awfully nice to live with servants about keeping fires stoked and having a conscientious valet who always kept his wrapper near.

His valet had actually been terribly put out when James had left for Gravesly alone, but he had only just employed the man, and he was not ready to go on assignment with some fluttering servant always about.

James glanced around Pru's shadowed room. His breeches were slung over the back of a chair, and he grabbed them and pulled them on, then shuffled around looking for his boots. It was a damn nuisance, really. He needed to remember to go into his own room and find his robe and slippers.

He called out once more to his wife, then lit a candle and started for the first floor. The house felt eerily quiet. The storm had died completely that morning, and now there was not even a speck of wind.

James pushed through the door to the kitchen, but the room was dark and empty of any human form. He stopped for a moment and listened again, worry starting to nag a bit at the back of his mind. Worry, and something else he did not quite want to name.

With a shake of his head, James ducked through the kitchen and went out the back door to the garden. The cold air kissed his bare chest, and he shivered. It did not look like there was a light in the barn, but James decided to check anyway. He went quickly to the old dark building, the door creaking loudly when he entered.

The blanket he and Pru had used the night before still lay on the floor, the empty bottle of wine was still on the crate where they had left it. Gooseflesh rose on James's skin when he remembered how he had emptied the last drops of wine on his wife's white belly and licked them up with his tongue.

He looked around, and his mind finally registered that it was terribly quiet in the barn. Devil was always quiet, but he had realized last night that Beauty liked to whinny. James let the door bang shut behind him as he went to Beauty's stall. The horse was not there.

James stood for a moment, staring at the stall, his heart thumping against his chest like a mallet. He closed his eyes, then turned on his heel and strode out of the barn. Without letting himself think anymore, James ran back to his room and dressed, then returned to the barn and took Devil from his stall and headed toward town.

Artie did not run out to meet him when he rode up in front of Harker's. The place seemed deserted, actually. He rode Devil around the back, dismounted, and led his horse into Harker's barn. The place was packed.

Beauty stood munching oats in one of the stalls. James felt himself go numb. He pulled his pistol from its holder at his side, left Devil standing in the middle of the barn, and quietly went to let himself into Harker's.

The door was not locked. James shook his head as he pushed his way into the inn. The front room and public room beyond it were deserted, but now James could hear the rumble of voices. He followed them to a back room, and then down some narrow, steep stairs and into a well-lit cellar crowded with men.

No one noticed his entrance, for they were all

faced away from him. They were all looking, in fact, at his wife. Prudence stood on an upturned box, hands on her hips, her delectable body clothed in breeches and a coat.

She was speaking to the men, giving directions, but James could barely hear her, because a great roar had started in his ears. He stared at his wife for a full minute, his mind rushing back in time and seeing, again, the slight silhouette of a man standing in a boat as the *Defender* gurgled her last breaths.

James knew in that moment that he was now looking at the very same person he had spied that dark night.

"The Wolf," some deckhand had whispered.

He noticed then that the roaring had died down, but so had the voice of his wife. He looked into her face, their gazes locking. And then he glanced around the room and saw that every person had turned to stare at him.

He looked back at Prudence, then he turned sharply and walked slowly back up the stairs into the back room of Harker's Inn.

He had known. Deep down, he must have suspected something from the first moment, because now he was not as shocked as he should have been.

James sat down heavily on a chair, his mind running over details that now made such sense. The cart, that huge cart and Clifton. James shook his head. And then there was his wife's body. She had muscles. Where other women were soft and delicate, his wife's arms were strong, her stomach flat and muscled.

James suddenly felt an intense urge to break something.

"James."

He closed his eyes. This was not a good moment for his wife to make her entrance.

"James, it's not . . ."

"Yes, it is." He stood and walked away from her voice. He had to put distance between them. She had betrayed him utterly. And the people of Gravesly. James stopped at the thought.

God, the people of Gravesly had made an ass of him. And to make it worse, he had begun to feel like he had finally found somewhere he could be accepted.

"James . . ."

"Shhh!" he hissed sharply, and whirled around to face Prudence. She stood just past the top of the stairwell, looking incredibly beautiful for one of the most wanted men in England. Even in the face of her betrayal, James itched to reach out and touch her.

Obviously he was possessed by the very devil to think such a thing. "It has all been a charade, then? You wield quite a bit of power in this small town, *Lady* Farnsworth, and not much honor."

Prudence stood a bit straighter. "And what

charade would that be, James?" She propped her fists on her hips. "Do you think I have ordered the entire town to be nice even though they are all truly hard-bitten criminals just waiting to stick a dagger in your back when you turn around?"

James felt as if his heart would cave in on itself. That Prudence could not even understand the depth of his hurt made him want to shake her.

"Oh, yes, that is it. And can you believe that every single person in this town is such a good actor? I say they should all tread the boards, don't you think?"

James tried to make himself breathe evenly. "Well one of you should, most definitely."

"I was going to tell you, of course."

"Of course," he said coldly.

Prudence huffed a breath of obvious frustration. She took a few angry steps toward him, then stopped. "You talk of honor as if you own the attribute," she said, her voice shaking. "Well, Captain, you do not know what honor is until you do all that you do for the honor of others, not just yourself."

They glared at each other.

"Yes, Captain Ashley, I am the Wolf. You will notice that the Wolf came into being two years ago, just about the time my husband died. I have led the smuggling activities in this area since then, and most recently I dispatched your ship to the bottom of the sea." Prudence advanced on him again. "And I am also, lest you forget, your wife."

James had never despised a person more than in that moment. He stood slowly and clasped his hands tightly behind his back, truly afraid that he just might reach out and strangle Prudence Farnsworth Ashley.

It *had* been a bunch of lies. Of course the respectable Lady Farnsworth had not ever wanted to become his wife, not him, the Most Delectable Laughingstock of London. She had not wanted him. The town of Gravesly had not brought him, an outsider, to their bosom.

No, he was still very much an outsider, very much the laughingstock.

"Come, James," his wife said on a sigh, her soft brown eyes pleading. "I am glad you know, finally. I have been wondering how I might tell you, and this"—she fluttered her hands in the air—"is not how I pictured it, but it is out, and I am glad."

She took another step toward him. "I know you are angry now, but I am sure that once you think on this you will understand. I know that you have come to like the people of Gravesly. And they cannot live without what I have done for them."

James could barely hear Prudence for the roaring that had begun to rumble in his head. He was reliving every moment of isolation he had ever lived through, and there were many.

Once again his feelings and his manhood could be ripped to shreds because he, as a bastard, did not matter.

"James, you accomplished your goal. You came to find the Wolf." Prudence held out her hands and smiled. "And you did."

James shuddered. "Stop speaking, wife, for you make light of something that you do not understand."

"Oh, do stop being so dramatic, James."

James took one step forward, wanting more than anything to shake her, but he stopped before he reached her. "You should take your name more seriously, dear, for you show absolutely no prudence whatsoever in your actions, deeds, and words. Have you ever," he continued before she could speak, "been unsure of your place in the world?"

Pru's delicate brows furrowed.

"No, or the question would not perplex you so. You have always been someone's daughter, someone's wife, or someone's keeper. You make light of that, act as if it were a burden, but you have never been without a title or a place. Even if I had not married you, you would still be a peer, Lady Farnsworth. A peer in a small town that shunned you, but a peer nonetheless.

"I, on the other hand, was born a bastard. I do not even know my father's name. The only thing I've ever known is that through my actions I could demand respect from those who would never give it to me just because of who I am.

"But even that is constantly ripped from my grasp by you people who think it is such fun to play with the emotions of those you deem below you."

Prudence glanced down, breaking their intense eye contact. "I never thought of you as below me."

"Speak truth, Prudence. I am a bastard, an officer in the Royal Navy. And you are a peeress." The anger building in James's chest rose, threatening to choke him. He took a deep breath and clenched his shaking fists at his sides.

All his life he had known the frustration he felt at that very moment: of not knowing exactly who he was, of feeling very much like he belonged nowhere. "I am sick of trying to make a name for myself. You people slap me down at every turn."

James stopped and stood silently for a moment and then, suddenly, smiled. He had thought that evening of speaking with Prudence about spending time in London, having her help him become respectable in the eyes of the ton. Well, now, there would be no talking about it. He would just do it.

"I truly no longer have to try so hard, do I? I am married to a peeress, after all."

Pru looked baffled.

"I think, dear wife, we should retire to London on the morrow."

"Oh most definitely not, James. I cannot leave Gravesly."

James cocked his head to the side. "Do not tell me, Prudence, that you suffer under the illusion that I would allow you to continue your work as the Wolf?"

Prudence swallowed audibly. "But I must, James. You do not understand. The work I do as the Wolf has kept people alive; it has kept this town alive."

"You do realize, dearest, that every single thief, murderer, and cheat has a reason for what they do? And, believe me, 'tis never because they are lying, greedy cheats. No, it is always because of some other person's downfall or need."

"So you think I'm a lying, greedy cheat?" Prudence folded her arms in front of her and tapped the toe of her boot on the floor.

"You, darling, are a criminal, and any other person caught doing what you have done would be hanged. But, of course, as your husband I shall protect you. I am sure you realized that when you seduced me into your little trap."

Prudence gasped. "I never . . ."

"Come, Prudence, no more lies." James closed the small distance between them. He could smell her scent: that light floral cleanness that had addled his senses since he first entered this woman's home. "But I most definitely will not allow you to continue in the role you have been playing. And we *will* be going to London, Prudence, unless you want me to bring Clifton to the attention of the magistrate in Rye."

"You wouldn't!"

"With pleasure, actually, if you do not comply with my wishes."

"You are horrid."

"You have no idea how horrid," James said, and cupped his hand behind Pru's neck. "You are no longer the Wolf, dear, but Mrs. James Ashley: soon to be the toast of London. You have gotten what you want from me, and now I require something from you." James lowered his head and took his wife's mouth in a bruising kiss.

# PART II

## London

# Chapter 15

**T**renton Albert Von Schubert, the second earl of Wimsley, was in a horribly foul mood, and it was causing much distress throughout his Mayfair town house. The upstairs maid had boxed the ears of a lowly scullery maid, the lord's valet had slapped the face of a footman, and the butler had dumped his breakfast on the floor and stated that the cook had not an inch of talent for making anything edible.

Wimsley sat ensconced in his favorite chair before the fire in his study, his gouty foot propped on a stool.

Viscount Leighton eyed his grandfather from his perch beside the beastly man.

"Are you on top of the Grave Matter, boy?"

Richard rolled his eyes. "Must we talk in code, Grandfather?" He leaned over and glanced beneath the chair. "I'm rather sure there are no spies about."

"Shush, boy!"

"Really, Grandfather, do call me Leighton." Richard flicked a speck of lint from his peach-colored waistcoat. "I am surely no longer supposed to endure being called 'boy,' am I?"

Wimsley leaned forward with a grunt. "I shall call you any damned name I wish, boy, and you will answer," he yelled, spittle flying from his mouth.

"Now then." Wimsley pushed himself back in his chair, the wig he insisted on wearing hanging too far over his right ear. "You deal with the Matter, boy. And you do it discreetly. The shipment we were supposed to receive yesterday never came. You promised that woman had the situation in hand even with that upstart down there causing problems, and now he turns up back in London married to her and putting it about that the Wolf is taken care of. I'd say she most definitely does not have the situation in hand."

Richard laughed, then jumped from his chair when Wimsley reached out to slap him. "You're getting slow, Grandfather," he said.

Wimsley frowned darkly. "Exactly my point, you prancing imbecile."

"Now, now, Grandfather, must we start calling names?" Richard went to the side table and helped himself to his grandfather's best brandy.

"You just make sure that there's nothing to worry about with the Grave Matter."

"Of course, Grandfather." Richard knocked back his entire glass of brandy and poured another.

"I knew it'd come to no good when that woman took over for her husband."

"Yes, Grandfather."

"Oh, shut up, you kowtowing peacock."

"As you wish, Grandfather."

Wimsley's jowls turned purple. Richard placed his empty glass next to the crystal decanter of brandy. He did so love these little tête-à-têtes with his grandfather. Good brandy and small apoplectic fits, what could be better?

"With that woman in London and the rumor that the Wolf has been taken out, the town is ripe to be plucked, boy. But 'tis our town and our profits that will be taken out from under our very noses unless we get on the problem immediately."

"We? I'm assuming you mean me."

"Don't be impertinent with me, boy." This last was yelled so loud that Wimsley went into a coughing fit. The old man's face went a horrible shade of blue. Richard stood waiting, as he always did when this happened, to see if perhaps this time his grandfather would fall over dead.

One could always hope.

His grandfather finally wheezed in a few breaths of air, his face returning to its usual splotchy red color. Richard went back to the sideboard and poured his grandfather a drink.

Wimsley accepted the offering with relish. "That Ashley fellow, he's the source of the problems."

There were always sources for his grandfather's problems: always someone to blame.

With a grunt Wimsley slapped his empty glass on the table beside him and settled back in his chair, his thick brows drawn together over his bulbous red nose. Richard could not help but grimace at the sight.

"Think of the scandal if society found out exactly to whom the Hero of England has hitched himself." Wimsley laughed. "The good Captain Ashley would be devastated."

Richard stared at his grandfather for a minute. He had realized early on in life that Trenton Albert Von Schubert was a bit touched in the head. The man was just plain hateful and mean, and it had turned him into a fat bore. But ever since Captain Ashley had entered the arena of his grandfather's interests, there had been a whole new twist to Wimsley's spiteful outbursts.

"Seems to me you'd be devastating yourself as well," Richard said.

"Well, of course, I would never do it, boy. It's just a nice thought."

A log on the fire broke in half, spewing sparks. "Well," Richard said brightly, "as always, Grandfather, it has been a pleasure." He strode toward the door.

"I'm not finished with you yet, boy. There's the matter of your finding a wife."

Richard stopped and sighed. He had truly hoped to miss the marriage lecture this fine morning.

"I'll cut you off, boy, unless you have a bride before the end of the Season."

"Please, Grandfather, that threat is getting rather old, is it not?"

Wimsley banged his fist on the arm of his chair. "I will not die until I am assured that this title will continue in this family!"

"Lord, does that mean you shall live forever? God help me."

Poor grandfather looked as if he would never breathe normally again.

" 'Tis your duty, boy, to make sure the title stays in the family." The old man shook his head rather violently. "This is all your father's fault. That man should have wielded a stronger hand when you were young."

"I don't remember seeing 'that man' more than twice before I was fifteen, so it wouldn't have mattered what he wielded now, would it?"

"You were too often in the care of women, that is your problem!"

Richard laughed. "Right, Grandfather, you have finally pinned down the exact origin of my problem. Of course, you could be wrong, fancy the thought. Maybe my whole problem is that I ate too many sweets. Or, perhaps it is all because you have driven me into a life of lust and idleness."

Wimsley choked, the veins at his temples bulging. "I have done nothing of the sort. Your problems have nothing to do with me at all."

Richard grinned. "You are so right. I would definitely lay the blame at the feet of my nanny. Or, now that I think of it, perhaps it was all my tutor's fault." Richard sighed wistfully. "Dear Mr. Larson, such a lovely young man. He had good hands, as I remember."

"Get out!" Wimsley screamed, his voice cracking and then wheezing. "Get out!"

"Yes, sir." Richard bowed to his grandfather and left. He took a deep breath when he reached the hall. He had been having these conferences with his grandfather since he could remember, and though they were rather tiring, he would miss them when the old man finally died. Richard loved to shock, and it was so very easy with his grandfather.

He knew, of course, that the only reason his grandfather even allowed him to breathe his same air was that Richard was the old man's sole heir. Richard was rather sure that his grandfather would have had him meet with a convenient accident if he had a brother.

Richard stopped in the front hall as Holmes

rushed off to retrieve his hat and coat. The butler returned and nearly threw the clothing at Richard. Poor man was scared of him, always had been.

With a chuckle, Richard thanked the cowering Holmes and walked out into the sunshine. He grinned at the world in general. He had the promise of lunch with a particularly lovely companion to look forward to, the sun was actually warm, and his grandfather was probably prostrate on the study floor clutching his chest. All was well with the world.

"Of all the . . ." Pru slapped the paper her husband had just handed her onto his massive desk. "This is preposterous!"

"They are rules, Prudence, to which I expect you to adhere."

Prudence blinked. "Adhere to your rules? *Your* rules? Who exactly do you think you are?"

"Your husband."

Pru made a face.

James stood slowly from his seat behind his desk and leveled a frosty stare on her. "I own you, Prudence. You are now mine. And I can and will command you to keep my rules."

Prudence stared at the man who had become her husband. Her honorable, sweet Captain Ashley had turned into the very devil. "Your rules are intolerable, James Ashley."

"I don't care, really, what you think of them, just so you live by them," James said without showing any change in his emotions. He turned away from her then and went to pour himself a drink. "Now, as I was saying, I have appointed you a social secretary."

"A keeper, you mean."

"As you wish." James drained his glass and placed it carefully back on the crystal tray. "I will have my secretary confer with yours each day on the social invitations I want you to accept. At two o'clock, you will ride in the park with your groom, you shall never leave this house without him in fact, and then you will be in the sitting room to accept guests from four until six every day. We will have supper, together, in the dining room. You will go to those social activities I have outlined and come straight home."

"But . . ."

"You will come straight home, Prudence." He turned and stared out a window at the street, keeping his hands clasped behind his back.

Pru drew herself up and clenched her fists. "I must have time for myself."

"Of course, in the mornings you may sew, read . . ." James waved his hand in the air without turning around. "Anything you wish that will occupy your time."

"That is not what I meant."

James turned quickly on his heel and pinned

her with a look his enemies had probably backed down from often. "I know what you meant, Prudence. That part of your life is over now. I will not accept any criminal behavior from my wife."

"But you do not understand, James." Prudence braved her husband's fierce demeanor and went to stand close to him. "Without me, Gravesly will fall to another. Even before I left, the Marley brothers from Pevensey were seen at Harker's. The Marleys are horrible men, James. They kill anyone who gets in their way."

James took a deep breath and held it for a moment. Prudence said a little prayer that she would be able to crack through the man's stubbornness on this subject.

"Gravesly was there hundreds of years before you got there, dear wife, and it shall be there hundreds of years after you leave this earth. Shocking, but true, the world does not revolve around you."

Prudence could only stare at the man, her jaw slack.

James crossed the small expanse between them and lifted her chin with his finger. "You are now Mrs. James Ashley, and will act as I want you to act. We will be a superior couple without a trace of scandal to our name. That means, Prudence, that you are no longer to associate yourself with the Wolf or Gravesly, and especially I will not tolerate any clandestine dealings in untaxed goods."

"And to hell with Mrs. Witherspoon and the Sawyer children."

"You will learn to school your tongue and your temperament, Mrs. Ashley," he continued without acknowledging her statement. "I do not want to hear loud voices or bad language; nor do I enjoy arguing."

"Is this a monastery or a house?"

James did not even flinch. "I will visit you every night until we conceive an heir."

"How exciting," she said, and shoved his hand away from her face.

He folded his arms across his chest and continued as if she had not said anything. "You will be completely faithful to me until you have birthed me two boys and at least one girl."

"A girl?" Pru ignored James's other ridiculous statements for a moment. "Why do you want a girl?"

"My grandson will be a lord."

"Oh." Prudence nodded. "Enlighten me, dear husband. I thought you did not trust the peerage, but now you say you want to marry your daughter into their circles? I do not understand."

"Our daughter will marry an earl or a duke, no less."

What a stubborn, horrible man. Pru narrowed her eyes on her new husband. "You are quite the dictator, are you not? I am sure this must have been how you acted with the men on your ship, but I was never privy to this side of your personality. You must excuse my chagrin."

"I shall treat you with respect, Mrs. Ashley, and I expect the same in return. Please do not speak to me with such insolence."

Prudence felt like screaming; instead, she drew in a deep breath. "Mrs. Ashley," she said quietly. "I am Mrs. Ashley." She laughed dully.

"Yes," James said, his voice like ice. "So sorry it doesn't quite meet your standards, *Lady* Farnsworth."

Pru shook her head. "Nothing would meet my standards, James. Don't you understand? I wouldn't want to be the wife of a duke, or the wife of the king for that matter. I want to be me, and I want to be worth something for myself. And I had that, dammit!"

She stepped closer to her husband, frustrated because his face showed no comprehension of what she was saying. "I am the Wolf. I took care of my cubs, I took care of people, I meant something, I was important. And it was me. It wasn't my husband, it wasn't because I was the daughter of a peer or the wife of a peer. It was me!" Pru thumped her chest with a closed fist. "Me, the Wolf. I had my own name, and my own reason for being on this earth. And it was good."

Her husband frowned, and she hated him in that moment. What she had just said was something she had kept to herself completely. She had just told this man her reason for being, and he frowned.

"I do not want to be married, James. I did it to save the people that I promised to help, but I most definitely did not want to be married again, or ever. I never wanted to take another man's name."

"But you have," James said.

"Yes, as a last resort, but does it mean that I have to give up everything that I am?"

They now stood with their toes nearly touching. Prudence glared up at her husband, and he returned the look with a steely stare. "I fear that you don't understand, dear. I have a signed confession from your dearest Clifton in my possession."

"You wouldn't."

"You know that I would."

Silence thundered in the large room. And then Prudence shook her head. "Why?" she asked quietly.

James looked away from her.

"All of this." Pru gestured about her at James's huge den. "It is all about what you told me on the way to Brighton, is it not?"

"I don't know what you're talking about."

"Is this about finding your place, James?" Pru asked. "Will the demise of Gravesly be what it finally takes for you to enjoy London? Will taking away everything I live for make it possible for you to be happy, finally?"

Her husband turned his gaze back to her. "Do not speak of what you do not understand," he said distinctly. And then he left her.

Her hand shook as she smoothed it along the banister that led up the grand stairwell in the middle of James Ashley's home. Prudence had thought that they were entering a palace as the gates to Ashley House had swung open. The coach, which had arrived at Chesley House to transport them to London, had been quite a shock as well. The only thing it lacked to be fit for the king was a crest on the door.

In fact, a crest was the only thing missing from the gates in front of Ashley House to make it a ducal mansion. The servants running about the place did not wear a certain color or livery proclaiming them a part of a peer's household either. They all wore black.

It all rather reminded her of a funeral, really.

Prudence sighed as she went to her room. It all seemed like a strange dream. Captain Ashley, her Captain Ashley, had turned into a stranger with hard eyes and a commanding manner.

She had entertained thoughts of softening him as they made their way to London. She was sure he had not meant everything he had said in Gravesly.

The man knew the people of Gravesly, had played with the children. He had made love to her and touched her. He could not stay angry and hurt forever.

Then he had handed over his list of rules like the captain of a ship handing orders to his first mate. And she did not know this man that was her husband at all. Of course, it was not as if she had really ever known Captain Ashley.

Perhaps the need to think she knew him, especially after the incredible night they had shared, had made her blind to the fact that this man was a stranger to her.

She was terribly afraid, also, that this new side of Captain Ashley could stay very angry and hurt for a long time.

"Lady Pru."

Prudence glanced up at the familiar face of Clifton and felt an incredible urge to cry. She stopped in the hall and sighed instead.

"Oh, dear, Clifton, what have I done?"

"You did what you thought you had to," he said softly.

"Yes, well, now I need to do something to fix it all."

Clifton cocked his head toward the door to her apartments. Prudence nodded and led the way into her sitting room, closing the door behind her.

"He holds you with threats that he will turn me in to the magistrate," Clifton said quietly. "I think you should call his bluff."

"I fear it is not a bluff."

"Then so be it."

"No!" Prudence shook her head. She turned away to pace the length of the room that was bigger than the kitchens at Chesley House. "No, I will not do that, Clifton."

"The Marley brothers will take over Gravesly, Lady Pru. And they will act fast with you gone."

"Then we shall act faster."

Clifton did not answer, and she knew exactly what he was thinking. Their actions were very much curtailed at the moment. She was now forced into a role that made her slightly nauseous: attending balls and routs and riding in the park. The grand lady of Ashley House.

"Mr. Watson," she said suddenly, snapping her fingers. Prudence whirled around. "I can find Mr. Watson."

Clifton's brows were bunched together over his nose. He was obviously unhappy with Pru's new plan. But Prudence was very used to that.

"The man probably moves in the same circles that James wants to be a part of. I shall find him. He will help us, Clifton, for his interests are at stake as well."

"And what do you plan to do, Lady Pru? Walk up to every man of the *ton* and ask them if they helped start a smuggling ring in Gravesly?"

Prudence frowned at her butler. "I do not appreciate your sarcasm, Clifton."

The man rolled his eyes. "I do not like this at all. I am going to turn myself in."

"Don't you dare, Clifton Rhodes. I will never forgive you."

Clifton's barrel chest rose and fell on a silent sigh. He turned away from her, shaking his head. "I will give you a week."

"Excuse me?" she asked.

"One week." He went to the door without looking at her. "If you haven't found Mr. Watson, I will turn myself in and Captain Ashley will have nothing to threaten you with. You will be able to go back to Gravesly." Clifton opened the door quietly and closed it behind him without even glancing at her once.

Prudence blinked at the closed door for a moment, wondering if the entire world had just turned upside down. The honorable Captain Ashley was truly the devil, and her dutiful servant was giving her ultimatums. What would happen next?

With a sigh, Prudence dropped into a chair and stared at her hands. They shook, still. She clasped them together and closed her eyes.

There had been a moment, a small moment in time the morning after their wedding that Pru had thought that all would be well.

Never in her life had she touched another human being as she had her husband. And though she harbored secrets, she had naively believed that something special had passed between them, something that did not happen for most people.

It certainly had never happened for her with Baron Farnsworth.

So she had thought they would be able to get through the problems that lay ahead. She had thought that she would, perhaps, enjoy taking this man's name for her own.

Now she realized that was complete poppycock. "It was lust," she said into the silent room. "That was all. He is not what I thought."

Prudence swallowed the sobs that rushed up her throat with that pronouncement.

Still, though she said it out loud, Pru could not quite make herself believe it entirely. She had always been a very good judge of character, and she definitely prided herself on a sharp mind.

She could not have been so wrong about Captain Ashley.

He was hurt. Of course he was.

But surely he of all people must understand that there were obligations one had to uphold when one was in charge of the destinies of others.

Surely, he must understand. He *would* understand.

Prudence leaned forward and propped her forehead in her hands. She missed Gravesly terribly, and it had been only two days since she'd left. And she was afraid, so very afraid, that her little town would never be the same again.

A tear slipped unbidden down her cheek. She rarely cried, but she knew that sometimes it was a good way to clear her mind of fear and pain.

And so she stood up quickly, went into her bedroom, and threw herself facedown onto her bed. Muffling her cries with a huge down pillow, Prudence sobbed her way through the afternoon.

Of course, she did not give in to complete despair. She knew that when she finished, she would feel much better and be ready to face the *ton* and find Mr. Watson.

# Chapter 16

J ames lay on his bed, his hands behind his head, staring at the ceiling. He could hear his wife crying in the room adjacent to his, though he was rather sure she would have stopped immediately if she knew.

She was not crying for attention as he had heard a few women cry in his life. No, the sobs that emanated from his wife's room were soul-wrenching tears of frustration and hurt.

At the moment, James was fighting the horribly urgent need to go in and console her. He wanted to put his arms around her and promise to make it all right.

Which made him very angry with himself. She deserved this, didn't she? The woman had betrayed him utterly. The whole town of Gravesly had made a laughingstock of him, really.

So, why couldn't he feel the same distant coldness for Gravesly that he could conjure in an instant for London and the ladies of the *ton* like Lady Jersey?

Why indeed?

James shook his head and forced himself to stand. He would leave the room, the house. He would go away so as not to be weakened by his wife's sobs. James stalked toward the door, but stopped with his hand on the handle.

His wife's cries were muffled, faint; in fact, he would never have heard them if he had not lain down for a short nap. It was only in complete silence that he had made out the sounds.

And then it had taken him a moment to figure out what they were.

She did not cry loudly so that he could hear and feel terrible. For, if she did, he knew that he would not feel anything but contempt.

James closed his eyes, gripping the handle to his door, the way out, the road to silence and sanity and strength. And then he turned and went to the door connecting his room with his wife's.

He stood there for what seemed forever. He could not show weakness, and if he entered her room now, he would be weak. He knew that.

The scene in his study had been difficult, no matter his feelings of betrayal. He had not enjoyed acting the tyrant to his wife, seeing the light

in her eyes fade. Knowing that by taking away
Gravesly, he took the meaning from her life.

But he could not go on with his quest and allow his wife hers as well.

James turned away and forced himself to leave
the room.

He hadn't come. The morning light touched
her eyelids, and the first thing that came to Prudence's mind was that her new husband had not
come. With the memory of his outrageous re-
quests the night before, Pru was quite happy he
had decided to stay away. And yet, as she
dressed, a picture of his large, callused hands ca-
ressing her nagged at the back of her mind.

"Stupid, frivolous thoughts," she muttered to
herself.

"Ma'am?" Her maid skittered backward and
almost dropped the brush she was using to dress
Pru's hair.

"Nothing, Mary, I am just talking to myself."
She was very unused to having servants bowing
and rushing about to make sure her every whim
and pleasure was obliged. No matter that it
sounded rather decadent, in truth it was annoying.

"I am sure my hair looks fine." Prudence
waved the girl aside. Pru finished her toilet
quickly and went downstairs. She let out a sigh of
relief when she opened the door to a deserted

dining room. Plates of food sat on the sideboard. Pru picked up a piece of bacon and munched on it as she continued through the servants' door. A footman on the other side dropped the plate of eggs he carried and stared at her in amazement.

"Oh, so sorry, ma'am." He bent quickly to clean up his mess.

"Goodness, I'm sorry for startling you." Pru knelt to help the man, and he jumped back like she had just taken off all her clothes.

"Please, ma'am, you will ruin your gown." He recovered his senses. "I'll go to the kitchen and get one of the maids to do this."

"Yes"—Pru looked at the coagulating mess on the floor—"I think it will need a mop." She stood and brushed at her skirts.

"The kitchen staff is terribly good at what they do, Mrs. Ashley. I am sure they can deal with this on their own."

Pru stiffened at the sound of James's voice. The footman blanched and backed away, mumbling something about a mop.

Pru turned slowly. "Good morning, husband mine, you did not attend me last night. I gathered from your rules that you would be at the deed of getting an heir every night until I started increasing."

James held out his arm. "I do not usually conduct conversations in the servants' hall. Please accompany me back to the dining room, Mrs. Ashley."

With a disgusted sniff, Pru laid her fingers gently on his elbow. "So, I am to be Mrs. Ashley now?"

"I do believe you demanded that title when you thought your butler was to be thrown in prison." He pushed open the door to the dining room and allowed her to go ahead of him into the room. It was amazing how he could effect such pristine manners yet inflect such a tone of malice to his words.

"Please sit, I shall make up a plate for you."

Prudence sighed. She did not want to sit at a table and eat with this horrible man who resided in the body of Captain Ashley. But she did as he asked and sat. She watched the man pick up a plate, her eyes, of course, going to his long fingers.

How she loved her husband's hands.

Truth be told, she was rather put out that James had not come to her room last night. Since the hard kiss he had given her at Harker's, James had not touched her at all.

His rules were abhorrent, but she had at least hoped that with the forced intimacy, perhaps she could find the old Captain Ashley hidden within this man who seemed possessed by the devil.

He put a plate laden with food in front of her without saying anything, and went back to fix his own plate. The footman from before entered with another platter of eggs, deposited them on the buffet, and stood aside, hands behind his back, chin in the air.

How she missed Chesley House and the warm breakfasts she would share with Delilah and Clifton in the kitchen. She sighed and speared one of her eggs with a fork. She would surely never get used to this life that her husband wanted so badly.

"I have booked passage for Clifton," James said as he sat at the other end of the long dining room table.

"Excuse me?" Pru asked.

"I think it best that Clifton go to the Colonies. I shall give him a nice fat pension, of course."

"The Colonies?"

"Well, the United States, if you must."

Pru blinked at the chameleon her husband had turned into.

"And, of course, I will keep the signed confession in a safe place, so you must not think that you may return to your former pursuits just because Clifton is living on another continent. They have courts there as well, you know." The man actually smiled and took a bite of his toast.

Pru wanted to fling her egg across the atrociously long table and hit the dear man smack on his nose.

"You cannot be serious."

"Yes, actually, I can, and I most definitely am."

Pru banged her fork down next to her plate and stood, shoving her chair back so hard that it crashed to the floor. The footman cringed.

"You cannot just order people to leave the country at your whim!"

James stood as well, except he did so calmly and slowly. He turned and nodded to the footman, who nearly ran from the room. "Please, Prudence, I have asked you not to raise your voice in the house. And I would appreciate it if you would not yell at me in front of the servants."

Pru shook her head in disbelief. "I am not your child, James. I am your wife."

"And I expect you, then, to act like an adult."

"Well, that would certainly be easier if you started acting like a human being."

They stared at each other in silence for a moment. And then James took up his napkin and wiped his mouth. "Good day, Prudence," he said, and went to the door.

"Don't you dare walk away from me, James Ashley!" Prudence took two huge strides to reach her husband before he left, and grabbed his arm.

He stopped, his gaze tracking a hot path from her face, to her fingers wrapped around his arm, and back to her face. "Let go of me, Prudence."

"With pleasure," she said with disgust.

"Monday next, Clifton will leave for the Colonies. That is the end of it, Prudence."

Well, that just meant she truly had only a week to find Mr. Watson and come up with a brilliant plan. At this point, she was running out of hope for any plan that could help her, even if she did manage to find the mysterious Mr. Watson.

She looked up into James's glacial gaze. "Are you truly this shallow, then?"

He blinked, and she thought she saw some emotion flicker in his eyes.

"The fate of Mrs. Witherspoon does not matter as much as what a bunch of society matrons think of you?"

James laughed, but the sound held no humor. "You underestimate people, Prudence. Mrs. Witherspoon can take care of herself, of that I'm sure."

"Are you, Captain? And you are willing to risk her life on that?"

"Really, Prudence, I rather think you are being a bit, what did you call me at Harker's, overly dramatic."

"Do not take lightly something you do not understand, Captain."

"Touché, Prudence," her husband said, and left her without another word.

The man was going to drive her to Bedlam, surely. She waited for a moment, schooling her emotions so she did not go back into the dining room and break every piece of china in reach. And then she went out into the hall. She was not sure what she would do, but she had a vague idea of finding Captain Ashley and strangling him.

"Mrs. Ashley?"

Pru looked over at a tall, thin man standing outside of her husband's study. "Yes?"

"Mr. Jenkins, ma'am." He advanced, stopped in front of her, and nodded. "I've been retained by your husband to act as your secretary."

"Ah." Pru smiled, not a real smile, but a tugging of her lips that obviously relayed exactly how she felt about her husband and his wonderful idea of a secretary.

Mr. Jenkins cleared his skinny throat. "I have your schedule made out for you." His long, spiderlike fingers slid a paper from a leather portfolio in his arms. "You will be attending three different soirées this evening." He held the itinerary out to her.

Pru folded her arms in front of her and stared at the piece of paper. "Three? How thrilling."

Mr. Jenkins frowned, looked at the schedule then back at her. She finally took pity on him and took it from him. He sighed heavily, and Pru smiled at him, a real smile this time. The poor man. He was just doing his job.

"Thank you, Jenkins. I will do as I am commanded." Pru turned to go up the stairs.

"Um, excuse me, Mrs. Ashley, but there is one more thing."

"Of course there is, does the captain want me

to meet with someone? Perhaps he wishes me to perform tricks for a party of his cronies. Or, maybe, I must do acrobatics at one of the delightful soirées which I am to attend this beauteous eve."

Jenkins looked like he wanted to run screaming from the room. "No, Mrs. Ashley." He worked his jaw and ran bony fingers through his dark, thinning hair. "I am to inform you that Chesley House is to be put up for sale."

"Ah, yes, my house, Chesley House. My dear husband is going to sell Chesley House." Pru took a deep breath and smoothed a hand down the front of her dress. "My husband, of course, gave you the thankless task of telling me, Jenkins. I would quit now, if I were you. Your employer is an absolute tyrant as well as a spineless toad." Pru clenched her fists at her sides, effectively wrinkling her schedule to oblivion, then marched up the stairs without even dismissing Jenkins.

Pru threw the crumpled paper in her hand across the room when she reached her chamber. Then, for good measure she turned around and slammed her door as hard as she could. The entire wall shook, and a bit of plaster fell from the ceiling. Pru took a deep breath. She felt a little better.

Unfortunately, she was still married to a man who would put Napoleon to shame, the arrogant, overbearing ass. He thought he was going to sell her house, did he? Well, she would just like to see the man try.

She kicked at her bedpost, bruised her toe, and cursed. "Bloody hell." Pru sat on the edge of her mattress and stared at the wall.

Prudence stood among the throngs of people at yet another ball. She had gone to her required three soirees the night before. Captain Ashley had accompanied her to the first, introduced her around, making sure to mention the name of her parents and Baron Farnsworth, and then let her go on alone.

She was starting to recognize people, now, after only two nights. It seemed she was quite a hit, for everyone wanted to know intimate details about the woman who had married the Most Delectable Man in England.

Now she knew why James hated the name so. If she heard one more woman titter behind her fan as she said it, Prudence just might do something drastically unladylike.

She flipped open her own fan and waved it before her face. It was damn hot. There were far too many people in one place, and half of them were dancing, making the heat even worse.

Lady Trent continued her treatise on the merits of using lemon as furniture polish, and Pru resisted the urge to drop dead from boredom.

Of course, it did not help her mood at all that

her plan to find Mr. Watson seemed nearly impossible as she stared out at the masses of people in the room. She had no idea what the man looked like. In fact, she could be absolutely wrong in assuming that he was even a peer, though, she was rather sure that he was.

On top of the futility of her search for Mr. Watson, Prudence was also becoming increasingly frustrated. Her husband had still not found it necessary to come to her bed.

Not that she would ever allow him the pleasure of her body, of course, but it would be nice if he would at least show the interest of trying.

"There is a book, fascinating, truly, about getting tea stains out of every kind of fabric imaginable," Mrs. Parker said. "I was thrilled when I found it at the lending library Tuesday last."

Lady Trent nodded sagely. "Ah, yes, I think I know of which book you speak, Trudy."

Prudence decided that she really had to quit this particular group, or she would probably say something shocking just to elicit some excitement.

"Excuse me," she murmured. "I am feeling the heat. I think I shall take some air."

"Of course, dear," Mrs. Parker said. "Now, about this lemon business, Winifred, how many of the fruits would you need to do, let's say, this ballroom?"

Prudence backed away, wound her way through the throngs of people to an open doorway, and plunged outside. She could make out a very beautiful garden in the moonlight, and so Pru went across the veranda and made her way down the stairs.

The dark night enveloped her, and she let out a sigh of relief. She was sick to death of people constantly staring at her and wanting to ask her questions about Captain Ashley.

Pru took in a deep lungful of fresh air and grimaced. She could not quite get used to air that actually had a texture, filled as it was with soot and sour smells. Spying a bench, Pru stalked deeper into the garden and plopped down on the cool, hard seat.

It was a lovely garden, at least what she could see in the dark seemed very well kept up. Prudence closed her eyes for a moment and enjoyed the silence. She could make out the slight scent of roses. Obviously, they were not close, but they were somewhere, and they smelled divine. A lovely change from the overcrowded ballroom. A lovely change from most of the scents of London, actually.

How she missed the sea. She wanted to kick herself for taking Gravesly quite for granted. Of course she never reveled in the beauty of the place or the sweetness of the people until she had both things stripped from her.

Damn James anyway.

Pru leaned over, propped her elbows on her

knees, and dropped her chin in her hands. How on earth was she going to clean up the mess she'd made of her life?

"Prudence!"

Pru jumped and toppled over backwards into the hedge. "Damn you, James," she hissed, thrashing about. She heard a ripping sound and rolled her eyes. "Now you've gone and ruined my dress."

She felt her husband's large hand wrap around her arm and pull her free of the clinging bush.

"Did you have to sneak up on me like that?" She pushed away from James and started picking leaves from her bodice. "You scared me near unto death!"

"Sh!"

"Excuse me?" Prudence stopped and planted her fists on her hips. "Did you just shush me? Because, I must tell you, James, no one in my life has ever shushed me."

"Well someone ought to have a long time ago."

Prudence blinked through the dark at her husband.

"It is not at all the thing to be out here alone, Pru. People will wonder."

"Lord but their lives must be a huge bore to make wondering about me out in the garden interesting."

"Please, Prudence . . ."

"Oh, go please yourself." She glared at him.

"What are you doing here anyway?" She had not seen her husband since he had left her at the first soirée the night before. She rather thought that he had not slept at Ashley House at all.

"I had meant to come collect you for a dance," he said, "but I could not possibly take you back in now. You look as if I've compromised you under a bush."

"That's not bloody likely."

"Really, Prudence, must you continue to try to shock? 'Tis like dealing with a child."

Pru made a sound of disgust. "And what else would you expect, James, when you act the over-bearing guardian?"

They stood silently glaring at each other for a long moment. And then Prudence sat back down on the bench with a sigh.

"James," she said, "we are married. I do realize that neither of us truly wanted this outcome, but here it is. Could we not make the best out of this situation?"

"I am not changing my mind about Clifton."

She really wanted to scream. "Well, I will tell you right now, James," Prudence said instead, "I will not allow you to sell Chesley House."

"Let us speak of these matters in the privacy of our home, Prudence."

"Our home? That monstrosity you call a home is most definitely not mine, and it never will be. I shall never feel at home there." Prudence felt tears burn the backs of her eyes. "The only home I shall ever know is Chesley House."

"Don't cry."

Pru stood again quickly. "Yes, sir!" She pretended to salute her husband.

He shook his head and looked away from her. "If we can come to some agreements, I will not sell Chesley House."

"Really?" Pru asked wanting more than ever to slap James's gorgeous face. "So you have found another thing to use in getting my complete compliance to your frivolous plans."

"They are not frivolous."

"Right, they are just shallow and idiotic."

Silence met her statement, and Pru felt a twinge of guilt. She really did not enjoy being angry and mean, and it bothered her that James's new persona had brought such things into her life on a constant basis.

"What is happening, James?" she asked now. "Can't you see the jeopardy Gravesly faces without me? Doesn't that bother you at all?"

"I think, Prudence, you overestimate your importance. Gravesly will be just fine."

Prudence pushed her husband out of the way and paced. "No, it will not, James." She stopped and stared dejectedly at a bush. "And you should not make Clifton leave the country," she said.

"I do not trust Clifton. I do not trust you, for that matter."

"Then I guess I shall be the next to be banished from England."

"No, you will follow my rules and stay in London as my wife."

Blood pounded in her temples. She whirled around. "Really? Well, then, the least you could do is make love to me!"

"Sh!"

"Do not shush me, James."

"Then do not yell things of a personal nature in public."

"James," Pru managed to ground out between her teeth as she grabbed her husband's cravat and pulled his face close to hers, "if you are so exacting with your rules, shouldn't you be coming to my bed nightly?"

James said nothing, but took an audible breath.

Prudence thought of their wedding night. It now seemed to be from another lifetime. And, suddenly, she just wanted it back, even if it wasn't real. "I am an unhappy woman," she said to her husband. "You have bullied me and threatened me, and you have made me very angry. I am worried about Gravesly, upset about the departure of my devoted butler, and extremely tense about this new life you have decided I must lead. Now, I happen to know that having intimate relations does not make everything happy and wonderful in a marriage, but let me tell you, dearest, it goes a long way in reducing tension. If you want me to continue going to these little parties and actually keeping a smile on my face, you will give me a tiny taste of the only happiness that you can give me, and fast."

"Really, Pru, this is all rather sordid of you, don't you think?"

"You have seen nothing yet, dearest husband."

The man looked thoroughly shocked, but Prudence was nearly going crazy with desire, anger, and frustration, and the only thing she had the possibility of diffusing was the desire. Except that her husband had suddenly decided that it was all too easy to keep his hands off of her.

Odious man.

"Must I remind you, Prudence, that you have absolutely no leverage with which to make deals?" her husband asked softly. "I can have Clifton thrown into Newgate with a moment's notice."

Prudence narrowed her eyes and let go of her husband's cravat. "Are you truly this shallow, James? I just really cannot fathom it. You would trade a man's life, a town's livelihood, for a place in society?"

James straightened away from her, a muscle jerking in his jaw.

And she knew in that instant that there was something going on behind her husband's mask that went much further than just needing to be accepted by society. And, of course, she should have realized that a long time ago. She remembered his cryptic remarks in the coach on the way to Brighton.

"You speak lightly of something you don't understand," he said darkly.

Prudence nodded. If she could understand, she knew that she would be able to reach James Ashley. And then she would have the key to taking back control. "You have said that exact thing to me before, James. Perhaps you should explain it to me so that I might understand."

James turned away from her. "I shall go bring the carriage around and meet you at the back gate so that you will not have to go through the ballroom." And he left without another word.

# Chapter 17

**P**ru stamped her foot. She had never stamped her foot in her life, but this situation definitely called for the stamping of feet. It could perhaps even call for the gnashing of teeth for that matter.

That would have to come later, though, for now she had company. Pru took a deep, calming breath. "Do come out from behind the tree, sir, it is so very uncouth to skulk."

The dark outline of a tall, gangly man moved and came toward her. "And here I thought I was doing such a good job at my skulking."

"You are rather horrible at it, actually, Viscount Leighton. I do hope it is not something you must do often."

"No, I do try not to most of the time."

"Well, good, then."

"You are very straightforward, Mrs. Ashley, as I must confess that I overheard your conversation with your husband."

"Yes, well, I do like to let people know what I expect."

"Of course, and I admire that completely. But, if you would permit me, I do think I could be of a bit of help to you in your predicament."

Pru frowned. "Which predicament would you be referring to, my lord?"

"I am sure you will have to excuse me for being a bit forward, but the predicament of wishing your husband to pay attention to you," the man stopped and cleared his throat. "Well, pleasuring you, shall we say?"

Pru laughed. "And you find *me* straightforward, my lord?"

"Refreshingly so."

"Hmmm." Pru contemplated Viscount Leighton. "So, my lord, am I to surmise that you have had experience with the predicament in which I find myself?"

"Mrs. Ashley, I understand men, that is all that is truly needed here."

"And you wish to help me?"

"I would love to."

"Why, my lord?"

The man smiled, his mouth wide and his teeth very white. "I believe wholeheartedly, Mrs. Ashley, that the world would be a far better place if we all just enjoyed each other. I do wish to help you in your quest to do this very thing with your husband."

Pru was sure there was more to the viscount's offer than he let on. "I must admit to being a country bumpkin, my lord. I have not even been in London a week. But I'm rather sure that this conversation is strange, is it not?"

"Not, actually. I have heard stranger."

"Really?"

"May I drive you in the park tomorrow, Mrs. Ashley, say about three o'clock?"

Prudence tapped her finger against her skirts for a moment. "Surely there is something terribly improper about this."

"Surely . . ." The viscount nodded. "But I do not enjoy being proper, so I don't usually try. May I come round at three, then?"

Prudence shrugged. As the viscount was the first halfway interesting person she had met, she found that she did want to go driving in the park with him. "I think I might enjoy that, my lord."

"Think? Ah, you wound me."

"Something tells me, Viscount Leighton, that your armor is probably thicker than that."

"How very perceptive of you." The viscount grinned wickedly and bowed once more. "Until tomorrow then." And he turned on the high heel of one of his bejeweled shoes.

* * *

James stood at the window of his study drinking. It was three o'clock, and he was pretty sure that he would be falling down drunk by five. He watched as Viscount Leighton handed Prudence into a jaunty cabriolet.

Viscount Leighton of all people. He was just the type James really did not want to associate with. Yes, the man was quite chummy with the Regent, and his grandfather, the earl of Wimsley, was some distant relative to the king, but, really, the viscount was quite on the very edge of respectability. And, being that James was himself at the very edge of respectability, he had hoped that his wife would associate herself with people who were more firmly entrenched.

James went to pour himself a fresh drink. With another gulp of whiskey burning his throat, he could freely admit that he was also a bit jealous. Viscount Leighton was one of those people who was so assured of his place in the world, that he never even thought to question himself. The man dressed and acted as if he had not a care in the world. And, of course, everyone found that attractive.

Another long pull from his glass of spirits, and James said out loud to the quiet room, "I want it myself, desperately!"

He slurred the 'n' sound in the word *want* and amended his estimation of complete inebriation to four o'clock. "Acceptance, is it so much to ask for?" he said to the portrait of his maternal grandfather, which hung over the large fireplace.

The painted face stared down at him with the same benign smile James had seen his entire life. He had never known his mother's father. From what he could figure out from the scant information he had scrounged up from a few servants of his mother, the man had died of a broken heart when James's mother had run off with her lover.

No one seemed to know the identity of the lover, but James's mother had returned to her father's funeral with a large belly, no husband, and, most importantly, no marriage papers.

She had often told James that she would reveal his father's identity sometime in the future when James was old enough to understand. But she had died suddenly of malaria when he was ten. And though James had scoured his mother's personal papers, he had never found one hint of who he really was.

Still, he knew that whoever had made his mother pregnant had taken her to London with him, and then had not married her. James had figured out on his own that his father was probably a peer in England.

His mother had been a very wealthy woman, so it was not lack of money that made her impossible to marry. Obviously his mother's bloodline had not been quite pure enough for the likes of the anonymous man.

And more obvious than that even was the fact that his father had not wanted a son born of that bloodline. The glass in James's fist broke suddenly into a thousand pieces. He watched as if from outside his own body as a deep cut in his palm oozed blood.

Closing his eyes, James dropped the broken glass on the carpet. "Who am I?" he whispered.

James knew, as he had known all his life, that he must answer that question to be whole.

" 'Tis a simple thing, really, Mrs. Ashley. All you must do is seduce your husband." Viscount Leighton slapped the reins in his hands gently against the two horses pulling his cabriolet. "And I am the perfect person to teach you the tricks of such a trade."

Prudence stared at the man beside her. "Really, my lord, do you expect me to believe that? You are going to teach me how to seduce my husband? Let me guess, you will do so by seducing me, and then I can go try out all I learn on the captain. Am I right?"

"Goodness no." Viscount Leighton made a face. "I do not seduce, I woo." He glanced at her and waggled his blond brows. "But I can certainly teach you how to seduce a man."

"And you would want to do this because you are suddenly my very best friend?"

"Of course not," the man laughed. " 'Tis like everything in life, Mrs. Ashley. I need something from you, and I have decided to offer my services in this problem you face so that I might get it."

Prudence shook her head. She could think of absolutely nothing she owned that Viscount Leighton would need. "Why don't you just ask me for whatever it is you want from me?"

"Because this is so much nicer, don't you think? I can think of nothing I'd rather do than have my hand in a seduction. Now"—The viscount touched his hat to a gentleman rider and smiled— "tell me whence you hail, dearest. I have heard rumors that you have hidden your beauty in some horrid little fish-smelling town north of Brighton."

"Gravesly is not at all horrid."

"Ah, but it does smell of fish, am I right?"

Prudence could not help but laugh. "Yes, quite right. Some days are worse than others, though."

"Of course I am right, remember that." Viscount Leighton waved to an older woman ensconced beneath mounds of blankets in the back of an open carriage. "Now am I also to believe that you met the dear captain when he dispensed with the notorious smuggler who has blackened our coastline these last couple years?"

"Captain Ashley dispensed with no one," Pru said rather indignantly.

"Really? But smuggling is no longer a problem in Gravesly?"

"It never was a problem."

"True, I hear the Wolf had no problems whatsoever turning quite a heady profit."

Prudence frowned and pulled at a loose thread peaking out of a seam in her skirt. It bothered her to speak of heady profits. The profits were rather slim, actually, after 60 percent went to their London backer. And it was all done to keep people fed, not to adorn them in jewels.

And she had to admit that she missed it desperately. Prudence glanced at the people parading through the park in carriages and on horseback. She could not imagine living like this, with no purpose. Well no worthy purpose, at least.

Pru suddenly felt very much like crying again, because, truly, this was now her life as well.

"Now you have gone silent and morose. Did I say something wrong?"

Prudence looked back at her companion. "No, really."

"Well, then, shall we begin with our first lesson in seduction?"

"Can you give it here? Out in the park, I mean?"

The viscount chuckled lowly. "You still think that I mean to have my way with you, don't you?"

"I think you want *something* of me, my lord."

"Well, of course, I have already told you I do."

"Wouldn't it be ever so much easier if you just told me what it was?"

"Yes, actually, but I, unlike you, have mastered the art of seduction, and one of the most important skills in such an undertaking is being mysterious."

Pru grinned. "So you *are* trying to seduce me!"

"Mysterious, my dear, means not saying every single word that comes into that pretty little head of yours."

"Believe me, my lord, I can be mysterious."

"Well, try it with your husband."

"Yes, sir."

"And touch him."

Just the word touch conjured in Pru's mind a vision of her husband's hands. Oh, how she wanted him to touch her with those hands.

"Touch him as much as possible."

"Hmm?" Pru said, suddenly realizing where she was and looking over at the Viscount.

"And look at him like that."

Prudence glanced away quickly. They had left the park and were very near the mammoth building Captain Ashley called his home. She felt a bit melancholy. Viscount Leighton was quite enjoyable company, but she would much rather drive in the park with James Ashley.

That thought gave her pause. She hated James

Ashley, didn't she? The man was horrible, really, forcing her to leave Gravesly and her work there.

The viscount jumped down from his seat, and Pru realized that they were home. She glanced up and saw the outline of her husband standing at the window of his study. He tipped back his head as she watched and drank from a glass in his hand.

"Lord Leighton," Pru said, still watching her husband.

"Yes, Mrs. Ashley."

Pru glanced down at her companion. He stood with his hand out waiting for her to alight. She placed her hand in his and allowed him to help her down from his conveyance. "Do you know anyone named Mr. Watson?" she asked then.

The viscount blinked, obviously startled. "Mr. Watson, you say?"

Prudence nodded.

"I do, actually," he said.

"Really?" Prudence had not expected an affirmative answer. She had asked everyone she met about Mr. Watson in the last two days, and it was as if the man did not exist. Of course, Prudence was rather sure that he did not go by the name Mr. Watson, so, really, the viscount's Mr. Watson could be the wrong person entirely.

"I would so like to meet him," Prudence said.

"He's rather reclusive." Lord Leighton escorted her to the front door of Ashley House, which had already been thrown open, to reveal a maid, the butler, and two footmen awaiting her entrance.

Pru turned, laying her hand on Viscount Leighton's arm and looking up into his green eyes. "But you know him," she said. "Perhaps you could . . ."

She did not know Viscount Leighton all that well. She had been in his company only three times, but in that moment, Prudence could tell there was something wrong. The viscount was not one to become uncomfortable in any situation. That fact had been clear in the first seconds of meeting him in Brighton.

And right now Viscount Leighton was definitely uncomfortable.

He knew exactly who Mr. Watson was.

"I need to speak with him," she said.

The viscount nodded, glanced away from her, then regained his composure. "Are you going to the Lawrences' musicale tonight?" he asked, his mouth barely moving over the words and his face turned away from her.

Pru wished she had paid more attention to Mr. Jenkins that morning. She wracked her brain, and could swear she remembered the name Lawrence. Well, if she did not have that particular event on her itinerary, she did now. "Yes," she said.

"Ten o'clock in the alley behind the Lawrences'

town house." Viscount Leighton turned his beautiful face toward her and smiled hugely. "It has been a pleasure, Mrs. Ashley." He bowed, kissed her hand, and was gone.

Prudence stood staring after the man for a moment, wondering. Could the thing Viscount Leighton needed from her have something to do with Mr. Watson and Gravesly?

Perhaps she needed to do a bit of investigating and find out exactly who Viscount Leighton was.

Holmes looked particularly put out at having to take Richard's coat. "Thank you, my dear man," Richard said sweetly as the butler scuttled away from him like a frightened crab.

It lightened his mood a bit to torture the servant. He had experienced a bit of a black cloud hanging over his head since he had left Mrs. Ashley that afternoon.

The woman was quite melancholy, and Richard had actually decided that he rather liked her. It was difficult to continue in his role as spy for his grandfather when his own emotions were being tugged at.

He did hate that. For once he decided he liked a person, Richard tended to become disgustingly maudlin. He felt this was not too much of a character flaw since he was aware of it completely.

Still and all it did make this situation a bit dirty, didn't it? He sighed, pulled out his handkerchief with his thumb and forefinger, pinky delightfully extended, and wiped lightly at his brow.

"He will see you in the study," Holmes announced, standing rather farther away than was necessary.

Richard tucked his handkerchief back in his pocket and batted his eyelashes at the butler. He could not have been in a worse mood to see his grandfather, but it had to be done.

Taking a deep, cleansing breath, Richard pushed through the door into his grandfather's sanctuary. The man sat where he always did, his wickedly ugly leg propped up before him.

"God," Wimsley said before Richard had even set foot inside. "That ingrate has ruined everything, hasn't he?"

Richard smiled hugely and went straight to the brandy. "And which ingrate would that be, dearest grandfather? There are so many around these days it is hard to keep track."

"That piece of filth that married Lady Farnsworth." Wimsley spewed spittle, and Richard grimaced. Best to keep his back to grandfather as he drank his brandy.

"Well?" his grandfather prompted with a smack of his beefy hand against his chair arm.

Richard drained his glass before turning around. "Well what?" he asked.

His grandfather shook his head, looking rather like a bulldog stepping out of a bath, jowls flap-

ping and droplets flying. Lovely. Richard placed
his glass on the crystal tray and leaned against
the sideboard. His grandfather was in quite a
lather. A good day to keep his distance.

"Well, did you speak with that woman?"

Richard winced.

"He knows, doesn't he?" Wimsley yelled
whacking his chair arm again. "He knows. He's a
crafty one, I'll give him that. Like his mother."

His grandfather was speaking in tongues,
surely. "I hate to be a bother," Richard interrupted
Wimsley's incoherent grumbling, "but would
you mind keeping me informed of where this
conversation is going?"

"You," Wimsley yelled, pointing a shaking
finger in Richard's direction, "are absolutely
worthless."

"Thank you."

"How much does he know?" his grandfather
asked, grabbing at the cane that stood next to his
chair. "How much does he know?" The old man
grunted and wheezed as he pulled his gouty foot
from its perch and pushed himself to a standing
position.

Richard took a calming breath and kept quiet.
He had known all his life that his grandfather
was crazy, but this was quite a performance. He
had to infer that Wimsley was ranting about the
captain.

The little comment about Ashley's mother was

a bit perplexing. And the vehemenence of his grandfather's state was even more so.

With the "Grave Matter," as his grandfather insisted on calling it, Wimsley was always very businesslike. It was, after all, his main source of income. A tidy income at that.

He usually left his Bedlamite outbursts for more personal matters like Richard's refusal to marry.

"From what I can deduce," Richard finally said as he watched his grandfather hobble toward him, "the captain knows about Lady Farnsworth's clandestine activities. I would say, actually . . ."

Richard decided it was time to vacate his position by the brandy. His grandfather was making a beeline for the alcohol. Well, beeline was not quite an accurate term. The man was staggering and muttering and, every once in a while, lurching.

Very unappetizing.

"Pour me a glass, boy!" Wimsley bellowed.

Richard grimaced and turned back to appease the man, but kept well away from where his grandfather stood in all of his sweating, rotund glory.

Wimsley grabbed the glass and slugged it back, then held it out for some more.

Richard poured with pleasure. He saw every glass of the stuff as one more step his grandfather made toward his grave.

Wimsley drank the full glass down, and then threw it across the room, where it shattered against the wall.

Impressive strength, actually.

"He's after me."

Richard just nodded. He had seen his grandfather only a few days ago. It seemed rather extreme that the man should spend his life as a half-crazy blithering idiot and then complete the circuit in only three days.

Perhaps, though, when it was time for one to lose one's mind completely, it was just plain time. He definitely hoped his grandfather did not live too much longer in this state. The man would truly be unbearable now.

"Right, well, we all have our ghosts, right, Grandfather?" Richard bowed slightly. "I shall be on my way then."

"No!"Wimsley's sausage fingers closed around Richard's arm. Bile climbed in his throat. He would have to burn his coat.

"I want that spawn of Satan dead!"

Very well. "Grandfather," Richard said softly, "you are overwrought. I don't want you contemplating the Grave Matter anymore. I will take care of it completely."

Wimsley closed his eyes, his entire body shaking. "He knows about it all. He's trying to drive me to Bedlam."

"I rather think you've gotten yourself there

quite nicely," Richard said through gritted teeth as he watched his grandfather's fingers digging into his very most favorite velvet jacket.

And then a choking noise made Richard glance up just in time to see Wimsley's eyes roll back in his head. With drool sliding out of the side of his mouth, the man said something that sounded very much like the word "bastard," and fell over backward.

Definitely a sight Richard could have done without.

He stood for a moment looking down at his grandfather. Wimsley's chest moved, and Richard sighed. He glanced at the ceiling wondering if God enjoyed torturing him so much, then smoothed the creases from the arm of his jacket and stepped over Wimsley's inert form.

"Holmes!" Richard called as he exited the study. "Holmes, your master has ranted himself into a fit."

Holmes appeared, eyes as round as his little beetle eyes could get.

"I'd suggest you attend him." Richard gestured toward the room he had just vacated. "Send a messenger if he dies."

Surely that was too much to hope for.

Richard found his own coat since Holmes was making horrid noises in the study and every maid and footman in the whole damn house seemed to be streaming toward the sound.

He let himself out. Usually when he trotted down the steps from Wimsley's town house, Richard felt rather like singing. Today, he was just completely flummoxed. And he was also very determined to deal with Lady Farnsworth on his own terms.

Of course, that would be a very easy thing if his grandfather would just give Richard an early birthday present and leave his earthly confines.

# Chapter 18

**P**rudence had been wrong. The Lawrences' musicale was not on her schedule, and she had had to do quite a bit of wrangling with Jenkins to get the thing added to her itinerary at just the right time.

Fortunately, she had received an invitation. It just had not passed muster with the captain. Jenkins nearly went into an apoplectic fit when Prudence insisted that she wanted to go.

Poor man was probably still prone on his bed with a wet compress on his head.

The musicale had actually been very entertaining. Mrs. Lawrence had invited a German pianist to play, and Prudence had sat enraptured. The man obviously felt his music as well as played it.

She had also felt a bit melancholy as she sat listening to the lovely music the man was able to draw out of the small piano. She wished James could be with her, for she knew instinctively that he would enjoy himself.

Prudence thought of their brief conversation about music on their way to Brighton, which seemed now to have been a hundred years before.

The memory saddened her soul.

Prudence sighed as she wound her way through the crush of people and searched for the front door. It was nearly ten, and Prudence had already taken leave of her hostess. She had said her good-byes to the dozen or so people that she knew.

She was hoping to meet Mr. Watson face-to-face that very night, and so her mind raced with what exactly she ought to say to him. Perhaps the man could send someone to oversee the smuggling in Gravesly until she could persuade her husband to allow her to go back.

Surely he could not keep her away from her duties forever.

It was as if her thoughts had conjured him up, for he appeared through the front door just as she started into the foyer. Prudence retreated quickly and ducked into the room she had just vacated. She hoped he had not seen her.

She darted among the throngs of people and went through a pair of French doors to the garden behind the house. She would have to find the back gate and leave that way, or her husband would thwart her meeting with Mr. Watson.

Prudence ran out into the wet garden, hunching against the rain that must have started as she sat listening to beautiful piano music. Fortunately, it was really just a fine mist, so it took her a bit longer to get soaked right through to her chemise than it would have if the rain had been coming down in buckets.

By the time she realized that she would never find a gate in the dark, though, she was shivering, and the jaunty feather she had sported on her hat was a dripping mess hanging limply in her face.

Prudence yanked the feather out of her cap and threw it aside. How did Captain James Ashley always manage to ruin even the most basic of plans?

With a glance back at the welcoming light of the Lawrences' house, Prudence realized that she was going to have to climb over the wall. She leaned her head back and stared at the stone edifice. It was a good ten feet high, but it sported lovely handholds in the chinks between the stones.

The only problem she could see was the rain. It would make the going rather slippery. Pru shrugged and started to climb. That was when she discovered the other problem.

She was decked out for a party, not a clandestine mission. Prudence winced when she heard a fearfully loud and long rip. Another dress ruined most probably. She glanced down at herself when she reached the top.

Oh yes, definitely ruined, but it had nothing to do with the hole where the skirt had become detached from the bodice. The beautiful filmy material was matted to her body and bore the dark stains of dirt along the front.

With a shake of her head, Pru glanced at the alley below. She could not detect anyone, but it was quite dark. She turned, climbed down a couple feet, then pushed away and jumped the last few feet to the ground.

"Really, Mrs. Ashley, do I scare you so much that you have to run away from me?"

At the unmistakable sound of her husband's baritone, Prudence screamed. So much for priding herself on being the best at going undetected in the dark of night. The scream was quite bloodcurdling, and reverberated down the alley like a shot from a cannon.

James did not even flinch.

Pru stood with her hand against her hammering heart and just tried to breathe.

"My coach is at the end of the street," her husband informed her. "Shall we go?"

"Where . . . why?" she managed to sputter.

"I have dispatched Lord Leighton," James said sharply. "Saw him skulking about in the alley before I even entered the Lawrences'."

Prudence let out a disgusted huff of breath. "He is the worst of skulkers."

"Yes. I spied him out here and told him that I was going to pick you up so there was no need for him to wait for you."

"But how did you . . ."

"Know? I didn't." James took her arm and started down the alley. "I deduced it from the fact that you were in the house, and he was hiding in the alley obviously waiting for someone. You would be the only person in London, I'm sure, who would find it necessary to sneak away with Lord Leighton from one of your engagements."

They had reached James's coach, and he opened the door himself, yanked a blanket from the seat, and wrapped it tightly around her, and then he picked her up as if she were some trifling piece of luggage and deposited her in the carriage.

"Thank you," she said.

"Think nothing of it, Mrs. Ashley."

How very civil they had become.

"Home, Clark," James yelled, then pulled the door closed behind him. "Anyway, dear wife, I told Lord Leighton that he should not wait another minute since I was going to go into the Lawrences' musicale and whisk you away myself."

"Oh?"

"And so he left." James reached down and tucked the tail of the blanket around Pru's feet. "And then I entered the Lawrences' and watched you depart toward the back. Now, I guess I shall just have to accompany you everywhere you go until you learn to behave."

"You could have caught me before I went over the wall," she said. "It would have made things ever so much more civilized."

"Ah, and that would mean that you have decided to act civilized?"

Pru frowned. "I am nothing if not civilized, Captain Ashley."

"I beg to differ."

"Beg all you want, Captain. Just because I found a different way to help my people than winning battles against the French doesn't mean my intentions are any less civil or heroic than yours."

"The end justifies the means?"

"Exactly," she agreed.

"I have always believed that philosophy to be a pile of horse dung, if you'll excuse my crude expression." James leaned forward in his seat so that their faces were only inches apart. She noticed that his hair was very wet, and there were raindrops shimmering in his lashes. Her husband looked absolutely devastating.

She probably resembled a sewer rat. Was there no justice in the world?

"You know, dear wife, you do have choices here. There are legal ways in which you can help the people of Gravesly."

Frustration made Prudence snort, most unladylike. "So you are saying that I should just go knock on the Regent's door and tell him that his taxes are making it impossible for the lower classes to survive?" she snapped. "I'm sure he would go right out and put a stop to it all."

"I am saying that, though you abhor it, you have a respected name and now you have money as well. Perhaps you should use this time in London to make connections with politicians who could help you make a difference: a legal difference."

Prudence blinked. "It is not my money."

Silence stretched between them. "No, it is your husband's. But that makes you a very rich woman by society's standards."

Prudence tapped her toe against the floor. "Do you think, really, I could possibly make a difference?"

"You?" Her husband actually laughed. "Prudence Farnsworth Ashley, you could probably do anything you put your mind to."

And for some reason, that statement made Prudence feel more proud than she had ever felt in her life.

James couldn't sleep. He lay in his huge bed staring determinedly at the ceiling. He hated London, had always hated London, and especially hated London during the Season. He had a sudden, very odd yearning to be back in Gravesly of all places. He wanted to walk the cobblestoned main street and have tea with Mrs. Witherspoon.

Odd indeed.

Yes, he had felt betrayed when he left the little seaside town, but with a bit of distance, he had to admit that Prudence was very right. There really was no way on earth every single resident of Gravesly had pretended to be nice to him. They were not all good actors. They were just very nice people.

He hoped that he had gotten through to his wife this evening. He hoped that she might start expending her energy in a legal way to help the people of Gravesly, because he was not an ogre. He did not want the people to go hungry.

And probably Pru was also right in her conjecture that at this point the town did need smuggling to maintain its citizens' habit of eating three meals a day.

And also probably James should at least send Clifton back to the town to make sure the more violent-natured smugglers did not overtake Gravesly.

If nothing else, James could not allow such a thing because of the children. Sickly-poo did not have the kind of magic needed to save them all from the likes of the Marley brothers. James had gone off to the War Office that evening after depositing his ramshackle wife at home and done a bit of investigating. The Marley brothers of Pevensey were most definitely not nice people.

James let out a low groan. He was going to send his wife's butler back to Gravesly to make sure the smuggling all went smoothly. God help him. James pushed back his covers and sat at the edge of his bed. How had he come to this point?

The fury he had felt only a couple of days ago had burned down to a tiny bit of anger. The betrayal had all but died in the face of logical thinking.

James stood and paced across the room. He still had his own desires to think of, though. He wanted Prudence to stay in London. He did not want her involved in the goings-on in Gravesly.

He wanted to build a prominent family of society, and then he wanted . . .

James swore softly and dug his fingers through his hair. He would not think of it, for he could not put words to the need that roiled in his chest. It was almost as if he knew that if he ever really outlined his deepest desire, he would never have any chance of attaining it.

Closing his eyes tightly, James leaned his forehead against the cool wood of the wall. And then he realized that it was not the wall at all, but a door. The door that linked his suite with his wife's. He leapt away as if the thing had burnt him.

"James?"

He closed his eyes, trying not to breathe. Her

voice was there, just on the other side of the door.

"James, I can hear you pacing around in there. May I come in?"

God no. James nearly laughed out loud. Here he stood, a man who had faced Napoleon's cannons, and the little blond woman who was his wife scared him senseless.

The handle jiggled, and then turned. It was not even locked. And then she was there, her hair down around her shoulders, the flame of a candle playing shadows across her lips. Those lips were ever his undoing.

She blinked at him, her jaw dropping slightly so that she stood openmouthed.

James followed her gaze and realized that he stood in front of his wife quite naked. He felt heat surge up his throat. Fortunately, the only light in the room was Pru's candle.

James turned and self-consciously walked over and took his wrapper from where he had thrown it over a chair. He had to breathe slowly as he tied it about himself and faced his wife once more.

"Prudence," he said for no reason. If ever a woman was more wrongly named, it was his wife.

His wife. The thought that Lady Farnsworth was now his wife still came to him as a shock at times.

She had obviously regained her composure, for

she started right in on castigating him. "Really, James, I can hear you thrashing about, moaning. Why will you not take me to bed and be done with it?"

James cleared his throat. "Obviously, I did not marry the most romantic of women."

"Every mood has its time and place, and now I am just plain fevered. Really, James, you could not keep your hands off of me in Gravesly. Why on earth do you prolong the inevitable now that we can, by law and before God, have our fun?"

"I . . ." But James could truly think of nothing to say. *I cannot touch you, because I'd lose every shred of willpower and sanity.*

"We are obviously both upset with each other," he finally said. "Why complicate that with . . . with . . ."

"Lust?"

"Right."

"Does it complicate it?" Prudence asked. "Or might it just make it easier for us to get along?"

She took a step forward, and James took a step back. "Wait." He stared into his wife's face, trying to read her motivations. "Are you trying to divert my attention once more? Perhaps you are trying to soften my feelings toward you so that you might play me like a flute."

"Hm, flute, nice phallic image," Prudence purred, and James's breath became shallow. "Obviously, James, I want you to be nicer to me. You are being mean and hateful."

"Like Creon?"

"Well, let's hope you will never be that mean and hateful, but yes. You are letting the people of Gravesly lie on a battlefield to die while the vultures circle."

James had to laugh. "Really, Prudence, you are being a bit dramatic, are you not?"

Prudence frowned. "I think we should strike that word from our vocabularies. It makes me want to scream when you say it to me, so it must have made you angry as well."

James sobered. "Yes, it did."

Prudence nodded. Then they stared at each other silently.

"James," Prudence said finally, glancing nervously at her feet, "I realize that you probably will not believe me, but I am sorry for hurting you." She looked back up at him. "I lied to you about many things, but I never lied about my feelings for you. I was attracted to you from the moment I saw you ride up to my door."

James nodded quickly, and took his turn staring at Prudence's feet. They were awfully lovely feet. And they were quite bare.

That made him shiver.

"Are you cold?"

"No," he said, suddenly wanting nothing more

than to take one of Prudence's small white toes into his mouth. James shook his head almost violently and returned his gaze to her face. Which really did not help quench his need to take her now no matter her betrayal or their doomed life as a married couple.

They stared at each other for a moment, then Prudence silently crossed the space between them on her bare white feet and slid her arms around his neck. And he did nothing to stop her.

"We could keep each other warm, James," she said, and exerted a bit of pressure against the back of his head.

It was only a slight pull. He could have resisted, easily. He could have pulled out of her arms and sent her back to her room. Easily.

At least that is what he told himself as he decided to indulge for just one moment and taste his wife.

Her lips, those lush, full lips opened beneath his, and he nearly shuddered with desire. He slipped his hands around her neck and cradled her jaw.

Her skin was like spun silk against the roughness of his fingers, and he held her lightly, not wanting to hurt her.

"Take me, James," she said against his mouth. "Please."

His wife flicked her small tongue between his lips and pressed her body close to his. He felt the give of her breasts against him and groaned out loud.

"Yes," she murmured, her hands against his back, holding him to her.

James surrendered the world then, and entered the fantasy place Prudence took him to. He picked her up, strode over to the bed, placed her on the rumpled linens, and followed her down.

Prudence took his head in her hands and guided his lips back to hers, and he once again lost himself in her scent, her taste, her feel.

James felt her through her nightgown, his hands gliding up her belly to cup her breast, then sliding down the curve of her waist and around to squeeze her round bottom.

She slipped her hands under the parted opening of his wrapper and pushed the piece of clothing off his shoulders.

"Mmm," she said, and broke their kiss so that she could put her mouth against his neck, then his shoulder. He felt her teeth against him and flinched when she bit him.

"Sorry," she said with a little laugh, her gaze darting up to his.

James laughed as well. "Quite all right, my lady vampire," he said, and bent to nibble at her neck.

She groaned and arched toward him as he pulled at the ribbons that held her night rail closed. He nudged the material away with his mouth as Prudence hooked one of her legs around his.

He kissed her again, letting his hands explore his wife's body. He could feel her need building in the way she arched against him and moved her leg up his and then down.

And then up. James realized that his wife's foot was resting against his buttock. He reached around and held her there, pushing his groin against her fully exposed woman's place.

She made a startled sound of need, bucking against him, and he knew that he would not be able to hold off much longer. James grabbed at the hem of his wife's nightgown, pulling it up to bunch around her waist, yanked his wrapper out of the way, and entered her.

She was wet and tight, and he pulled her hard against him as they lay on their sides, completely connected.

She kissed his mouth and rocked against him, and he tasted her deeply. With one hand James held Prudence against him, and with the other he found her nipple through the material of her shift and rubbed his thumbnail lightly across it.

Prudence made a funny sound in the back of her throat and kissed him in a frenzy that excited James as he had never been before. He pushed into his wife, tasting her, then, sliding his hand down, touched her wetness with his finger.

She jerked against him, and he carefully

pressed his finger where he knew she would experience the most pleasure.

They found a rhythm together, never breaking their kiss or moving from their first position, and in moments James felt his wife contract around him, once, then twice, and then he poured his seed into her body with his own climax.

In the aftermath of their lovemaking, James felt as if he had just experienced a euphoric battle of sorts. He lay back, his member slipping from Prudence's body, and just concentrated on breathing.

Beside him Pru breathed heavily as she also lay on her back and stared at the ceiling.

And then she giggled.

James turned his head to stare at his wife. "What on earth is so funny?"

She turned to look at him as well. Pru sighed, her shoulders lifting, then dropping, and she smiled. Quite a contented smile James noticed with not a little pride.

"I am just so glad that we did that."

"Really?"

"Yes." Pru levered herself up on one elbow to stare down at him. Her gown gaped open, and James could see one breast peeking out at him. He wanted to reach out and touch it, but he could not find the strength.

"James, we need to talk."

His member had begun to find life once more as he watched his wife: her lovely mouth, and her nightgown hanging about her wantonly. But it now shriveled and died, and James closed his eyes.

"You know, I have no secrets from you anymore." Prudence stopped and cocked her head to the side. "Well, at least I have no important secrets."

"Exactly what does that mean?"

She ignored him. "I believe that it is time that you told me your secrets. You keep saying that I should not speak of something I do not understand. Well, I don't understand it, truly, James. You are like another person. You order me about and restrict my life. You act as if it is so important to be accepted by the *ton*."

"It is important," he said quietly.

"See, this is what I mean," she said. "Why is it important, James? There is no meaning to it. These people are basically worthless except for the fact that they were lucky enough to be born into the right families."

"You could never understand," he said.

"Why?"

James took a few deep breaths. She would never understand his needs because no one ever had. He had tried to explain long ago as a young boy to a few of his acquaintances.

Later, as a lovesick young man, he had tried to tell Melissa. They had all looked at him as if he were speaking another language.

In truth, he had never put his ultimate desire into words. He told Pru she didn't understand, and the irony of it all was that he did not really understand.

"I . . . it is difficult to . . ." James shook his head.

Prudence reached out and laced her fingers with his. James glanced down at their joined hands. "I don't know who I am," he said. There was so much more to it, but that is what it all stemmed from. He had never, even when his mother was alive, felt like he belonged anywhere.

He frowned and looked back into his wife's soft brown eyes. "I want . . . I mean . . ." No, he could not say what he *really* meant. "I want to prove myself," he said instead and shrugged. "You should understand, Prudence. It seems that need has motivated you as well."

She nodded slightly, a sad smile playing about her lips. "Yes, it has. But if that is what you truly want, you would have told me long ago, James. For as you have just said, I understand the need to prove oneself well enough."

James pulled his hand from his wife's grip, his heart beating much harder than it should. She was making him think of things he would rather not. She was making him think of his father.

The man who had ruined his life, really.

"My father promised to marry my mother," he heard himself say. "She never told me that, of course, she never spoke of him at all, in fact. I only know as much as I know because my mother was delirious the last few days of her life. She said a few words over and over, 'my lord,' and 'my husband.' " James rubbed at his temples.

His wife leaned over and kissed his lips. It was a soft, light, barely there touch, but it made him want to pull her into his arms and make love to her again.

"You want to know who your father is," she said simply.

James felt as if someone had just dumped him over the side of a ship. He hit stinging, ice-cold water, sank for a moment, then surfaced and took a deep breath of air.

"You want to solve the mystery of your birth, but you are a bit afraid, I'm sure. Part of you wants him to love you and embrace you, another part probably wants to kill him."

Oh God.

"Go," he said, his words sounding strangled and foreign.

"Oh, James." His wife said his name like a song, and a feeling of need that had nothing to do with his physical self tingled up his spine.

James rolled off the bed and turned his back on the sight of his nearly naked wife. "Leave, Prudence."

She said nothing, but she did not leave either.

He knew for the room throbbed with her very presence; the air held her scent, their scent.

"I will not allow you to divert my attention again from what I think is important, Prudence. And I will not listen to your words of lust and nonsense. You, dear, are the worst of connivers."

"Oh!"

James immediately felt horrible for the words that had spilled from his mouth. Of course, they were not what he truly felt.

He just wanted her to leave, needed her to leave.

James turned. "Prudence, I did not mean . . . that is to say . . ."

His wife stood quickly. "I do think you should not say anything at all, James." Gripping the top of her nightgown together, Pru stomped through the door between their rooms and slammed it shut so forcefully that a very large portrait wobbled on its mooring.

James shook his head and strode toward the door, but just as his hand curled around the knob, he heard the bolt on Pru's side slide home with a pronounced harshness.

Once more, James found himself standing with his forehead against the cool wood of the door. "I am sorry, Prudence, it was not what I meant to say."

But his outspoken wife had become very quiet indeed. James knocked his forehead against the door a couple times in pure frustration.

# Chapter 19

❧ ❧

**P**rudence did not sleep at all. At first she was so terribly angry with her husband that she lay on her bed fuming. She imagined every sort of horrible thing she could do to the man.

And then frustration hit, and she thought of the people of Gravesly and how she was letting them down. And she thought of Lord Leighton and Mr. Watson, and then perhaps she did sleep for she imagined that her husband and Lord Leighton were swimming in a lagoon with sharks and she was desperately trying to scream to them, but they did not seem to hear.

Sitting up quickly, Prudence stared into the dark of her room, breathing as if she had just rowed a boat out to the schooner. She sighed when it registered in her mind where she was and dropped back on her pillows.

She was rather sure she had figured out her husband. Actually, she was very sure. He had immediately gone on the defensive and attacked her after she voiced her opinion, and with all of her interaction with men in the last couple of years she had learned much about them.

Strange creatures, really. When faced with the idea of being vulnerable in any way, emotionally or physically, they went on the attack. She understood such a reaction from animals. Usually bigger animals were trying to kill them. But, really, it would be nice if men could learn that the human race was surely not on the same level as a pack of wild dogs.

Of course, she had resorted to her own weakness and let him hurt her feelings when he was really only trying to protect his own.

But she *was* human.

Pru threw her coverlet aside and jumped out of bed. It was time to pace.

James wanted to find his place. She remembered him saying this on their trip to Brighton. And, it seemed, he had it in his head that in order to do so, he would have to know his father. Prudence nodded and propped her hands on her hips as she walked.

She was not as sure about his need to be accepted by society. Pru took another turn about her room and snapped her fingers. "If he is worthy enough, his father will come to him."

Pru stopped her pacing for a moment and closed her eyes. "Stupid man," she said softly, wanting in that moment to run through the door connecting her room to her husband's and throw her arms around him.

But she would not do that, of course.

Pru linked her hands behind her back, turned on her heel, and walked back across her suite. At least now she understood.

This knowledge could help her immensely. Finally, she would know how to manipulate Captain Ashley.

She shook her head.

No, no, no, that is not what she wanted at all, not really.

Prudence dropped into a brocade chair that sat before the enormous fireplace in her room. So what *did* she want?

She thought back to the days before Captain Ashley had complicated her life with his presence. She had been very sure of herself then, so very sure that she wanted to be the Wolf and take care of Gravesly for the rest of her life.

She had known that she was happy. And then Captain Ashley had dipped his head under the doorway of her small house, and suddenly everything changed.

Her heart had decided that it wanted more.

But what exactly?

Prudence made a strangled sound and combed

her fingers through her hair. What indeed. She
wanted to make love to her husband. She wanted
James Ashley to hold her in his strong arms and
touch her with his lovely hands.

And she wanted him to love her.

Because she loved him.

"Damn him," she muttered. He had complicated everything.

Her dear husband had given her more things
to want. Unfortunately, given who he was, he had
made them impossible to have.

She would have to figure out what was most
important. And that was quite easy, really. There
was no way that loving a man came before people's lives. It did not have anything to do with her
need to have her own name anymore, either.

They had gotten to the point where a whole
town faced destruction.

"Think," she said out loud. And then she stood
again and resumed pacing. "Think," she said
again, and realized that she really must whisper,
so lowered her voice.

"No matter my ultimate wants, I need to concentrate on my immediate needs. I need to put
my own feelings aside. I need to meet with Mr.
Watson, and I need to soften my husband. So"—
Pru twirled on her heel and started back across
the room—"I will find Lord Leighton tomorrow,"
she snapped her fingers. "And I will send Clifton
to interrogate the man's servants." That was a

flash of pure brilliance. Prudence smiled hugely. "And I will try desperately to be patient with my husband even when he says things that make me want to bash him over the head with the hardest thing I can find."

Prudence did not realize it, but she did not have to whisper her thoughts. James had left his room a few minutes after his wife had slammed out in a huff.

"I have a problem," he said softly through Clifton's door about twenty minutes later. James heard movement, then his wife's butler filled his vision. Nothing like a man the size of a small country to make you tongue-tied. In the darkness James could just make out Clifton's round head and dark eye patch.

"You've woken me from a sound sleep to stare at me, Captain?"

James frowned. "No, man, I need to speak with you immediately on a matter of grave importance."

"Then speak."

James glanced down the hall. The walls in these downstairs rooms were probably as thin as sheets. "Meet me in my study in ten minutes, Clifton."

"Yes, sir," Clifton answered, obviously intrigued, for the man gave no more argument as he stepped back and closed the door.

James took the stairs two at a time back up to the main floor. When he reached his study, he sank into the chair he had only moments ago vacated, propped his feet back on the table in front of him, and curled his fingers around the still-warm glass at his elbow. Another swallow of fine whiskey heated his throat and splashed into his belly. One whole glass had already preceded this last.

Prudence was driving him to drink, truly.

Not only did he have to figure out the problem of her former life, but he had to figure out the problem of his future life. He had resigned his commission in the navy the first day back in London, feeling rather like he could not continue in good faith since his wife's former occupation had been one frowned upon by the king. He had also not gone the usual route of taking a job in the War Office. Again, he had not felt completely right about it.

Still, he had been playing with the idea of going into politics. Politics did not require complete honesty in the least. Also, a thought had occurred to him while he spoke with his wife in the carriage. Perhaps, he could persuade her to live in London as the proper wife of a politician and help the people of Gravesly through legal channels.

And perhaps they could do it together.

And perhaps they could live their entire lives like the first night of their marriage.

The thought was lovely, but probably completely without merit. Persuading Prudence to do anything that she did not want to do was a Herculean task if ever there was one.

"Sir?" Clifton stood in the doorway.

He stood. "Thank you for coming up, Clifton. Would you like a drink?"

Clifton shook his head curtly.

"Fine then, please sit with me." James gestured to the chair opposite him.

Clifton squinted toward the chair, then looked at James suspiciously.

"I am not going to bite you, Clifton. I just wish to speak with you."

The butler said nothing, but entered and carefully took the seat across from James. James sat as well, trying to think of the best way to broach the subject he needed to discuss.

"First of all, Clifton, may I have your word that our conference here tonight will remain in confidence?"

Clifton stared at him for a very long time in silence, but James waited patiently. The two glasses of whiskey actually helped him in this effort.

Finally, Clifton nodded slowly. "I will keep your confidence, sir, if doing so does not hurt Lady Prudence."

James shook his head. "It will not."

"Fine, then."

James fingered his empty glass. "I have decided not to send you to the Colonies, Clifton."

Clifton blinked, and James thought for one strange moment that the large man was going to cry. But then he sat up a bit straighter and belied this notion with the darkest frown James had ever seen on a human visage.

"I must admit"—James looked away from the butler—"to a certain soft spot in my heart for the people of Gravesly." James furrowed his brow and concentrated on the small wash of whiskey at the bottom of his glass. A beat of silence went by, and he could not help thinking of how desperately he wanted to believe that the people of Gravesly had felt the same for him.

Pathetic, really.

"Anyway, Prudence has informed me that the Marley brothers have been spotted in Gravesly, and that this could mean that they will try to take over the smuggling business of the town. Are her fears legitimate?"

He glanced up and saw that Clifton was very wary of James's questions. The man's one good eye could not possibly get any smaller and still be open.

"Yes," the butler finally said.

"I want you to go to Gravesly, then, and make sure that does not happen."

Clifton's blue eye was now as round as James

had ever seen it. "Is this a trick?" the man asked blatantly.

"No," James answered, and stood. He clasped his hands behind his back, widened his stance, and stood staring down at his wife's butler. "You have my word of honor that this is not a trick, Clifton."

The man nodded slowly.

"Now I want your word of honor that you will not attempt to continue the work you and your mistress were conducting before I found out."

Clifton shook his head. "What? Do you want me to go or don't you?"

"I want you to go to protect Gravesly from harm, but I do not want any smuggling to take place."

The man made a disgusted sound in the back of his throat. "If we do not get the business back up and going, the Marley brothers will take over no matter if I'm there or not. And anyway"—the butler stood as well—"we've got other problems besides the Marley brothers."

"What other problems?"

But Clifton had shut his mouth. Obviously, he felt as if he had said too much.

"Clifton, I am trying to help, truly. What other problems?"

The butler shrugged. "Well, there's our London contact. He hasn't received any shipments in a few days, and I'm sure the man is angry."

"Who is your London contact?"

Clifton truly clammed up now. "Don't know," he said succinctly.

James took a deep breath and rubbed his forehead with his thumb and forefinger. He had a horrible headache.

"Captain," Clifton said with a tone that had James glancing up sharply, "the smuggling gang in Gravesly will not listen to me. I could, perhaps, keep the Marley brothers at bay for a week or two by telling Harker and the others that Lady Prudence would be there soon. But they need a leader, a real leader. Someone they look up to. Someone they can believe in. Someone they know can keep the bad influences out of their operation.

"The baron knew that, and it is why, when he got so sick, he told me that I would have to get Lady Prudence to take over for him. It was hard for them at first since she was a woman, but they do need someone they perceive as higher than them in some way to lead them." Clifton shook his head slightly. "If you are truly worried, Captain, you need to send Lady Pru back to Gravesly."

This was the most Clifton had ever said to him, and it made James believe that he had at least garnered the man's trust. For the moment.

James nodded as if contemplating Clifton's suggestion. Of course, there was absolutely no way he would send his wife anywhere near Gravesly. It was ludicrous, really, to send Clifton.

He should go forth with his original plan, sell Chesley House, send Clifton away, and never let his wife back in the small town of Gravesly again.

Of course, that had been his plan when he had been burning with anger and betrayal. Both of those emotions had now smoldered down to his usual frustration and a bit of strong pique.

James furrowed his hand through his hair and nodded again. "I will think on what you have said, Clifton. But while I am deciding on my next course of action, I would appreciate your compliance with my wishes. I want you to go to Gravesly and do what you can to keep the Marley brothers away from the town."

"Of course," the man said.

Of course? Goodness, he seemed to have Clifton's loyalty suddenly.

"Good." James went to the sideboard, poured two glasses of whiskey, and handed one to Clifton. "To your success," he said, holding up his own glass.

Clifton looked a bit flustered, but clicked his glass against James's and drank.

Prudence Farnsworth Ashley sat in the kitchen of the earl of Wimsley sipping tea with the under-housekeeper. Her original plan of having Clifton gossip with Leighton's servants had been thwarted, yet again, by her husband. The man had sent Clifton off to pack up his things and say good-bye to the people in Gravesly.

And she had not even been given the chance to speak with Clifton before he left. Still, she hoped her butler would know to put it about that she was not gone, and that the Wolf would be back.

Then she had borrowed a cap and apron from Mary on the pretense that she needed them for a pattern to make some for her servants in Gravesly, locked herself in her room, and climbed a convenient trellis to the street.

She knew that servants gossiped incessantly, for when she lived in Gravesly, she gossiped with them. In fact, Delilah had once worked in the kitchens of the earl of Trent. Her cook had told her that the servants of London society knew every secret of the *ton*, and if there was ever something she needed to know about the peerage, a gossiping servant would be able to uncover anything.

So, Pru had become a servant. She had made her way first to the home of Lord Leighton where, on the pretext of looking for a job, she learned from a particularly chatty chambermaid that the man had close ties to his only living relative, the earl of Wimsley.

That bit of information sent Pru scurrying across town to the Wimsley mansion, aware of the fact that she had been gone from the house for a terribly long time and might be missed soon.

Now, using the name of the Leighton servant to get in the door, she sipped tea with another very talkative servant of Wimsley. It seemed the underground information lines of the servants of London were quite extensive and very interesting to say the least. She already knew the intimate details of the viscount's relationship with his grandfather.

Wimsley, she was told, was a raving lunatic. A tyrant as a master, he also yelled and ranted at Leighton and insisted in speaking in code even though all the servants already knew all of the man's deep, dark secrets.

This last bit of information piqued Pru's flagging interest, and she sat up a bit straighter in her chair by the fire.

"Deep, dark secrets?" she asked, leaning toward her companion conspiratorially. "I must say, that does sound interesting, now doesn't it?" She rolled her eyes and waved her hand in the air between them. "The people in my household are about as dull as dishwater, if you must know the truth. That Captain Ashley's never done anything more exciting than save us from the French."

"Ah, but 'e's a looker, ain't 'e?" she asked, with a wink and a slurp of tea.

Pru scrunched up her nose at this. Even the servants found her husband desirable. Was there anyone in this town unaffected by wide shoulders, stormy gray eyes, and dark-as-sin hair? Prudence sighed.

"See now, even you're a bit o'er the top for 'im, aren't you?"

Prudence hid behind her teacup for a moment, then waved her new friend to continue with her story. "So, tell me some of these deep, dark secrets," she said.

"Well, there's the stuff about some place down south, and 'ow 'e makes all 'is money, of course. But that's so boring it'd put you to sleep, I'm sure."

Prudence shook her head, but Livy continued on undaunted. "Now, the fun stuff comes with the older servants. There's a woman that's been 'ere since before Leighton was born. She says there was goings-on in those days to put a scandal on the name of Wimsley for a couple or three generations at least."

"Really?" Pru asked with feigned interest. "But surely the thing about how the earl makes his money is ever so much more scandal-ridden than something so long ago?"

Livy snorted and shook her head. "Oh, that's nothing. The earl is like most of the peers in this town, makin' money on the backs of hardworkin' people. And, o' course, lettin' them take the blame should anyone find out. No," Livy continued without even taking a breath, "the deep and dark secrets come when ol' Mrs. Winter starts her tales."

Livy sat back with a satisfied grin and folded her arms across her ample stomach. "Wimsley had not one, but two sons, which any of the people who 'ave lived in London for more than fifty years could tell you."

With a forced smile, Pru surreptitiously checked the clock on the mantel. She really had to get home.

"Now, his second son went on to India to make his own fortune and never came back."

Prudence just barely suppressed an irritated sigh. "Well that certainly has happened to a few poor souls, now hasn't it?" Pru said. "But having a secret source of income, now that . . ."

But Livy didn't seem to be listening. "The son never came back, but a pregnant woman did, claiming that the son was dead and she was his wife."

Pru suddenly found herself interested in spite of herself. "Whatever became of her?" she asked, and then realized that she had just fed the fire of Livy's gossip telling in the wrong direction.

Livy's eyes rounded as she waggled her brows dramatically. "Well now, 'ere's where it just becomes the juiciest bit o' knowledge you'd ever want to know. There's some connection between Old Wimsley and the girl's father that just made Wimsley fly into a rage like none other before it.

It's told round 'ere that after this particular fit, there wasn't a piece of porcelain to be 'ad in the whole house that wasn't smashed to smithereens."

"Goodness."

"Yes, and he sent that poor gel on her way, so 'e did. Sent her right on out the door as if she weren't carrying his grandchild at all."

Prudence blinked in consternation.

"Never 'eard of 'er or the child again."

"If this is so well-known, why on earth isn't it a scandal? I can't believe that no one in London ever whispered about it or decried Wimsley's actions."

With a disbelieving sound somewhere between a chortle and a snort, Livy frowned at her. "It's well-known by us, not them."

Prudence did not understand. "Us?"

Livy shook her head. "What, is the world so different in Gravesly that there's no us and them?" she asked with a harsh laugh. "Can't say as I ever knew that."

Us and them? Pru glanced down at her apron, and suddenly understood. "Oh," she said, comprehension dawning. "Of course."

Livy looked at her as if she had just sprouted wings.

Goodness, who knew that so much could be learned from the servants of the *ton*? She wished a long life to her second persona of Clarissa, special maid to Mrs. Ashley. Clarissa, it seemed, had the right connections to find out all kinds of interesting fodder. "So no one knows the name of the wife, or even whether the baby lived?"

Livy shook her head and shrugged. "No. I told you it was deep and dark now, didn't I?" A bell clanged on the board above their heads, and Livy's shoulders drooped. " 'E's wantin' me to do some foul thing, I'm sure." She stood. "You're a fun one to talk to, Clarissa. I like how you talk, almost like you're one of them." She giggled a bit. "Come back soon." And she disappeared through a massive wood door.

Pru closed her eyes for a moment, realizing that she had not been told anything that she could use. She had allowed herself to be taken in by a bit of servant's gossip and had completely forgotten to find out about what she really needed to know.

With a mental slap, Prudence vowed to be more consistent with her inquiries from now on. At least, though, she was rather sure that she was on the right track.

Lord Leighton obviously knew of whom she spoke when she talked of Mr. Watson, and his grandfather had some secret source of income from a place south of London. She had to conclude that either, or perhaps both of the men, were the mysterious Mr. Watson.

Prudence let herself out of the servants' entrance, climbed the steep stairs to the street, and hurried up the street. She kept her head down, of course, so that no one would recognize her. Unfortunately, that unwieldy position made it terribly hard to avoid running into people. Especially people of the upper classes who, she had discovered in the few hours she had spent as one of the lower classes, tended to keep their noses in the air and not give a second thought to anyone in their way.

Until now, Prudence had been able to avoid any serious injury, though she had been the recipient of a few harsh words and some old woman had found it necessary to whack Pru across the shins with her cane.

She was beginning to realize that she would not wish the job of London servant on her very worst enemy, and she was just vowing to give every single person in the Ashley household a raise when Prudence ran headlong into someone and landed smack on her behind in a stinking gutter.

She expected the man to keep going, seeing how most people treated the lowly working class, but he stooped down to help her, offering a hand encased in a fine kid the color of fresh petunias.

Prudence blinked from the strange-colored gloves, up a brocade sleeve, and into the very green eyes of Lord Leighton. With a wince, she glanced quickly down at her aproned lap.

"Mrs. Ashley, I presume," he said.

He had recognized her. How would she ever

explain this small caper? Wracking her brains for
a plausible excuse, Prudence put her hand into
Leighton's and allowed the man to help her up
out of the filthy gutter.

She wished, at least, that she had fallen onto
the relatively clean walkway. But now on top of
looking like a scullery maid, Pru smelled very
much like a necessary. Lovely.

Lord Leighton frowned down at her, then
glanced up at his grandfather's house not far
from where they stood. "I hope your husband did
not take you too much to task for the other
evening?" he asked.

"Oh no," Prudence replied, thinking it rather
ludicrous that they speak to each other as if nothing out of the ordinary was going on. "I presume
Captain Ashley believes I was indulging my rebel-
lious spirit. He is not threatened by you."

Leighton laughed knowingly. "I'm not surprised, dear. Still, I am glad he did not do anything terrible to you."

The viscount frowned down at her. "But, of
course, now I must ask you about this lovely
dress?"

Pru gave a tiny thought to just sprinting off
and leaving the viscount behind her, but she
knew that it would not solve anything.

And she certainly would have to engage the
man in conversation at some point.

"I was . . ." She stopped and wracked her brain

for a reply. "Well, this is a disguise, actually and, I . . ."

"Was ingratiating yourself with my grandfather's servants in the hopes of learning more of Mr. Watson."

Prudence actually smiled. "Yes, exactly."

He nodded. "Terribly innovative of you, Mrs. Ashley."

"I do try."

"Yes, you do. So, have you uncovered the grisly truth?"

"I know that your grandfather is Mr. Watson."

Leighton nodded, placed his hand on her back and guided her into the shadows of the town house beside them. "Smart woman, Mrs. Ashley," he said.

Smart enough to know that she might be in danger. Pru glanced up the street, and then back at Leighton.

He chuckled. "I am not going to hurt you. I could care less that you have found out the truth."

"So you just do your grandfather's dirty work?" she asked.

"I try, actually, not to do much at all. Wimsley does nearly all of it. He just uses me to scream at when things go wrong, and he asked me to find out what happened with the last shipment that never arrived."

"Right. That would be the one that James found and turned over to the magistrate in Rye."

"Ah."

Pru stared up at Leighton, still unsure that she could trust the man.

"This is not the best place to discuss such matters."

With a glance down at her attire, Prudence nodded in agreement. "No," she said. "Not very discreet, anyway."

"Shall we make another attempt at meeting?" he asked.

"I will be in the park with my groom this afternoon and shall foolishly leave my bonnet at home," she decided quickly. "When he goes back to fetch it for me, I could slip away."

"We should avoid the route du roi," he said.

"Oh yes, Rotten Row is not a good idea, either."

Leighton tapped one thin white finger against his chin, and said, "Perhaps we should enjoy Kensington Park?"

"Roger's Seat?" she asked.

"Perfect."

"Roger's Seat, then, four o'clock."

"I shall await the moment with excitement," Leighton effused. "Your beauty makes even the shortest of times apart difficult to endure, dearest Mrs. Ashley. I begin to believe that you are my muse. Surely, with the thought of our meeting in our future, I will pen a great masterpiece this very day."

Prudence snorted.

"My poetry falls on deaf ears. Well, then, until we meet again." And with a tip of his hat, Leighton strode off toward the front door of his grandfather's mansion.

# Chapter 20

Richard decided to skip his meeting with Wimsley. The old man would definitely have quite a fit, for he was expecting his grandson at noon. Such an ungodly hour, anyway.

Instead, Richard turned at the end of the street, waited for a moment watching the lusciously curved Mrs. Ashley scurry away in her maid's disguise, and crossed over toward his very favorite coffeehouse.

Once settled, Richard contemplated his situation. There were only a couple of reasons why he continued to indulge his grandfather's insistence that they see each other at all.

Foremost, there was Richard's rather sophomoric need to retain a link to his only living relative. But Richard had admitted early to himself that his childhood had made him quite maudlin and so desperately in need of family ties that it could someday be detrimental to his sanity.

But, again, since he fully understood this, he was very sure he could sidestep the problem of turning into a Bedlamite like his grandfather.

The second, and decidedly less important reason he made even the smallest attempt to stay in his grandfather's good graces was the same reason almost every young man of society did anything.

Money.

Of course, this reason had become less and less important as the years went by. He adored beautiful things, and surrounded himself with lush belongings as well as dressed himself immaculately, but he always lived within his means. And he invested wisely.

His personal fortune was nothing to sneer at. But, of course, it would not hurt at all to have his grandfather's inheritance.

Anyway, he did admit to a personal attachment to the home he had grown up in. The place just north of Yorkshire was not entailed with the earldom and therefore could be given to absolutely anyone who took his grandfather's fancy.

Not that any person of the human race had ever taken his grandfather's fancy, but Richard rather hoped Wimsley would decide to deed over Leighton Abbey to his grandson.

This hope tended to make it important to keep

appointments Richard made with his grandfather. But today, even Leighton Abbey could not make him face his grandfather's hysterics.

Richard checked through the windows of the coffeehouse for anyone of interest before pushing through the doors and choosing a table that would afford him a perfect view of the street. He ordered a scone with clotted cream, a lovely indulgence that made even the worst day so much better, and a strong coffee.

Good, good, good.

All he needed now was *Lady Whistledown's Society Papers*, and he would have heaven on earth. Unfortunately, he did not have the paper, so, ignoring the disgusted looks from other patrons, Richard settled back and propped his favorite Hessians on the chair opposite him.

He needed to think.

James watched his wife climb through her sitting-room window. She hefted her slight frame through on her strong arms, then swung over a very lovely leg. A bit of scooting and grunting, and she had her other leg through and was standing triumphantly inside her apartments.

"Hello, dear."

Prudence screamed.

James pushed himself away from the corner he had been inhabiting and came forward. He had assumed the disciplinary face that he used on errant seamen. But his heart thumped away painfully in his chest.

It hurt him that his wife defied him, and it scared him that it hurt.

"James," Prudence breathed, one hand pressed to her breast.

"Lovely cap, dearest," he said, noting the disguise. She must have been doing something that involved Gravesly and smuggling. It hurt, damn it.

"You have now managed to take another ten years from my life, sir. At this rate I shall die yesterday."

"Hmmm. Well, I must tell you, Prudence, I came to your rooms this morning to apologize."

"Apologize?"

"I am sorry that I hurt your feelings last night."

Pru blinked, then she shrank down into a chair, her hands in her lap, her head bowed.

James watched her silently as neither said anything for a good five minutes.

"I think I deserve to know exactly what you were doing today, Prudence," he said finally.

She shrugged, looking very small suddenly. "I had an idea last night, and I was going to send Clifton to explore it, but you have sent him away."

"And your idea?"

Prudence sat up straight and looked at him. He could see that she had gotten over feeling bad and was now going to berate him or let him know how shallow he was or something along those lines. James sighed.

"The people of Gravesly . . ."

James did not let her continue. He took the space between them in two large strides, grabbed both her arms, and pulled her to her feet.

"Damn the people of Gravesly, Pru. You defy me, you lie, you continue in illegal activities. Can't you see how serious this is?"

Her eyes darkened, and he could see that she was getting ready to lecture. It was amazing how well he knew this woman already. James leaned down and kissed her before she could say a word.

He felt her resist for a moment, then kiss him back as if the world around them did not exist.

James broke the kiss with a sigh, let go of his wife, and walked away from her. "I want you to stop this, Prudence. And it is not just my shallow character that says that." He turned back to stare at her. "You are not in Gravesly anymore, Prudence. If the authorities were to learn of your activities, you could be hanged."

She swallowed audibly. "Are you worried about me, James? Or are you worried of the beating your reputation would take if your wife was forced to stand trial?"

He did not answer her. He would not. "Does it matter?" he asked finally.

She lifted her brows and shrugged. "I guess

not." Prudence sat again, only this time, she kept her shoulders straight and her eyes on him.

"Tell me, James, about your mother."

"Excuse me?"

"James," Prudence said slowly, "I want to tell you something I heard today from a servant in the home of the earl of Wimsley."

Why on earth had his wife been speaking to a servant of Wimsley's?

"There is a story that his second son went away to India and never came back. Instead, a young woman showed up saying that the son was dead and she was his wife and carried his child. But the earl sent her away."

James did not want to think of it. "I am sure that happened to a number of women."

His wife nodded and looked up into his eyes. "Yes, I am sure it did," she said.

James turned away abruptly. He needed to move. He needed to get out of this room, out of this house. He strode toward the door and wrapped his fingers around the handle.

"Men," his wife said, with a sniff of disgust.

James did not want to listen to her anymore. She opened dark rooms in his mind better left closed. He turned the doorknob.

"You are all so afraid of being afraid, you can barely function, really."

Out, he needed out.

"James, stop."

And he did. He dropped his hand to his side and turned around.

Prudence had her bottom lip trapped between her teeth, and was looking at him with a gaze that made him suddenly think of his mother: the only person in the whole world who had ever loved him.

James felt suddenly as if he could not breathe.

"You want to know who your father is, but you dare not look for him for fear you'll be rejected again. So you have decided to live your life as one worthy of a father and wait for him to find you."

James stood as still as he could as the truth he had never even articulated to himself washed through his mind, through his body. "Yes," he finally said.

Prudence shook her head. "*He* is not worthy of *you*, James." She stood up, walked over to him, put her arms around his waist, and rested her head against his chest.

"You're right," he said softly. "I'm afraid of being afraid."

Prudence arrived at Roger's Seat early. She pushed herself up into the niche in the wall, swung her feet, and watched a mother bird feeding her babies in the tree over her head.

"My goodness, 'tis a goddess awaiting my arrival."

Prudence glanced down at Viscount Leighton and could not help but laugh as he swirled his greatcoat in an elaborate gesture and bowed as if he greeted a royal.

"My lord," she said with a nod of her head, but did not give up her perch in Roger's Seat.

Leighton turned and leaned his back against the wall beside her. "So," he said, crossing his arms in front of him. "I have pondered our predicament this afternoon and have decided that I should reveal everything to you. Including the fact that my grandfather is a raving loon."

"I had already deduced that."

"Yes, it isn't hard."

Leighton sighed rather sadly.

Prudence turned her gaze up to watch another small hatchling receive its dinner from its mother's mouth. "You said, 'our predicament.' How is this *our* predicament?"

"For all this"—Leighton gestured to his fine clothes—"I am a very simple man, Mrs. Ashley. I am led by my emotions, and I don't mind admitting it. I like you. I don't like my grandfather." He frowned and looked away from her. "I would like to help you, if I can. Because I have a feeling you need help."

Prudence laughed shortly. "Quite an understatement. Your grandfather needs the Wolf, and I have decided that I can no longer be the Wolf."

Leighton pushed away from his languid position against the wall and turned his eyes on her. "Hmm."

"Yes, that would put a damper on your income."

Leighton shrugged. "It doesn't really matter to me. It's not my income after all, just my inheritance. And I don't really expect to receive that anyway. I'm rather sure old Wimsley will find some way to remind me of what a terrible disgrace I am to the family from his grave."

"Then perhaps you really can help me."

Leighton smiled his beautiful smile. "Of course, Mrs. Ashley, I am at your service. I could never deny a woman in love."

Prudence blinked.

"This is all because you love the captain, is it not?"

She rolled her eyes, ready to deny such an accusation, and then realized there was no reason to do such a thing. "Yes, I love my husband."

And she was willing to give up her role as the Wolf for him. But she wasn't willing to let the people of Gravesly fend for themselves. She pushed off of her perch. "Shall we walk?"

"With you on my arm," he said, holding out his elbow, "I would walk to the ends of the earth."

Prudence placed her gloved fingers on his arm. "My problem is twofold. There is your grandfather to appease, and Gravesly to save."

"Neither an easy thing to do."

"Quite right."

They walked without speaking for a while.

"Money would appease Grandfather," Leighton noted. "Lots of it, I think."

Pru laughed. "Your grandfather already *has* most of my money."

"You could ask your husband."

"No."

"Right."

They continued their stroll.

"Could you find someone to take over the business for you? Clifton?"

Prudence shook her head. "Why do you think my husband asked me, a woman, to take over at his death? There is no one else." She stopped and turned to look at Leighton. "The situation in Gravesly is unique. We are the only smuggling gang that has been able to keep violence out of the equation. The town is safe for everyone. We have never killed any of the excise men or government agents. In fact, I really believe that is the reason we have been left alone for the most part."

"Until Captain Ashley happened upon the scene."

"Yes. Anyway, the people of Gravesly need a firm hand to keep them from becoming like all the other smuggling towns in the area, and my husband believed that having a strong person in charge, a person who cared and was looked up to as someone above the rest, was the best way to accomplish the task."

"And he was right, obviously." Leighton drummed his fingers against his leg for a moment. "You would need a peer, then, a peer with the best interests of Gravesly at heart who lives among them so they would trust him . . . or her." With a shake of his head, Leighton glanced down at her. "You are the only one."

Prudence sighed, her shoulders rising and falling. "I am the only one." Despair made her feel weak. She left Leighton and sank onto a garden seat at the side of the path.

"It is too bad Gravesly could not be like Brighton, really. Brighton is able to survive without smuggling because of the money spent there when the peers are in residence."

Prudence nodded as Leighton sat beside her. "And Gravesly is ever so much more pleasant than Brighton."

"Really?" he asked. "I would love to see it, then."

They sat silently, each mulling ideas until Leighton suddenly laughed. "Mrs. Ashley, what if you took the *ton* to see Gravesly?"

"Whatever do you mean, man?"

Leighton stood, his features animated as he laughed again. He did a little pirouette. "I have the most perfect idea, but we must start on it immediately." He grabbed Pru's arm and nearly launched her from her seat. "Come dear, we have work to do. And while we work, we shall think on the problem of Grandfather. Of course"—he winked at her—"we can always hope the man sticks his spoon in the wall. I've been praying for his death for years."

# Chapter 21

◦─◦◯◦─◦

Leighton's plan was working startlingly well.
In only two days, Prudence had become the
talk of the *ton*. She had to admit, of course, that
they had been interested in her before. She just
had not taken advantage of that interest.

Now, with the viscount's help, Prudence had
found someone to cut her hair, a daring do, actually, that was quite short and curly. She absolutely
loved it. And the viscount had directed her to a
modiste who had been able to fit her with a few
beautiful gowns and deliver them before the end
of the first day.

Prudence Ashley had hit her next ball looking
like the muse Leighton had called her and just
brimming with charm and excitement. The buzz
had begun, and now only three days later, the entire town spoke of what a beautiful woman Mrs.

Ashley was, how very interesting her conversation seemed, and how incredibly fashionable her clothes were.

She was a hit.

Leighton, as he said, had never had a moment's doubt that she could do exactly as he had outlined in his plan. And now, Prudence just needed to talk of Gravesly, and their plan would be on the way to complete success.

Of course, Captain Ashley had not really spoken to her since the day he had found her sneaking in her sitting-room window, but he had informed her that Clifton would be staying on in Gravesly and not be forced to leave the country.

This information definitely lifted Pru's spirits and made her believe that perhaps her dearest husband had a bit of a soft spot for her.

Unfortunately, that soft spot was not showing this evening. As he had said before, he now accompanied her to every one of her engagements, still outlined each day by Jenkins.

This, actually, had caught the morbid fascination of the *ton* as well. It was being whispered about that Captain Ashley was besotted with his wife and would not let her out of his sight. As this was quite a phenomenon, Pru could feel the eyes of nearly every person in the crush at the Belmont Ball turn toward them when they were announced.

"Really, James, I shall not run off to do anything horrible, I promise," she said to her husband, as they pushed their way into the crowded ballroom. "I will be right here when you return with my punch."

The poor man contemplated her for a moment, then bowed slightly. "If you are gone when I return, I will hunt you down like a wolf," he said softly, and turned into the press of people around them.

Prudence actually giggled, then set her attention to the women who had started to gather. A few, she noticed, had cut their hair just like hers.

Leighton had said that it would happen, but she had not believed him in the least.

"Oooh," said one of the younger ladies, a Mrs. Hampton if Pru remembered right. "Your husband looks absolutely dashing this evening, Mrs. Ashley."

"Shush, Leta," said Lady Rawley.

Mrs. Hampton, who could not be much older than eighteen, blinked and seemed to shrink two inches.

Pru linked her arm through Mrs. Hampton's. "He's lovely, isn't he?" she whispered so that only the younger girl could hear, and then turned to smile at the other women. Their circle became larger with each passing minute. There were a few brave men as well.

Perfect.

"Actually," she said with just a bit of a tremor traveling up her legs and knocking her knees together, "I am just thrilled with my husband. I am so glad that he came down to Gravesly on assignment."

"Of course, you could have come up here to London, Mrs. Ashley," Lady Rawley said. "And then, perhaps, you would have met him ever so much sooner."

"Yes, and it would have given others a chance at snapping you up!" one of the men guffawed.

A few of the older women frowned, but Mrs. Hampton giggled. "Actually," Pru said, sending up a little prayer of thanks to God for such a lovely opening, "it would have never happened here in London."

"Whyever not?"

Pru shrugged and sighed dreamily. "Gravesly is so incredibly romantic. Our love for one another could have begun in no other place."

"Gravesly? Romantic?" Lord Tilton asked disbelievingly. "Isn't it just a little port town?"

"Oh goodness, no," Prudence said quickly. "Gravesly is truly lovely. We're ever so grateful, really, that the people of London have not found it as they have Brighton."

"Is there anything to do there?" asked a very disbelieving Mrs. Hampton.

"Oh yes, I am so very glad its charms have

been kept secret for so long, so that it is not over-run like Brighton." Prudence crinkled her nose in disgust.

"No, our little Gravesly is lovely and quaint. Gravesly Bay is a very nice beach, and, of course, the waters are said to correct every type of ill."

"Really?"

"Yes, and everyone knows that sea air is very good for you," Prudence added.

"Yes, I've heard that," said Lord Tilton.

Prudence nodded. "And you know," she said suddenly, "Gravesly is going to have their big fair next week. I am planning to attend, of course."

"Fair?" someone asked.

"Oh yes," Prudence said. "It is wonderful. There are games and Mrs. Sawyer sells her incredible strawberry jellies and oh . . ." she made a small sound of pure enjoyment. "The cakes that the baker puts out are something every person should try at least once before they die."

"We never said anything about a fair," Leighton said the next day when she accepted him into the parlor at Ashley House.

"Nor did we say anything about you coming here," she countered glancing toward the door. "I'm sure the butler will announce your presence to Ashley. My husband is only in his study."

Leighton shrugged. "I have something to tell both of you."

"Both of us?"

Without answering, Leighton went to stand before the large fireplace. He stared into the dancing flames for a moment, then turned toward her.

"I have been investigating the story you told me. The one of the woman who claimed to be Albert James Von Schubert's wife so many years ago."

"That is his name? Your grandfather's second son was named Albert James?"

Leighton tipped his head slightly.

"Oh." Prudence backed up and sank into a chair.

"I had heard something of the story, though I had thought it to be a legend. With the details one servant gave me, I decided to see if I could find anything more. I thought, at first, that we could use the information to blackmail Grandfather."

"And now you don't think we can?" she asked.

"We could actually, easily."

They stared at each other. "But . . ." she prompted.

"But, I will let you decide if you want to take that course." Leighton casually slid the fingers of his right hand into the small pocket of his waistcoat. Then he pulled them out and clasped his hands before him. It was the first time Prudence had ever seen the viscount appear uncomfortable.

"My grandfather had a locked box buried in his garden. I found it one day when I was about ten." Leighton smiled slightly. "I was playing pirates and digging for buried treasure. Anyway, I tried to open it at the time, but it was rusted shut. My grandfather found me, of course. Gave me a whipping and took the box away."

"You have been playing pirates again, my lord?" Pru asked, though her throat had gone so dry, it was a wonder any words came out at all.

He nodded and pulled a thin packet from the inside of his jacket. "My grandfather is not just a Bedlamite, but the most evil man on earth, I think. These are legal papers proving the annulment of the marriage of Albert Von Schubert to Sarah Elizabeth Ashley. I did not find the original marriage papers, but this obviously proves they were married."

"Annulment?" Prudence felt as if her brain had quit working completely. She could not seem to understand what everything meant.

"From what I knew, what you found out, these papers and some discreet questioning of my grandfather's staff, I have pieced together a sad story. Suffice it to say, Ashley was conceived in wedlock, most definitely, but my grandfather had the marriage annulled after Ashley's father died so that Ashley was born a bastard."

"How? That isn't legal, surely."

"We are part German, Mrs. Ashley, distant relatives of the king of England. Wimsley can do anything he pleases."

"Oh."

Quiet filled the room then. Poor Leighton looked absolutely deflated. The strutting peacock had turned into a sad little pigeon. "It made me physically ill when I realized the extent of Grandfather's maliciousness." Leighton shook his head. "I've always known, of course, that he is really horrible, but . . ."

Pru just nodded. She knew, of course, that this information could make her free of Wimsley. With something this horrid hanging over his head, she could demand that he let Gravesly out of their contract.

But then she would have to wait for Wimsley's death to tell James the truth. And probably, then, James would never speak to her again for keeping such a thing from him.

"Do you want to tell him, or shall I?" she asked.

Leighton closed his eyes and leaned against the wall as if his legs would no longer support him. "I am so very glad you have decided to tell him."

"By him, I am assuming you mean me?"

Pru jumped, clenching her hands in her skirt.

Leighton glanced up and straightened away from the wall. "Ashley, we meet again."

"Always a pleasure, Leighton," James said, ice dripping from his words. Still, he came forward to shake the viscount's proffered hand. Her husband topped Leighton by a good foot, and his hand was large and brown against Leighton's slight white one.

Prudence felt a surge of pure lust as she watched her beautiful husband greet their guest. Neither the time, nor the place, but she just could not help herself.

Hadn't that been her problem from their first meeting? She did not know whether to cry or laugh at the thought.

Pru rubbed at her temples, then realized that Leighton was staring at her pointedly.

"Go ahead," she said.

Leighton nodded as Ashley glanced between the two of them, and then the viscount handed over the leather packet to her husband. "I want to apologize for the way my grandfather treated your mother, Captain," Leighton said softly.

James stood very still, staring down at Leighton's offering. "Excuse me?" he said.

"These are annulment papers, Captain, dissolving the marriage of Albert James Von Schubert and Sarah Elizabeth Ashley."

Pru could not see James, but she heard the hitch in his breathing. She wanted to jump up and hold him, but she waited to see what he would do.

"Von Schubert?"

"My uncle," Leighton said. "Albert is . . . was the earl of Wimsley's younger son. About thirty-four years ago, he was in the army stationed in India. He married a woman there, your mother, and returned home, but died during the passage."

James slowly extracted the leather packet from Leighton's grasp.

"I have pieced together this story, and I am not sure on some points. It seems, though, that your maternal grandfather did not approve of the match. They married secretly and left India without telling anyone. On this point, I have not been able to figure out exactly what the problem was, but Wimsley's maid told your wife that the earl had quite a fit when he found out exactly who your mother was. I can only surmise that for some reason my grandfather and your maternal grandfather were quite strong enemies."

James glanced at Pru, his gray eyes the color of dark rain clouds.

She knew she had to tell him the whole truth. "Wimsley is the London backer of Gravesly's smuggling ring. Leighton thought we could find something scandalous to blackmail him with so that Gravesly would be let out of the contract with the earl."

James just nodded.

"When your mother reached England, widowed and with child, my . . . our grandfather did the unthinkable." Leighton looked down at the floor. "He had the marriage annulled."

Pru wanted to cry for Sarah Elizabeth Ashley.

"I realize that you do not trust me after our experience in India together," Leighton said.

"What experience?" Pru asked.

"Nothing," both men said together.

Pru frowned, but Leighton continued. "I want to assure you, though, that Wimsley is no longer as influential as he once was, and his mind is not as sharp. I, on the other hand, command loyalties from people in high places." He took a step toward James, and said in a softer tone, "I will respect your wishes entirely. If you wish to fight this annulment in court, I will help. If you want to keep this whole thing quiet, I will do that as well. It is only fair that you make this decision now, since that right was so unfairly taken from your mother."

James just nodded.

And Pru began to cry. It surprised her, really; she had been trembling, yes, but keeping the tears at bay. And then suddenly something wet plunked onto her skirt and then another and another. Within seconds her face was wet with tears.

James turned, then stopped and watched her for a moment. He looked as if he might say something, but then he just shook his head and left without another word.

James took the stairs to his private rooms in a daze. He staggered into his sitting room, dropped into a chair, and stared at the wall, one hand wrapped around the proof that he was not truly a bastard, the other, palm up on his knee.

And he did not move until night darkened his window. And then he stood up, walked carefully over to a vase that sat on his mantel, picked it up, and threw it across the room.

It crashed against the wall and broke into a thousand small pieces.

His father, the father he had dreamed about his whole life. The father he had hoped would some-day show up on his doorstep professing pride and ownership of his son, was dead, had been dead for James's whole life.

Why hadn't his mother told him that much, at least?

James took up the matching vase and threw it at the exact spot the other had gone. The crash re-verberated in the large room nicely.

He could not blame his mother, though. A woman in such circumstances did not have many choices. And she did her best. And she had loved him.

Wimsley, on the other hand, was of the devil's own blood.

"James?"

James glanced up quickly at the sound of his wife's voice. She stood in the doorway that sepa-rated their rooms, her short hair mussed, her wrapper hanging about her shoulders.

Was it so late that she had been asleep? "I'm sorry," he said automatically. "I did not mean to wake you."

"I was not asleep."

They did not speak for a moment, and then Prudence closed the distance between them and took him in her arms. He stood stiffly, but his wife kissed his neck and his jaw and then tucked her head beneath his chin and held him against her tightly.

And it felt so damn good that he just let her hold him. And then, instead of saying anything, James leaned down and took his wife's full lips in a deep kiss that seemed to fill his very soul.

They kissed, and he touched her, everywhere that he could. He pushed his fingers through her short, springy hair. He had loved her long hair and had a moment of grief when he saw her new cut.

But now he knew that he would love his wife's hair in any form. And if she were to shave herself bald, then he would love her head. He laughed a little at this thought, and she moved as if to pull away, but he did not allow her to.

James deepened their kiss and smoothed his fingers around her face, touching her eyelids, her nose, her lips against his, her chin. And then he pulled her close, loving the feel of her body pressed to his.

He laid her carefully on the plush rug beneath their feet and peeled her wrapper and night rail from her. And then he worshiped her with his mouth.

James kissed the inside of Pru's elbows, he nibbled at her neck and licked the soft skin of her belly. He smoothed his hands along the inside of her thighs and wet the underside of her knee with his tongue. And then, finally, he took one small, white toe into his mouth and sucked.

She writhed beneath his ministrations, her moans like music in the night.

And then, after quickly shedding his clothes, he pushed his knees between his wife's thighs and entered her, and it truly felt like the world melted away from them. It did not matter. None of it mattered when he could come into the soft wetness of Prudence. They rocked against each other, kissing and loving and finding their release together.

And they slept together afterward in James's large bed until the dawn came.

James opened his eyes reluctantly when the first rays of sunlight streamed through the windows. The world was back.

Prudence turned over in bed to snuggle up to her husband, but he wasn't there. He must have awoken early.

She sighed, for she had quite hoped for a repeat performance of the night before. Just the thought made her shiver.

Prudence was not sure how everything was going to work out, but she knew with all of her heart that if they did it together, they would be okay. Because she loved him.

And she was rather sure he loved her, too.

And that felt so good, Prudence wanted to jump out of bed and sing.

James pushed open the door of his bedroom and stood looking down at her.

"You're dressed," she said with a pout.

He did not smile. "I am going to confront Wimsley."

Prudence pushed up to kneel on the bed. "Confront him? What are you going to say?"

James took in a deep breath. "He has to pay for what he did."

Pru nodded tentatively. Something about her husband's demeanor scared her. "Yes, what he did was truly awful."

"And I have the means to bring him down."

"Bring him down?"

"I have already seen Leighton this morning. He has agreed to get together the proof needed to show the world that the great earl of Wimsley is actually making his money by smuggling untaxed goods into the country."

Prudence felt as if someone had just hit her with a grapnel. "But . . ." she blinked several times and tried to keep breathing. "But to bring Wimsley down means that you will take Gravesly with him." And her as well. But she did not add this. Of course her husband realized it.

"I will protect you."

"You can't, James. Wimsley is not the type just to let this happen to him. He will tell the world who I am."

"That doesn't matter anymore," James said dully. "I have no one to prove myself to. I do not care if scandal hovers over me for the rest of my life."

"But what of Gravesly!" Pru crawled off the bed to stand before James. "Harker will surely go to jail. And I will, too."

"I can protect you," James said stubbornly.

Prudence made a disbelieving sound and shook her head. "You are not thinking right, James. Yes, you have the means to have Wimsley thrown in jail and humiliated in front of his peers. But if you exercise those means, you shall ruin the lives of every family in Gravesly."

James blinked, but did not look at her. "So be it," he said.

Prudence felt her chest constrict and her throat tighten. "Fine," she said then. "But I will not stay by your side while you do this horrible thing, James. I am going back to Gravesly to do every-thing I can for those people, because *they* are my family." She pushed her husband out of her way, rushed into her room, and slammed the door be-hind her as hard as she could.

# Chapter 22

~~~⟆⟅~~~

**T**he butler told him the earl was out and slammed the door in his face. He was getting that reaction rather a lot these days. James rubbed at his temples.

There was a tiny part of him that wanted to turn around and leave. He wanted to leave London, leave Wimsley, and back to Gravesly, go back to his wife.

But he could not. His heart ached for his mother, for his father, for himself. And he knew that he would never be able to live with himself unless he brought the great earl of Wimsley low.

James straightened his spine and banged the knocker once more.

The butler took his time, but answered the door finally. "Do you wish to leave a message, sir?" he asked with a sneer.

"Yes." And James pushed past the tiny man without any effort whatsoever.

"Hey there, now!" the man yelled, but James strode down the hall, opening doors as he went. It did not take him long to find Wimsley. The man stared up at him with round, angry eyes when James threw open the door of what seemed to be a library.

"Wimsley," James said.

Wimsley sat on a chair before the fire, his foot resting before him on a stool. He did not get up, he did not move, in fact. But his rounded eyes squinted into slits. "Get out," he said.

James laughed, a horrible sound. "I have a feeling we are replaying a scene that probably took place in this very room thirty-four years ago." He stepped into the library and shut the door on the sputtering butler. "Only, I am not a small, mourning woman with child, am I?"

"I shall have you jailed. I shall call the magistrate."

"Good, I am sure he will be interested in exactly how you come by your income, Wimsley."

The man shoved himself out of his chair then, his foot thumping to the floor as he grappled with the heavy gold head of his cane. "I will not stand for this!" he yelled when he finally righted himself.

"You have no choice, I'm afraid."

"Damn you."

"I return your sentiments completely," James said calmly.

His grandfather's face had gone quite purple. The man leaned heavily on his cane, and that implement shook with its owner's rage.

"God, you are as smug as he was," the man spat. "So sure of himself, so stuffed with himself, the lowly commoner!"

James held his breath for a moment. Was the man going mad?

"He had nothing, and she chose him, just because he walked around with his chest stuck out like a bloody peacock." Wimsley shook his head, then stood straight and threw his cane at James.

The stick clattered to the floor only a couple of feet beyond the earl. The old man sank onto his chair, wincing and grabbing at his leg.

"I am the earl of Wimsley, boy," he said then. "You can't do anything to hurt me. You are a nobody."

"I am your grandson."

"You are a bastard!" Wimsley screamed the last, his voice high-pitched with an edge of hysteria.

"Why?" James asked quietly.

"Because!" Wimsley glared at him. "There was no way I would ever allow the seed of that man to take my name!" Wimsely pointed a sausage-like finger at him. "Your grandfather took the only woman I ever loved. She was worthy of so much more. He was a nothing, but he took her anyway."

James understood. All of this, the reason his mother had been disgraced, the reason he had lived his life without a name or family, was because the man ranting before him had not gotten what he once wanted.

"You make me ill," James said.

And Wimsley laughed. He fell back against the cushions of his chair laughing as if he had lost his mind.

And James knew that he did not need to bring Wimsley low. "You are a pathetic excuse for a man."

But Wimsley only laughed harder.

"Your heir betrayed you," James said. "Leighton has given me proof that you profit from the sale of untaxed goods. He gave me leave to use it in any way I wished."

Wimsley's laughter sputtered to a halt. "Nothing will happen to me, you imbecile. I am the earl of Wimsley. I'm not some low-blood shopkeeper like your grandfather."

"My grandfather could have bought you twenty times over."

Wimsley sneered. "Oh yes, quite a brain for business, that low blood. He made quite a success of himself here in England, but then he stepped above himself and wooed the only woman I ever loved. And I ruined him. I am the reason your dearest grandfather had to take his money and his family and leave for India." Wimsley huffed another wheezing laugh. "An eye for an eye, you know."

James did not want to spend one more second in the room with such a vile creature. He turned on his heel.

"Your wife is going to jail, Ashley. I'll make sure of that as well."

James stopped. He turned, then, wishing he could kill the man. "My wife will be going nowhere but home, Wimsley. If you ever bother her, or anyone else in Gravesly for that matter, I will go to court and fight the annulment of my mother's marriage."

"Bah!" the old man said. "You have no proof."

James arched his brows and smiled smugly. "I have the annulment papers, which certainly prove my parents were married. And I have my birth date, which proves they were married when I was conceived. I most definitely have proof." Before the man could contest this last statement, James continued, "And it really does not matter, does it? The entire world would know about your perfidy. Not only that, dear man, but they would know how a beautiful woman chose a lowly shopkeeper over the great earl of Wimsley."

James looked down his nose at his grandfather.

"I would say, man, that you would be in for a great lot of embarrassment."

Wimsley snorted and heaved and generally made sounds like a pig routing for food. And then he turned an even darker shade of purple.

"Right then," James said. "I shall leave you to the devil." And he did.

She had heard nothing from her husband or Leighton, and she did not care. At least that is what she told herself. Prudence was very busy, anyway. She had a fair to organize.

Of course, she was not sure if anyone would show up. She was not sure if the magistrate would be coming for her soon. She was not sure of anything, really.

But she knew that she at least had to try to make this fair a success, because the townfolk of Gravesly were in need of something other than smuggling to support them. And rich peers spending their money in town would be just the thing.

She hoped the plan would work, because she would probably be hanging from a gibbet in the near future.

Prudence sighed as she threw the brake of the wagon and clambered down.

"Aya, Lady Pru," Tuck said with a smile, and jumped up to take the reins.

Prudence waved listlessly and climbed the

stairs to Chesley House. She was so angry with her husband, she wanted to throttle him. But she still missed him terribly.

Love was so horribly unfair. Why couldn't she just hate the selfish ingrate?

She yanked off her bonnet when Mabel opened the door. "There's that paper you like so much on the table," Mabel said, putting out her hands to receive bonnet and gloves.

Pru glanced over and saw that *Lady Whistledown's Society Papers* had been delivered. She picked it up listlessly and perused the columns nonchalantly. And then she snapped to attention.

"Holy Mother of God," she whispered.

"Excuse me, Lady Pru."

Prudence looked up at Mabel and blinked. And then she laughed. And then she twirled around and did a little dance. "Oh, Mabel," she cried, "we're in the paper."

Mabel looked completely confused.

"Lady Whistledown has mentioned the Gravesly Fair. Of course, she is making fun of us and calling it a bumpkin affair, but she mentioned us." Pru threw the paper in the air. "And she has sarcastically mentioned all the stumbling idiots who will attend!"

"And that is good?" Mabel asked, obviously not understanding at all.

"It's more than good, dear. It's wonderful. The people she mentioned who are coming set all the rules. If they're coming, all the others will follow. Mabel," Pru threw her arms around the surprised maid. "All of London will be here tomorrow."

Gravesly could not possibly hold another human being. The road into town was lined with the most elegant carriages James had ever seen. He felt a smile pull at his lips. Prudence's plan had come to fruition.

His wife was truly a woman of rare abilities.

He knew she would probably be in town, but he turned up the rutted road toward Chesley House. He did not want to go into Gravesly. Not now, anyway.

The small white house came into view, and James felt as if his heart must have swelled because his chest felt tight.

A rider cantered around the house and came toward him.

Clifton.

The butler slowed and tipped his hat, and then he did the strangest thing ever. He smiled. "Captain," Clifton said, "welcome home." And then the big man continued on his way.

James stopped, his hands shaking. Home. With a shake of his head, James shoved his heels into Devil's withers. He wished it would be. He hoped. If Prudence would ever forgive him.

And then she was there. James swallowed as he rode up to Chesley House, where his wife stood on the top step. "Whoa," he said, pulling Devil to a stop.

Prudence stared at him for a moment. And, slowly, she smiled. "It's quite a party in town. Would you like to escort me?"

He blinked.

"The Londoners are quite taken with Gravesly. Mrs. Hampton has told her husband that he really must buy a summer home here."

James smiled slowly, then laughed. "Well, I guess your plan has worked."

"Yes." She bit at her bottom lip. "Will I be allowed to see it to its fruition, or will I be going to jail soon?"

With a shake of his head, James dropped to the ground and took his wife in his arms. He held her so tightly, she whimpered, and he had to loosen his hold. But he did not let go.

"I will always protect you," he said.

"So there is something to protect me from, then?"

He laughed softly. "No, I think, actually, that I have taken care of it. I told Wimsley that the moment any magistrate comes to Gravesly to arrest my wife or anyone else, the world would know every embarrassing detail of his past."

"There are embarrassing details?"

"The whole scandal would be embarrassing enough, but there is also a little known fact that my maternal grandmother rejected the earl of

Wimsley so that she could marry a low-blood shopkeeper."

Prudence giggled. "That is embarrassing."

James buried his face in the softness of his wife's hair. "Wimsley is a pathetic, sad, lonely man. I did not need to bring him low. He's done the job quite well all by himself."

Prudence leaned back, looking up at him with her beautiful, warm eyes, her teeth working her lush bottom lip. He wanted to take her there on the steps of their house.

"Are you all right, though, James?" she asked.

"And why wouldn't I be," he said sternly. "I have the most beautiful wife in Christendom, a lovely home overlooking the sea, and I will never be alone again.

"I am home, dearest," he whispered. "I have a family, and I am home."

Prudence smiled widely, then threw her arms around him. God, it felt so good to have her against him.

"I love you, Mrs. Ashley," he said.

"I know, Mr. Ashley," she replied.

# Epilogue

*One year later*

**R**ichard stood beside James and Prudence, watching as Clifton finally married Leslie Redding. He smiled at the huge butler as he turned with his new bride to leave the chapel. The man's face was absolutely ashen.

"So, you have drafted the bill, I hear," Prudence whispered, and Richard nodded.

"Yes, but we've still a long way to go until it passes."

Pru grinned at him. "But with you and my dear husband in the House of Lords, I could not ask for better connections."

Richard leaned down and kissed the babe in Pru's arms.

She shooed him away. "You'll wake her, Wimsley."

Richard frowned. "Please, I've asked you not to call me that. So many people do now."

"Well, that's what happens when you become the earl of Wimsley," James said, taking the sleeping child from his wife's arms.

Richard glanced over at James and scowled. "Just because I've given over to you the best name there ever was doesn't mean you can be snippy."

The new Lord Leighton laughed. "I am never snippy. And I already told you that I certainly did not want to become your legal heir."

"Too bad."

The two men laughed together and started down the aisle of the church.

The people of Gravesly clamored to address James. They patted Abby's head lightly and smiled up into James's face as if he were the king of England. Richard stood back a little to let James be feted.

He glanced over at Pru then and smiled hugely. He adored her completely, and he loved his cousin with a fierceness that he had never felt.

Richard let James get ahead of him and dropped back to put his arm around the beautiful Lady Leighton. "It could not be a more lovely day for a wedding," he said. "And I did think that the bride's gown was quite smashing."

"It had better be since I made it."

Richard laughed as they finally strolled into the sunshine. The birds were singing, the weather was warm, and his family was well and filled with love. All was right with the world.

*♋ Coming next month . . . ♋*

## Avon Romantic Treasure
*Claiming the Highlander* by Kinley MacGregor

To end a long-running feud proud Maggie convinces her clan's women to deny their men *everything*. But warrior Braden MacAllister might get her to change her stubborn mind . . .

## Avon Contemporary Romance
*The Dixie Belle's Guide to Love* by Luanne Jones

What's an ex-beauty princess to do when she suddenly finds herself without a man? Why, eat all the cookies she can and loll about the house in a comfy pair of sweatpants . . . until the sexiest man in town comes knocking at her door.

## Avon Romance
*The MacKenzies: Jared* by Ana Leigh

The MacKenzies are a proud breed of men and women—as wild and untamed as the land they call home. Now, meet Jared, the sexiest, strongest of them all . . .

*The Lily and the Sword* by Sara Bennett

Lily finds herself married to her mortal enemy, Radulf, the King's Sword, never dreaming that she could fall in love with such a man . . .

*Avon Romances—*
*the best in exceptional authors*
*and unforgettable novels!*